Hope for Valhalla

◊ ◊ ◊

Hope for Valhalla

a novel

by
mike whicker

a Walküre imprint

This is a work of historical fiction

ISBN: 978-0-9844160-9-7

printed in the United States of America

For

Sandy Whicker

Part 1

If Castro had never taken over in 1959, Cuba would have become the "Republic of Las Vegas."

> — *Meyer Lansky,*
> *Mafia mobster,*
> *1973*

Chapter 1

New York City
02 October 1946

Paul "Fat Paulie" Villano sat at a table in *Louis's Sicilian Ristorante* in the Bronx. This was a 'mom and pop' restaurant started and run by Louis and his wife who emigrated from Sicily in 1924. Although small with only nine tables, it was a popular eating place for locals and members of the New York Mafia because of its authentic Sicilian bill of fare. The veal was considered by many as the best in New York City.

As soon as Villano entered and had been seated at a table by the sole waiter, Louis emerged from the kitchen to greet and pay his respects to his frequent customer who he knew was a mob enforcer.

"Good evening, Mr. Villano," Louis said pleasantly and with a strong Italian accent. "Will it be just you dining with us tonight?"

"No," Villano answered. "Two more men will be joining me, Louis."

"Motto bene. I'll send out some wine and bread while you wait."

In the early '40s, Paul Villano had been a member of Albert Anastasia's Murder Inc. and had taken part in at least a half-dozen hits for Anastasia's group of murderers, yet Fat Paulie was not a member of the Vincenzo Mangano family where Anastasia served as an underboss. Instead, Villano served as a top soldier for the Joseph Bonanno family. Like Mangano, 'Joe Bananas', controlled one of the five families that oversaw the city's organized crime. In fact, Louis, the restaurant's owner, was a distant cousin of Bonanno from the old country and his restaurant was one of the few privileged businesses in the Bronx that was not required to pay the mob a monthly 'protection tax.'

In addition, *Louis's* was not among the many Italian restaurants around the city, and other U.S. cities, that were forced to change its name or bill of fare because of anti-Italian sentiments in the early days of the war. Some German and Italian restaurants had been the targets of vandalism or even a Molotov cocktail in the dead of night. Everyone knew *Louis's* was a popular mob restaurant so it was left alone.

The two associates Villano was there to meet worked for the Mangano family. That is one reason Villano choose this particular restaurant for the meeting. *Louis's* was well within Bonanno's turf.

Fat Paulie arrived fifteen minutes early for an 8:00 p.m. dinner with his former colleagues. It was now 8:15 and they still had not arrived. Fat Paulie was not happy. He hated it when someone didn't show up on time. He had already drank a half carafe of the house red wine and eaten a full basket of baguettes. Of course, Villano hadn't gained his nickname erroneously. At just 5'8" but 290 pounds, Fat Paulie could handle generous portions of food.

Finally, his two old allies arrived. 'Checkers' Grosso and Tony Carlevano walked through the front door and made their way to Villano's table.

"You're late," spouted Villano. "Where have you cocksuckers been? I'm starving."

"Fuck you, you big fat fuck," Checkers said. "It might save that fat heart of yours an attack if you waited on a meal once in awhile."

Longtime partners in crime, the men allowed each other's mutually vulgar insults.

When the waiter saw that the other men had arrived, he stepped over for their orders. His name was Carlo and he was engaged to Louis's daughter who worked in the kitchen. Louis wasn't thrilled about the relationship; Carlo was from Naples, not Sicily, but because of his daughter's non-stop pleading, Louis agreed to ensure Carlo a job in the States when he entered the country six months ago. Carlo was a good waiter; Louis had to admit that.

Checkers and Tony ordered the veal braciola, Fat Paulie the rigatoni and sausage.

"I thought you always ate the veal here," Tony said to Villano.

"I've had veal the last three times I've been here; time for something else. Louis's wife makes a gravy that is also one of the best in the city," Fat Paulie was referring to the restaurant's marinara sauce.

While waiting for the food to arrive, the men shared some humor from the past.

"I still laugh my ass off when I remember that Harlem pimp we had to take care of," Villano laughed. "It was you, Checkers, me and Mickie the Limp. You weren't in on this one Tony. Did Checkers ever tell you about it?"

"No, I don't think so," the young man answered.

"It was just before the war, I remember that. Anastasia gave us the job. The pimp had been holding out on his dues to Lucky. The cocksucker had been warned. He knew he was in trouble and he went underground. It took us three weeks to find the fuck. You remember all this, don't you Checkers?"

Checkers smiled. "Oh, yeah, how could I forget? Those were good times."

"Anyhow, Tony, we finally found out from one of his whores that the idiot was holing up in a barn in Jersey operating from there. I could stop right there and the story would be funny enough—a Harlem pimp running his operation out of an abandoned barn in the woods in bum-fuck New Jersey. The guy didn't even have a telephone. To do business he had to drive to a gas station."

All the men laughed.

"So one night about midnight, or a little after, we take a drive: me, Checkers, and Mickie. We left the car about a mile from the barn so the pimp doesn't hear us coming. Then we have to traipse our asses a mile though the woods. Mickie the Limp had a club foot. The heel of one of his shoes was three inches thicker than the other one. He fell on his ass about six times on the way through the woods."

More laughter from the men.

"Finally we reach the damn barn and there is a light on. Mickie falls again, making noise, and the light goes out. We make it to the barn door and go inside. The inside was blacker than a crow's ass but we knew the guy was in there. We had to use our flashlights, which made us sitting ducks, and the guy starts shooting at us. I think he was behind a hay bale or something; we could only see the flashes from his gun. There was a bunch of barrels and old rusty farm shit so we all ducked behind whatever we could find.

"Of course we couldn't see his black ass in the dark, but when we heard the pimp's gun click empty, I took Mickie's flashlight so the

5

asshole would think we were all staying put. Mickie had lost his gun while falling on his ass in the woods, so as the dumb shit pimp reloaded, Mickie grabbed an old rusty rake and tried to sneak up on the guy. So here we go. The guy spots Mickie at the last minute and starts running around the barn with old Mickie chasing the guy with a rake. Funniest thing I ever saw. Mickie was so slow he couldn't catch a two-legged dog. Finally, after Checkers and I got in our laughs, we opened up and one of us plugged the pimp in the leg. We still don't know which one of us plugged him. He goes down screaming and Mickie finally catches up to the guy and starts whacking him with the rake. Probably took him twenty whacks before the stupid ass was dead. Mickie was so tired he fell backwards on a bale of hay."

Both Tony and Checkers laughed loudly.

"What did you do with the body?" Tony asked.

"Checkers hiked back to our car and drove it up by the barn. We loaded the fuck in the trunk and drove back to Harlem. We dropped the body on the sidewalk in front of a nightclub the guy used to run his business out of as a warning to anyone else who tries to do business without giving the family in charge of that territory their cut."

After Carlo brought out the meals and more wine, the men tucked in and began discussing the reason for tonight's meeting.

"What's Don Mangano's decision about giving Joe Bananas a piece of the new Cuba business," Paulie asked between bites of Italian sausage.

"He doesn't feel your boss is offering enough," Checkers answered.

"What? Joe is offering a million dollar buy in and protection. What the hell does Mangano want? Joe's balls?"

"Mangano feels he has plenty of protection already, and the decision on the dough was made by Meyer Lansky. You know he's in charge down there in Cuba."

"Lansky, the Jew fuck," said Paulie. "So how much does he want?"

"We'll have to get back to you."

"There will be a big problem between the families if Joe gets cut out. You know that, right Checkers?" Paulie said menacingly.

"Mangano realizes that. Nobody wants a war. Don Mangano is going to talk to Lansky personally."

"Well, tell him to make it snappy. Joe Bananas isn't known for his patience."

Checkers nodded. So far, the younger Tony Carlevano had just listened.

A few more details about Cuba were discussed then at the end of dinner Fat Paulie began rehashing more funny stories from the past (at least stories that appealed to a gangster's sense of humor).

When it was time to leave, Paulie said, "Dinner is on me. So you'll get back to me soon on a deal for Joe, right Checkers?"

"Right. I'll tell Don Mangano something needs to be done."

"Good."

Paulie paid the check and the three men rose and walked out together. Paulie's driver had parked across the street. Since he was a novice gangster, having just joined the Bonanno family a few months ago, he was not yet fully trusted so he was not included in the conversation. He had waited in the car the entire time. Tony had driven Checkers and had parked down the block.

As soon as the three men emerged out onto the sidewalk, Tony pulled out a .45 and shot Paulie in the back of the head. Brain matter spewed out of Villano's forehead then he dropped dead on the walk. Both Checkers and Tony unloaded several more rounds into the body.

Villano's young driver saw what happened, scooted across the front street and exited the car from the passenger side. He ran for his life and ducked down the nearest alley.

Checkers Grosso emptied one more shell into Villano's body and said, "Thanks for dinner, Paulie."

Chapter 2

Havana, Cuba
Thursday, 10 October 1946

Even on this autumn Thursday, the Mediterranean sun beat down on Havana making those walking the streets feel as if they traipsed across a colossal frying pan.

However, there were places one could find respite from the searing heat.

The Hotel Nacional, just two miles north of Old Town Havana, was by far the largest hotel in Havana with 457 rooms, and 16 large suites. It stood on a high hill overlooking the sea, offering guests not only the sea breeze, but a window air conditioner in every room. Built in the 1930s, the hotel's overall look was art deco as one would suspect of that decade. The Nacional also offered guests a large casino, not surprising since the hotel was the brainchild of the American mobster Meyer Lansky.

In fact, Lansky and three of his colleagues from the New York mafia: Lucky Luciano, Benjamin Siegel and Albert Anastasia currently sat in the Salon de la Historia, a special room off the Nacional's lobby where the New York mobsters often met. The salon walls were adorned with life-sized murals of gangsters intermingled with celebrities and movie stars.

A waiter delivered two bottles of fourteen-year-old Glenfiddich Scotch and a large plate of fried red and green bell peppers. A humidor of Cuban cigars sat on a shelf beside the table.

When the waiter left the room, Luciano started things off. "We had some trouble last night. Some sucker lost his wad at the roulette table, got drunk, and began running his mouth that the games were fixed."

"Which sand dune is the dumb bastard buried under this morning?" Siegel asked and everyone laughed.

"You know we can't whack some jerk like that, Ben," Luciano answered. "Bad for business. I had a couple of our guys take him for a ride. They gave him a good once over, warned him to never show his rat face at the casino again, then they threw him out of the car near some swamp."

Albert Anastasia, the head of Murder, Inc. and known as the "Lord High Executioner," poured everyone a dram of Scotch. "So why the meeting, Lucky? We're not here to talk about some tourist fuck with a big mouth."

Luciano deferred to Meyer Lansky.

"We need more floor walkers," Lansky said. "Good looking broads who will latch on to the money bags and get them to gamble more. We're way short in that area and it's hurting business. Too many rich suckers are placing small bets and then leaving to watch the topless broads in the floor shows."

"Bring in some of our whores from New York," Anastasia suggested. "What's the big deal?"

"These women have to have some class and know how to dress and talk intelligently to these guys, Albert," Lansky answered after he put a slice of pepper in his mouth and took a sip of Scotch. "Street prostitutes looped on drugs won't fly."

"So where do we get these broads, Meyer?" Luciano asked.

"I'm working on it. I've got four who might fit the bill waiting outside the room. They're all foreigners with accents; the accents give them more class." Lansky pressed a buzzer on the wall beside the table.

"Yes, boss," was heard through the speaker.

"Aldo, send in the women."

"You got it boss."

In a moment the door opened and Aldo flagged in the women. He left and shut the door.

Four attractive women in cocktail dresses such as would be required for their prospective jobs stood together. Some seemed a bit nervous to be in the presence of such notorious men. Two of the women were Latino twins, another was black, and one was a blonde Caucasian.

"Would you like a drink, ladies?" Meyer asked.

None spoke but all shook their heads 'no'.

"But you do all drink, right? We can give you tea for whiskey or brandy, but if your mark insists on ordering for you and gets you something like a martini, the bartenders will water it down for you but you'll still get some alcohol. My people filled you in on your duties, right?"

All of them nodded 'yes'.

You'll get a small salary but you can make a fortune in tips if you latch on to the right guys and play your cards right. Your job is to get the money bags to gamble more. That's understood, am I right?" Lansky asked.

All of the women again nodded.

"These broads don't talk much," said Anastasia. "How are they going to work the suckers?"

"They'll be just fine, Albert," said Ben Siegel. The ruthless gangster with a movie idol face smiled at the women. "Tell us a little about yourselves. The twins there; what's your story? Where you from?"

One of the twins took charge. "We are from Brazil, from Rio de Janeiro." The woman's accent was Portuguese. "I am Lina. This is my sister, Lizete." Both women had the dark Latino skin, dark hair and eyes as many would expect of native-born Brazilians. Both were rather short, about 5'3" but with full figures and very busty.

Luciano leaned over to Anastasia thinking he was being discreet but said loudly enough that all could hear, including the women, "Great tits."

Anastasia changed his focus to the third woman. "What's the deal, Meyer? We're hiring the Coloreds now?"

"She's French," Lansky shot back, growing tired of the boorish behavior of the group in general. The Cuban operations were Meyer Lansky's brainchild and he was in charge. Despite his associates being murderers and racketeers, Lansky knew each man had the capacity to impress people with their charm when the occasion presented itself— all except perhaps Albert Anastasia. "Let's show a little class around the ladies, gentlemen," Lansky admonished the group. "Albert, to answer your question, next week we have a large group of French Moroccan high rollers who have booked several suites. And regardless of that, some white men go for Negro women." No questions were asked of the attractive French woman so she said nothing.

Finally the men got to the blonde. She was taller than the others and sturdily built, like a female pole vaulter or Olympic swimmer.

"What's your story, sister?" Luciano asked.

"I was born in Germany but my mother was British and I lived in London during the war." The woman's British accent was undeniable.

"Why did you decide to come to Havana? The cigars?" A couple of the men chuckled.

"I got into a spot of trouble in London and figured it was time for a fresh start somewhere else."

"What trouble was that?" Siegel asked.

"It seems I borrowed a bicycle without the owner's permission. A Bobby saw me and took out after me on his bicycle. He happened to ride into the side of a lorry while chasing me. He wasn't hurt too badly, just a broken leg, but now they have a warrant out for me for 'endangering a police officer while committing a crime.' That comes with jail time in England. I didn't want to go to jail so here I am."

"Let me get this straight," Lucky Luciano said. "You stole a bicycle and a cop runs into the side of a truck while chasing you?"

"Yes, sir, that's basically it."

There was a brief pause then the four men broke out into riotous laughter.

"I like her already," said Siegel, still laughing. "What's your name, darling?"

"Erika."

Chapter 3

Washington, D.C.
Saturday, 12 October 1946

Leroy Carr and Al Hodge sat together in a rear booth in the Mayflower Hotel lounge. Carr was the CIA's deputy director and Hodge, also with the new agency, had been Carr's friend and right-hand man since their days together during the war when they both worked for the OSS. Both had offices at the Pentagon, but they often used the Mayflower lounge as a meeting place if they wanted a drink or a meal while discussing business. A gin and tonic sat in front of Carr, a whiskey sour in front of Hodge. In the center of the table a bowl of mixed nuts was already half emptied by the cashew and hazel nut loving Hodge.

"Al, you look like a squirrel chomping on his winter stash," said an amused Leroy Carr.

"Yeah? When I was a kid my father and I went squirrel hunting every fall. Maybe that's why squirrels are good eating. It's the nuts."

"You never told me you were a squirrel hunter when you were a kid."

Hodge grew up in Tennessee. "I'm a crack shot with a kid-size .22 rifle. Dad and I put a good dent in the gray squirrel population in the Smokey Mountains. Don't be climbing a tree in the woods if I'm around."

"I'll be sure and remember that," said Carr.

"So what's the latest, Leroy?"

"She got a job as a floor walker at the Nacional. It's not much, but her foot is in the door. We need to come up with a plan to get her closer to the inner-circle."

"By the 'inner-circle' I assume you mean Meyer Lansky."

"She said at the meeting when she was hired, besides Lansky; Luciano, Bugsy, and Anastasia were there. So any of them will work."

"Anastasia? He's just an under boss who gets rid of people. What was a thug like him doing there?"

"Good question. I have no idea. But that's not our concern. The mob is the FBI's problem. Our mission is to find out if the communists are in cahoots with the mob. Cuba legalized the Communist Party in '38, and three years ago the Russians moved in. We know the communists are trying to influence everything from the mob-run labor unions in New York, to the powers-that-be in Hollywood. With Batista now out of power in Cuba, we have to find out if there is a working relationship between the mafia and Soviets in Cuba."

"Batista, that guy is as big a racketeer as any of those mafia guys," Hodge commented.

"Agreed, but he held a check on the communists. Until he's back in power, the U.S. has no ally in Cuba. Not one with any real power, anyway. That's why we have to get Erika closer to the inner-circle of the Nacional.

"Pack your bags, Al, and work on your Mambo. You're going to Cuba."

Chapter 4

Havana, Cuba
Thursday, 17 October 1946

Erika's assigned shift was the hours from eight in the evening until four o'clock in the morning—the busiest time. Six days a week.

Since she had been hired one week ago, she had spent her working hours wearing slinking cocktail dresses in the Hotel Nacional casino flirting with the high-rollers, doing what she could to keep them at the tables. That was her job. Luckily, she did not have to pick all the men herself. Floor walkers like Erika sat in a private room until summoned by men whose job it was to watch for cheating gamers or dealers, and identify such targets as high rollers who could use some female companionship. The high roller would be pointed out to her and she'd go to work. While out on the casino floor, the women were allowed and encouraged to move to another mark if they thought they could be more productive.

She had learned a great deal about various games of chance over the past week while placing chips down for men at a roulette table, throwing the dice for another rich man at a crap table, or sitting beside and acting impressed by a mark who was determined to prove his gambling skill as he played black jack or Caribbean stud poker. Erika had been offered money by some of the big spenders to join them in their hotel room. Fortunately, she had an automatic excuse for turning down these offers. House rules prohibited the floor walkers from accepting such propositions. The women prostituting themselves were forbidden by Meyer Lansky not for any moral or legal reasons, but out of the need to keep the women around and ready for duty on the floor. If the floor walkers wanted to make some extra money in a guest's hotel room while off duty that was left up to the individual woman.

She had seen Lansky in the casino a few times, usually playing host to various nefarious looking men and their girlfriends (mob wives were normally left at home). She knew Bugsy Siegel was still staying in the hotel; she spotted him go into the casino bar yesterday.

She had not seen Lucky Luciano or Albert Anastasia since the day she stood before them with the other three women hired on that day a week ago.

Currently, Erika was on the arm of a tall, middle-aged Texas oil man complete with the accent, a white cowboy hat, string tie, alligator skin cowboy boots, and a large dram of rye whiskey. He, of course, also bought her drinks for which he paid full price for liquor but was only tea. For the past hour, he had given Erika chips to place when some other player controlled the dice. She almost always placed the man's $100 bets on the "Don't Pass" square, meaning she was betting against the dice tosser. Whenever the stickman pushed the dice to the oil man, he placed the bets himself and she rolled the dice. They had started out poorly, losing nearly $3000, then Erika got on a hot streak throwing the dice and had brought the oil man back to about even. Floor walkers were not admonished if one of their marks ended up a winner (as long as it didn't happen too often). Casino managers knew they needed some winners now and then. It was not good business for everyone to lose all the time. The word would get around and business would drop off.

Floor walkers were not supposed to act like casino employees but to give the illusion that they were there just to have a good time. But only the most novice of casino gamblers swallowed that ruse. Most experienced gamblers, like the Texas oil man, knew Erika worked for the casino. When some associates of the oil man came to the craps table, the man withdrew from the game. Apparently the men, who all dressed like rich Texans, had come to Havana together.

He turned to Erika. "Thank you, little lady," he said to her as he handed her a $100 chip. "My amigos and I are going to dinner. I'd be happy to have you join us but we'll just be discussing business back home and I'm sure you'd be bored stiffer than a new saddle."

"I had a brilliant time," Erika told him, "and thanks for the tip." She always spoke with a British accent. Although she was from Germany, Erika had learned English from her British mother so it came naturally.

"My pleasure. Adios."

There is a good guy, Erika thought. He knew why she was there but both had had fun and he hadn't tried to get her in bed like some of the others. She was glad she had gotten on the lucky steak and he had at least not lost money.

After a floor walker split from a high roller for whatever reason, the women had been instructed to walk around the casino floor looking for a new mark. If none were found, they were to report back to the waiting room. It didn't take long for Erika to spot her next encounter. Al Hodge was dressed to the nines and sitting at a black jack table.

"Would you like some company?" she asked Al as she slid onto the stool beside him.

"You bet. What are you drinking?"

"Brandy," she answered.

Al flagged a waitress and ordered her drink along with another Scotch on the rocks for himself.

"My name's Al," he told her.

"Erika, nice to meet you."

For the next hour they both played their parts. She would tell Al when to stay or take another hit. She intentionally chose to hit too high which caused him to lose a considerable amount of money. They both knew this would look good for her with the casino watchdogs constantly lurking around. No conversation passed between them about the mission because of all the ears around the table and some spectators behind them waiting for a seat to open up.

Finally, after the hour at the black jack table, Al said he was taking a break to go to the bar and handed her a chip for a gratuity. She thanked him and departed. Erika went to the ladies room. Along with the chip was a small note taped to it, smaller than the chip itself.

Meet me at the Café del Lugo
492 Paseo del Prado
tomorrow at noon

Chapter 5

Havana
Next day—Friday, 18 October 1946

One of the many coffee cafés in Havana serving the world famous Cuban coffee, the Café del Lugo was about a three mile drive, and southeast, from the Hotel Nacional. Erika took a bus halfway then switched to a taxi, always keeping an eye out. There was no reason for her to think she might be followed, Meyer Lansky and his cohorts had no idea who she really was, but it was standard procedure for both parties to be on guard when having a clandestine meeting. Better to be safe than sorry.

When she arrived a few minutes before noon, Al Hodge was already sitting at one of the café's sidewalk tables reading an English language version of the Havana Mensaje, one of the daily newspapers. Naturally, a cup of coffee sat on the table in front of him.

Erika sat down and said, "Hello, Al."

Hodge, still not looking up from the newspaper, returned the greeting. "Hello, Erika. There's an ad here that claims to have a heckuva good sale on shoes at a store not far from my hotel. I might have to check that out." He finally folded the newspaper and laid it on the table. A waiter appeared with a coffee for Erika. The coffee did not have to be ordered. All of the café's customers were started out with a cup.

"Where are you staying? Can you tell me?"

"Yep, same place as you are."

"You're staying at the Nacional?" Normally, Hodge would avoid staying at any hotel where Erika stayed.

"I'm a rich gambler, remember. That's where rich American gamblers stay when they're in Havana. Plus, it will allow us to meet easily. We won't have to sneak around and meet at cafés all the time. You can give the impression that I've hired you to come to my hotel room if anyone asks. The floor girls can do that on their own time, right?"

"You've got good intel, Al."

"We sent down a scout to gather what information he could as soon as you let us know you had gotten one of those jobs. So fill me in. Anything to report?"

"Nothing yet. I haven't seen Luciano or Anastasia since the day I was hired."

"Anastasia is back in New York," he interrupted. "The passport people let us know when those characters come in or go out of the country. But you say you haven't seen Lucky Luciano? He's got to still be here. He's not allowed back into the States. Cuba allowed him in but there was a lot of objection among government factions. Luciano is probably lying low in some beach house trying to stay out of the limelight."

"I saw Bugsy Siegel go into the casino bar a couple of nights ago."

"Was anyone with him?"

"No. Not even a female companion. I've seen Meyer Lansky a few times but he's always hobnobbing with guys who look like fellow mobsters. I haven't recognized any of them."

"We have to find a way to get you closer to one of the big shots. Siegel would be the best bet if he sticks around for awhile. He's quite the ladies' man. But don't call him Bugsy. The word out is he hates that nickname."

"My thoughts, too. About getting close to Siegel, that is. The opportunity just hasn't been there."

"How about the good old femme fatale approach?" Hodge threw out. "You've always been good at that. Next time you see Siegel alone, give him a flirt."

"I'm not doing that anymore. I could flirt, but then he'd want me in bed. My days of doing that are over."

"Why?"

Erika shrugged but did not answer.

"Don't forget the mission objective," Hodge reminded her.

Erika looked at him with amusement and a bit of impatience. "Al, have I ever forgotten a mission objective? In a nutshell, we're not after the mob. We want to find out if the communists have any influence with the mob's dealings. Getting a toe-hold inside the mob would be the best way to do that. Satisfied?"

18

Al nodded. "I'll talk things over with Leroy about a plan to get you closer. Meanwhile, if you come up with something let me know. I'm in room 621 under the name Harold Walker. Calling or coming by my room won't be suspicious. As one of the hotel girls, you're just making some extra dough on the side."

Erika picked up a menu. "Can we eat now? I haven't eaten anything since a light dinner before my shift last night."

Chapter 6

Washington, D.C.
Next day—Saturday, 19 October 1946

Al Hodge flew from Havana to Miami in a small Fairchild UC-86 overhead wing that cruised at 145 miles per hour. Only 228 air miles between the two cities, his flight was short—about an hour and a half. Hodge's pilot was a CIA "shuttler" whose job it was to perform short hop clandestine flights. During the war he had flown British Lysanders—the small "moon planes"—under the radar to deliver British SOE agents and American OSS operatives from England to secluded fields and meadows in Nazi-occupied France. Those flights took place in the dead of night. There was no need for that much security today and the aircraft lifted off from a private airstrip twenty miles west of Havana at one o'clock in the afternoon.

Leroy Carr's pilot was an Army-Air Force captain. He and Carr had a much longer distance to cover from Washington, D.C. Even though the Army Lockheed Electra Junior cruised at a faster 225 mph, the 925 mile flight took him just over four hours. Carr had a packet of information and photographs for Hodge. This demanded a face-to-face instead of a telephone conversation.

They kept it simple and just met in an airport bar. Carr and Hodge had met in airport bars many times; in fact, both had been in this particular bar before. As with other airport bars, businessmen wearing suits often met there for between-flight exchanges of ideas and information. No one would pay them any mind.

Carr drank gin and tonics, Hodge usually whiskey on the rocks, but since it was mid-afternoon and both men would fly back to where they came from immediately after their meeting, both ordered a Falstaff beer. They waited to begin their conversation until after the waiter delivered the beer.

Carr pushed a folder across the table to Hodge.

"Here's some intel and photographs of known Russian agents and American communist sympathizers we know are in Cuba now, or have been there recently," Carr explained. "You'll have to let Erika see this as soon as possible. Tell her to let you know immediately if she sees any of them hanging around the Nacional. There are also some photos of gangsters we know have made trips there—under bosses and lower level guys she might spot."

Hodge nodded. "I'll study it tonight and get it to Lehmann tomorrow."

"I'd have made two copies, one for each of you, but we can't take the chance that a housekeeper or anyone else might run across it in her room. She'll have to look it over and give it back to you. She has a sharp memory so hopefully the photos, or at least most of them, will stick."

"She's got the memory of an elephant. We've learned that from past history, that's for sure," Hodge replied.

"So what's the latest, Al?"

"Nothing to get excited about. As I told you on the phone last night, she has seen Bugsy and Lansky around but has had no opportunity to intermingle with them. And by the way, she says she's done with the siren approach."

Carr thought for a moment. "I bet that has something to do with her husband's death on the last mission."

"You know her, Leroy. She's not going to change her mind."

"That's a sensitive thing, having female agents giving their bodies up to a mark. We're not going to try and change her mind. That's a decision she has a right to make. Perhaps it's time to bring in Zhanna Rogova."

Hodge threw up his arms. "Damn it, Leroy. Tell me you're joking!"

If Erika is done playing the siren, we'll have to use a different approach. Don't panic, Al. It won't be as bad as it was during their last mission together. Erika and Zhanna developed a working relationship in Poland.

"If you say so, Leroy."

Chapter 7

Fort Huachuca, Arizona
Tuesday, 22 October 1946

Zhanna Rogova completed the mandatory CIA field agent training at Fort Huachuca two weeks ago, but since that time she had been held there until Leroy Carr decided what to do with her. There was some thought of using her as a drill instructor at the "Farm" – the CIA's new training facility at Camp Perry in Virginia. But until Carr made up his mind, she would idle away her days in southern Arizona.

During the war, the Russian Rogova had earned the reputation as the Red Army's top sniper. Early in 1945, just before the war ended, she was transferred to SMERSH (the Soviet version of CIA counter intelligence) where her duties included hunting down and eliminating Russians caught spying for the Allies or other countries. While working for SMERSH, her reputation grew beyond expert sniper to ruthless and deadly assassin.

With her jet hair and spellbinding eyes, Zhanna would have been considered attractive were it not for the gruesome rope burn that encircled her neck. After being captured by the Germans outside the Korsun Pocket in 1944, she was hanged by the SS. The SS preferred to hang people slowly, and luckily for Zhanna the Pocket was overrun by Soviet troops who cut her down before her hanging reached its goal.

One reason Leroy Carr had held Zhanna at Fort Huachuca was that Erika Lehmann would also be a trainer at the Farm when not on a mission, and Zhanna Rogova and Erika Lehmann had a history together. One filled with turmoil. In spite of this, Carr felt the two intimidating women had established a working rapport during a recent mission in Poland. The CIA deputy director was counting on that relationship when he ordered Rogova to be flown from Fort Huachuca to Washington.

She arrived in D.C. just after dawn, flown in overnight on a military cargo plane. It was now nine o'clock in the morning as the former Soviet operative was escorted by two MPs into Leroy Carr's

Pentagon office. Carr thanked the MPs and asked them to wait outside his door.

"Have a seat, Zhanna. I see you successfully completed your initial training at Huachuca this time." It was Zhanna's second try at Huachuca. The first time she had failed, not because the training was too difficult for her, but because of her brusque attitude toward the instructors.

"Yes, I finished nearly a month ago. Why was I held there so long after my training was complete?" Zhanna's English was now pretty solid, although she spoke it with a heavy Russian accent. "You told me I would be an instructor at your new training center in Virginia once my processing and training was finished in Arizona." Zhanna could not pronounce the Native American word 'Huachuca' so she always avoided it.

"I'm moving things along as quickly as I can," Carr replied. "But that's not why I had you brought here today. I'm considering another Shield Maiden mission."

'Shield Maidens' was the code name for a group of four CIA agents. Led by Erika Lehmann, the group included Zhanna, Kathryn Fischer, and Sheila Reid. Those first three women worked for the CIA. Reid was an Army major and Carr's executive assistant. Their first mission together a few months ago when they were tasked to rescue Hedy Lamarr from the Soviets was successful. It was during that mission that Erika and Zhanna, the German and the Russian blood enemies, had developed the esprit de corps Carr had to count on.

"Another mission with Erika?" Zhanna asked.

"Yes, I don't know if Kathryn and Sheila will be involved, and if they are to what extent. That will depend on how the mission progresses. But with Erika, yes. She's already working on site."

Zhanna looked at him.

"Cuba," Carr answered her silent question.

"What's in Cuba?"

"A lot of good cigars," Carr said flippantly. 'Seriously, high-ranking members of the New York Mafia have recently taken up operations there, and several top dog Soviets and American communist sympathizers have been coming and going. We're concerned there might be a connection. That's what we have to find out." Carr was careful with the details, telling Rogova only the basics that she would need to know going in.

Zhanna said, "I know about your American gangsters—Al Capone."

"Capone has been out of the picture since he was shipped off to Alcatraz in the early 30s. He's out now but dying of syphilis at his estate in Florida. He doesn't have much time left. No, it's an entire set of new characters that we're now dealing with."

"When would I start?"

"Are you and Erika going to be able to work together without the problems of last time?

Zhanna shrugged. "I will not be the one who starts such problems. But if Erika chooses to do so I will not back down."

"That's only slightly reassuring, at best," Carr stated. Then came the warning. "You know what we can do if you don't cooperate. We can deport you back to Russia where most likely you will be immediately executed."

"You have reminded me of that many times, Mr. Carr."

"Just so we understand each other."

"When do I leave for Cuba?"

"On Thursday, the day after tomorrow."

"I assume Erika's and my job will be to lure certain marks into bed and get what we can from what you Americans call 'pillow talk.'"

"Not this time," said Carr. "We're taking a much different approach. You'll be fully briefed tomorrow."

Chapter 8

Havana
Wednesday, 23 October 1946

Two Hotel Nacional security men held the man down as Benjamin "Bugsy" Siegel brought down a hammer on the back of the man's hand. The man screamed and Siegel repeated the process three more times until the bones in the man's right hand were reduced to splinters.

"If I ever see you in the hotel again, next time I'll do the same to your head, you piece of shit," Siegel told the man. "Take this rat out back and throw him in a dumpster," Siegel ordered hotel security. "See if he can climb out with one hand. Better yet, take him for a ride and dump his ass out in the boonies somewhere. He can walk home trying to hitch a ride with a thumb that looks like a fat guy's limp dick."

The man has been caught counting cards at a blackjack table.

As soon as Siegel left the storage room where the man had been attended to, he was intercepted on the casino floor by Saul Weinstein, one of Meyer Lansky's aides.

"Mr. Siegel," said Weinstein. "Mr. Lanksy would like to see you right away. He's waiting in his private dining room."

Siegel nodded. When he reached the room, Lansky sat alone with a glass of milk and a pear in front of him.

"Milk and a pear, Meyer?"

I'm getting old, Ben. The stomach isn't what it used to be—an ulcer. But I didn't want to talk to you about my health report. You know that Fat Paulie Villano was taken out last week in New York."

"Yeah, I heard. I assume it was by Anastasia's men and that you gave the go ahead."

Lansky nodded. "Villano was one of Joe Banana's top lieutenants. Hopefully this will serve as warning to Joe to get his nose out of our business and stop insisting on a cut of our action. He's done absolutely nothing to help us set up shop here and he has no right to hoard in. Now he's offered a million dollar buy-in, which I consider an insult considering the tens of millions we came up with to get a foot hold down here."

"You know Bonanno with have to save face with some sort of retaliation."

"That's why I wanted to talk to you," said Lansky. "I've already notified our family in New York to be on the lookout, and we're going to increase security down here for me, you and Lucky."

"Where is Lucky? I haven't seen him in awhile."

"He's staying in some cottage on the beach about forty miles west of here. Since his Italian visa to enter Cuba is only temporary, we all feel it's best he's not seen around here too much. Since Batista got ousted in '44 and has not been replaced, this is a country without a leader. We have too much invested to take the chance it becomes the Wild West with gun battles every day. Customers will be afraid to come around."

◊ ◊ ◊

[that evening}
Erika stood next to one of the casino bars doing her job to look pretty for the next Daddy Big Bucks she would escort. Two hotel security men stood together down the bar, but close enough that Erika could overhear their conversation.

"Did you hear the latest?" one man said to the other.

"I don't know; it depends on what is the latest."

"Lansky and Siegel want to increase security—for themselves and for the hotel."

◊ ◊ ◊

[later, same evening]
Al Hodge was on the phone with Leroy Carr who was at home. Erika stood by.

"Sounds like a good option to our original plan, Leroy."

"I agree, this would get them closer to the inner circle than our plan to try and get them in as chauffeurs."

"By 'them' you're including Rogova, right?"

26

"Right. I'm briefing her tomorrow. Sounds like you and I have an all-nighter revamping this thing. Bugsy is the one we want to go after. Lansky has health problems and rarely leaves the hotel. Siegel is out and about more. Let's put some thoughts together and call me back in an hour at my office."

Chapter 9

Havana
Friday, 25 October 1946

The plan had been revised, and Zhanna Rogova arrived in Havana late last night. She stayed the night in Erika's room, one of the small rooms set aside for certain hotel employees located just over the boiler room. The boiler was not needed this time of year to heat the hotel rooms; in fact, that was rarely needed in Cuba even during the winter months, but the boiler also produced hot water for the rooms and the kitchen so it ran constantly. This made Erika's room swelter. Windows were kept open and ceiling fans running.

Because of their past history, the two women's reunion was not a joyous one, but reserved and kept professional.

Over breakfast in the hotel's breakfast cantina, the new plan was discussed.

"So you are certain this 'Bugsy' man leaves the hotel at eight in the evening?" Zhanna asked.

"On Friday nights, yes. It's a poorly kept secret, all the floor walkers know about it. He's quite the womanizer, and word is he meets up with a woman at a bar a few blocks from the hotel. Apparently she's married so their meetings are discreet."

"I assume you've talked to Hodge and everything is in place," Zhanna added.

"Supposedly so."

◊ ◊ ◊

[that evening]
At eight o'clock, Erika and Zhanna stood outside and a few yards down from the casino main entrance. Erika was wearing one of her cocktail dresses, Zhanna regular street clothes as would be commonly seen in Havana. Both were smoking brown Cuban cigarettes.

The women had lingered there, leaning against the building for about twenty minutes when finally Bugsy Siegel and two of his

Neanderthal-looking bodyguards emerged from the entrance and turned their way.

As Siegel approached, he looked at Erika and stopped. "I know you, don't I?" he asked Erika. "You're one of our floor girls"

"Yes, Mr. Siegel, I'm Erika. You hired me a couple of weeks ago. I'm working tonight. Right now I'm on a break."

Siegel looked at Zhanna. "Who's your friend?"

Zhanna wore a brightly colored neck scarf to cover her scar.

"This is my friend from Russia, Zhanna," Erika replied. Zhanna took a deep drag on her cigarette and blew the smoke in Siegel's face. One of the bodyguards stepped forward but Siegel put his hand out to stop him.

"A spicy broad, I like that," said an amused Siegel. "Do you speak English?" he asked Zhanna.

"Yes, I speak your English."

"You should see me about a job as a floor walker; you could work with your friend."

Zhanna loosened her scarf to reveal her hideous neck scar. "You do not want me as one of your floor women."

After seeing the scar, Siegel nodded then turned back to Erika. "Darling, we should get together sometime. I'll buy you dinner."

Just then a speeding car fishtailed around the corner and squealed to a stop where they all stood. Four men flung open car doors and emerged shooting. Siegel's bodyguards attempted to draw their guns but one was hit in the shoulder and the other knocked unconscious. Zhanna stabbed one of the attackers with a dagger she had tied under her pant leg, stabbing him in the torso. Erika jumped into the fray and knocked down and disarmed two of the men. She dislocated one of the men's shoulders, causing him to scream out in pain.

Bugsy Siegel lay prone on the walk and began to rise and pull his gun. Erika shouted, "Stay down!" and raced over and wrestled the gun away from Siegel. After Zhanna had used her knife on another attacker, the men decided to abort their mission. They all quickly dove back into the car, helping their wounded. Erika picked up another gun and with Siegel's in one hand and an attacker's gun in the other, opened up on the car as it sped away. She intentionally placed her shots high on the rear windshield so as not to hit any of Al Hodge's men ducking low inside.

"Let's get you back in the hotel," Erika told Siegel.

"No, not yet. My car is just down there. It's best to get away from here for awhile. You never know what else they might have planned.' Siegel flipped the keys to Erika. "You drive."

"What about your guards?"

One had a gunshot wound, the other was still unconscious.

"Leave those Schmucks there," Bugsy sneered, "They don't deserve our bother. Someone will see them and eventually call an ambulance. That's good enough for them, the worthless fucks."

They loaded into Siegel's new cream-colored Cadillac convertible. Erika and Zhanna in the front, Bugsy, used to being chauffeured, sat in the back.

"Where to?" Erika asked.

"Just get this thing going. Head into Old Havana. Make several turns along the way. I'll keep an eye out for a tail."

"Nobody is going to tail me for long; I know all the tricks," Erika responded.

"Were did you learn how to avoid a tail?" he asked. "And where did you learn to fight and shoot like that?"

"I was an agent for the German Abwehr during the war."

"Abwehr? What's that?"

"German military intelligence; I was a spy."

"You said when we hired you that you came from England. I remember because of your accent."

"My mother was British and I learned English from her. I did come here from London, I didn't lie about that, but I had been there only a few months."

"And what's the story on your friend?"

"Zhanna was a sniper and an assassin for the Soviet army."

"A Nazi spy and a Russian assassin." Siegel leaned back in his seat and said no more, just staring at the back of the women's heads.

Chapter 10

**Washington, D.C.
Saturday, 26 October 1946**

Leroy Carr was on an early morning telephone call with Al Hodge in Havana.

"How'd it go, Al?"

"Despite the fact Rogova stabbed two of our guys and Lehmann badly dislocated another agent's shoulder, it went fine," Hodge said sarcastically.

"That wasn't supposed to happen. The fighting had to be real, but avoid significant injuries. Zhanna was supposed to push her knife through clothing but at an angle so skin wasn't broken. How are the men doing?"

"They'll be okay. She at least avoided areas with major organs and didn't push the blade in too far. They got stitched up last night. The guy who will take the longest time to heal is Wilkerson. Erika did a number on his shoulder. He'll be in a sling for weeks."

Well, at least no one was killed, Al. We can be thankful for that."

"I guess you're right, Leroy. When you team up Lehmann and Rogova, worse things could have happened—and normally do."

"Did they tell Bugsy who they really were?"

"Yes. Erika told him she was a German spy during the war and Zhanna a Russian assassin.

"Okay. Things seem to be in place. Keep me informed, Al."

[Hotel Nacional, Havana—later that afternoon]
"It had to be one of Bonanno's crews," said Meyer Lansky. "We talked about he would retaliate for Paulie Villano."

"That's what I figure," Siegel responded. "Stupid move to try a hit down here. He should have waited for one my trips back to New York."

Lansky nodded. "Old Joe Bananas was never known as the sharpest tack in the five families."

"I'll have Albert hit them back."

"Not now," said Lansky. "As I said before, we can't afford a war right now. Our situation down here is too dicey. You'll have time for that later. Just beef up your personal security. Those two broads you told me about, the ones that saved your ass, the German and the Russian. Put them on your staff; they might come in handy since they speak those languages, but don't call them 'bodyguards.' It will raise too many questions. Call them your 'personal assistants' or some crap like that. And have a couple of male bodyguards around that look the part. We'll get you some better men than those two jokers that where with you last night."

[that evening]

Like nearly every night, tonight Erika was at work in her short cocktail dress on the casino floor. When someone tapped her on the shoulder, she turned, expecting to see to an older man with deep pockets (her normal clientele). This time it was a man in a gray flannel suit—a member of the hotel security staff.

"Mr. Siegel is giving you the rest of the night off," the man said without expression. "In one hour, meet him for dinner at his table in the Copa Showroom. Just tell the maitre d' that you are guests of Mr. Siegel."

"Guests? That means more than one."

"He wants you to bring your friend with you. The one from last night. He said you would understand."

Erika nodded. "Very well. Thank you."

Now she had to find Zhanna. Erika checked their room, and the hotel bars and restaurants. Erika was hoping Zhanna hadn't left the hotel. Finally she found her on one the verandas off to herself, smoking a Cuban cigar.

"Zhanna, I've been looking for you for twenty minutes," Erika said as she approached Zhanna's table.

"Why?"

"It's show time in the Copa."

Chapter 11

Copa Showroom, Hotel Nacional
Same day—Saturday, 26 October 1946

Erika and Zhanna went to their room and quickly changed clothes. Erika squeezed into another cocktail dress but this one had a longer shirt and was more suitable for dinner than the mini dresses she used during her floor walker duties. Zhanna also donned a dress and her ever present neck scarf. The women quickly touched up their makeup and headed down to the Copa room.

The Copa was the main showroom at the Nacional. Two smaller showrooms featured secondary acts, but the headliners always worked the Copa. Frank Sinatra, Tony Bennett, and Henny Youngman were just three of the famous entertainers who had headlined at the Copa in the past few months.

A large stage festooned with silk runners at first drew the eye's attention. The enormous dining area sported white linen covered tables that tiered upward from floor level. The premium tables sat at floor level just in front of the stage and the rest staggered on levels two feet higher as they rose to the rear. This allowed every diner an unobstructed view of the stage.

Tonight's headliners were showgirls flown in from the Moulin Rouge in Paris, but the show was yet to start and the stage sat silent when Erika and Zhanna arrived. The room was about half full of people drinking or already dining. As instructed, Erika told the maitre d' they were guests of Mr. Siegel. He grabbed two menus and led them to one of the front row tables; Siegel had not yet arrived. The maitre d' held their chairs while they sat. He told them a waiter would be by shortly for their drink orders.

Bugsy arrived with a curvy blonde on his arm before the drink waiter. "Hello, ladies."

Erika returned the greeting. "Hello, Mr. Siegel." Zhanna nodded.

Siegel didn't bother introducing his lady friend. Instead, he pulled out a wad of cash and handed it to her. "I've got some business to discuss, Doll. Why don't you go shopping and I'll see you later tonight."

The woman took the money, kissed Siegel's cheek and departed without saying a word.

Apparently Siegel's presence convinced the drink waiter to hop to it, and he walked up to the table as the mobster sat down. The man lit the table's candle.

"We don't need menus," Siegel told the waiter who held three of them in hand.

"What are you drinking, ladies?" Siegel asked. "You might want to try the martinis. Best this side of New York."

Erika ordered a brandy; Zhanna ordered a martini, but asked for vodka.

"I'll have a double Laphroaig on the rocks," Siegel told the waiter. "And tell the bartender to not take a nap before he makes the drinks."

"Yes, sir, Mr. Siegel. I'll bring them right over."

Before Siegel could pull out a pack of cigarettes and offer Erika and Zhanna one, the drinks arrived. Siegel held a gold and diamond encrusted lighter for the women as they lit up.

The food waiter showed up but Siegel told him they were going to have a couple of cocktails before dinner and he would summon him when they were ready to order food.

"Thanks for coming tonight," Siegel told Erika and Zhanna, as if they had a choice. "We talked some in the car last night but I don't remember thanking you for what you did. So thank you. It was surprising to say the least to find out one of our floor girls was a trained Nazi spy with the hand fighting and shooting skills that you have, Erika." Siegel prided himself on remembering names. "And that you had a friend who was a Russian sniper and assassin during the war."

There was a pause as Siegel waited for a response. Finally, Erika said, "That was Zhanna's and my past life. We are trying to move on. That's why we came to Cuba."

"Why Cuba? Are you on the lam?"

"Zhanna is wanted by the Russians and I'm wanted in the United States," Erika answered.

"What for?"

"We'd rather not talk about it."

"What for?" Siegel asked again firmly.

"I'm wanted for murder in two states," Erika answered.

Siegel laughed. "Who isn't?" He seemed to get a great kick out of his joke.

Siegel addressed Zhanna. "Zhanna, you haven't said a word. What's your story?"

"I left Russia and SMERSH without permission."

"SMERSH, what the hell is that?"

"I eliminated people for that organization."

"So, the Ivans' version of Murder, Inc."

Zhanna didn't comment.

"Let's order some food. I hope you two ladies are hungry. May I order for you?"

Without waiting for a reply, Siegel flagged over the waiter. "Bring us three large porterhouse steaks with lobster and all the trimmings. And another round of drinks. How would you like your steak cooked, ladies?"

Both Erika and Zhanna ordered medium rare; Bugsy medium.

"Women who eat a steak medium rare, I love it," said Siegel. Putting on his best front, he had yet to refer to them as 'broads' or 'dames.'

The floor show started. A magician first appeared on stage followed by a juggler. Then the girls of the Moulin Rouge took to the stage. Most were topless but with colorful and elaborate costumes with plenty of feathers and tall hats that drew as much attention as the women's breasts.

Bugsy, Erika, and Zhanna each had one more drink then two waiters delivered the food. The steaks were enormous; the candlestick centerpiece was moved aside and the three whole lobsters and a large bowl of salad were placed in the middle of the table. One of the waiters sliced a loaf of warm, freshly baked bread and the other placed a baked potato and sautéed mushrooms on each person's plate. Bugsy ordered some wine for the table.

All three began eating and conversation was sparse. When the women were almost finished, Bugsy took a sip of his Scotch and finally got down to the business of the night.

"I want both of you to work for me as bodyguards. I'll refer to you as my assistants. Erika, I know your room is not the best. I'll move you and Zhanna into a two-bedroom suite on my floor. The job means you'll have to travel with me back and forth to the States. Erika, I can protect you from the cops, and Zhanna from the Russians. The pay is good, a lot more than you're making now as a floor girl, Erika."

Leroy Carr was already protecting Erika in the States. The part where Siegel said he could protect Zhanna from the Russians was what perked both women's interest although neither showed any outward reaction. This was the mission to determine any links between the communists and the Mafia.

Erika looked at Zhanna who said, "No."

Lehmann knew this was a cagey move by her partner and she had to give her credit for playing her part well. Erika turned to Siegel, "Mr. Siegel, we appreciate your offer, but we'll decline."

Siegel looked shocked. "Why?"

"Like I said, we are trying for a new start."

Bugsy Siegel was not a man used to being declined on an offer. "I would hate to see the people searching for you find out where you are," he said with a subtle tone of menace. "You will give me one month. After that, I promise you can walk away with no hard feelings or problems from me or my associates. You'll start tomorrow. More wine?" Siegel raised the carafe. "Oh, and I have a soufflé coming for dessert."

Finishing off the soufflé kept them there until the show ended with the famous Moulin Rouge Can-Can.

Part 2

Lorelei : a siren of Germanic legend whose singing lures Rhine
River boatman to destruction on a reef.

— Merriam Webster's Collegiate Dictionary
Tenth Edition

Chapter 12

Hotel Nacional, Havana
Next day—Sunday, 27 October 1946

The original four New York mobsters who had hired Erika as a floor walker once again sat around Meyer Lansky's private conference table in the Hotel Nacional: Lucky Luciano, Albert Anastasia, Meyer Lansky, and Benjamin Siegel. Hiring members of a crew was not taken lightly and this had drawn Anastasia back from New York and brought Luciano out of cover from his hideaway on the west coast of Cuba.

Luciano started. "I spoke with Mangano last night before I flew down this morning, Siegel. The Don is not on board with two women being brought into a crew."

"He hasn't met the women," Siegel retorted. "I'll smooth things over with the Don."

"Tell us again about these two dames," Lucky said.

"I told you everything already. Erika, the blonde we hired as a floor walker a few weeks ago was a German spy during the war. That's where she learned her combat skills. The Russian, Zhanna, was a sniper and assassin for the Russkies."

"And they are both wanted?" Lansky added.

"So what?" How many guys on our crews haven't done time or are currently being investigated for one thing or another? I've seen what these women can do. They saved my life."

"I don't tell you guys who you can or cannot hire on a crew," Siegel continued. "I asked for this meeting as a courtesy out of respect. The women are in my crew. Subject closed. By the way, I'll be taking the women and my male bodyguards to Las Vegas in the next few days. They need me there to supervise some construction at the Flamingo."

The other mobsters saw that Bugsy had made up his mind. Lansky moved on to a different subject. "Albert, what's the latest out of the Bonanno family about the attempted hit on Ben the other night?"

"They're all still saying they had nothing to do with it. That none of their men have ever been to Cuba and we can check the passport records department."

"I don't buy it," said Siegel. "It had to be Bonanno in retaliation for Fat Paulie Villano. Bonanno could have hired outside help for the hit to cover his ass."

◊ ◊ ◊

Just after lunchtime, Erika and Zhanna were moved from Erika's tiny utility room reserved for hotel employees who did not have local homes. They were moved to a swank two-bedroom suite on Bugsy Siegel's penthouse floor. The two bedrooms would allow the women a measure of privacy. Siegel showed up just moments after they moved in. He gave the bellmen who moved their luggage a generous tip. One of the bellmen had delivered a new set of expensive leather luggage for each woman, a gift from Siegel.

"What do you think, ladies? A bit nicer and roomier than your room down by the boiler, wouldn't you say, Erika?"

"Very nice," she answered. "And definitely a lot cooler."

"Here's how things are done with all my bodyguards," said Siegel. "You're on call 24-hours-a day. That doesn't mean you can't go out and have a life, but I expect you to tell me where you will be at all times. Sometimes my need for you can come up quickly and I don't want to have to send out a pack of hillbillies with bloodhounds to find you. Are we clear about that?"

"Yes, Mr. Siegel. May I ask about the luggage?"

"Tomorrow I'll spend most of my time clearing up some business here at the hotel, then on Tuesday we leave for the States." He handed each woman $300 in cash. "We'll stop for a couple of days in New York before heading out west. You can buy some clothes in New York. I have many associates among the Jews in the garment district. I'll set you up with one of them. You'll get a lot for your money. As far as the clothes you buy, make sure you look sharp, but as respectable business women, not as gold diggers. We also have to get you a piece so be sure your clothes are such that you can wear a shoulder holster or a holster in your pants behind your back. Do you have any particular handgun you prefer?"

Chapter 13

New York City
Tuesday, 29 October 1947

Yesterday, Siegel sent his two male bodyguards, Saul and Nico, ahead to New York. Saul was Jewish like Siegel, Nico an Italian from Sicily. Their primary job was to rent Siegel's room at the Waldorf=Astoria and watch it during the night so the FBI didn't have access to plant bugs. The male bodyguards would stay in Siegel's suite; Erika and Zhanna in a room directly across the hallway.

This morning, Siegel and his two female "associates" left Havana at nine o'clock and after a brief layover in Miami, boarded a Boeing Stratoliner and touched down at La Guardia at just after four in the afternoon.

"How long are we going to be in New York, Mr. Siegel?" Erika asked as they disembarked.

"Three nights. We'll lay low tonight in our hotel. You can order room service. Tomorrow you two can get your clothes and I'll have one of my men get your guns. Tomorrow night we'll go out on the town. I want to visit some old friends. The next night we have a sit down with Joe Banana. Vito Genovese called for it to try and clear the bad blood between the Bonanno family and ours."

The women shopped for clothes on 5th Ave the next day. While they were out, Erika called Leroy Carr, filled him in, and gave him the names of Saul and Nico.

"What are their last names?" asked Carr.

"I don't know. Siegel introduced them only as Saul and Nico."

"I'll see if we have anyone in our files with those names associated with Siegel. In the meantime, be careful and check in at every opportunity."

When they left the Waldorf that evening, Saul did the driving with Nico riding shotgun. Bugsy and the women sat in the back of the spacious, burgundy '46 Cadillac limo—a car that fit the flash of Bugsy Siegel.

Earlier that day, Siegel handed over handguns to the women. Erika had asked for a Beretta semi-auto and Zhanna a Smith & Wesson .38 snub revolver.

The night was taken up by Bugsy and the group going around to several of his old haunts frequented by mobsters with Bugsy and his old cohorts engaging in a lot of back slapping and lighthearted vulgar name calling.

There was only one incident during the night but it was a significant one.

At a small bar called Roma in the Bronx, one of Bugsy's old buddies inquired about Erika and Zhanna.

"Ben, do you bang these broads one at a time or do them both together?" The man was extremely large, at least 6'5" with multiple scars on his face.

As the laughter from the others started, the man said, "What do you say you give me a crack at them?"

Zhanna picked up the man's drink and threw it in his face. He jerked back and grunted, then rose from the table to confront Zhanna. Others rose and Erika pulled her pistol. Saul and Nico also pulled out their guns.

"Back off, Frankenstein!" Erika shouted. "I don't think anyone here is bulletproof."

"These women are my associates," said Siegel to the enormous man with liquor dripping from his face. "I think you might want to reconsider your remark."

The man sat down. "I meant no disrespect, Ben."

"Good. Then that's settled." Siegel signaled his four bodyguards to lower their weapons.

◊ ◊ ◊

[Thursday evening]
The meeting between Joe Bonanno and Bugsy Siegel took place at a restaurant in Brooklyn called Bruno's. Erika and Zhanna were not privy to the conversation and they stood for nearly two hours with

Saul and Nico outside the small private dining area. Along with them were four of Joe Bonanno's body guards.

After Siegel finally came out of the room, they all loaded into the Cadillac and headed back to the Waldorf. Siegel offered no comment about the meeting and Erika knew she couldn't ask questions on such a matter. The main comment from Siegel concerned their next journey.

"Tomorrow we leave for Las Vegas. Right now the town is just a hick gas stop along the highway but I'm building a hotel and casino there that will make the Nacional look like a flea bag."

Chapter 14

Grand Central Station, New York
Wednesday, 30 October 1946

The PA voice for Grand Central Station was always loud and clear. A bell sounded, signaling important information was forthcoming.

"THE 915 TO CHICAGO, WITH A STOP IN CLEVELAND WILL DEPART IN TWENTY MINUTES. ALL PASSENGERS PLEASE PROGRESS TO TRACK 13 FOR FINAL LOADING."

Bugsy and his two female bodyguards had already settled themselves into a first-class cabin on the Super Chief. Bugsy had stops to make in Chicago and St. Louis—meetings with fellow mobsters investing in his new hotel in Nevada. They would spend a short night in Chicago before boarding their train to St. Louis. After that, they would fly to Los Angeles (apparently more business) and finish the journey to Las Vegas by car.

Once again, Saul and Nico had been sent ahead, making connections to Las Vegas. Erika and Zhanna assumed this must be standard procedure for the mobster to send a front team ahead anytime he was on the move. It gave the women some satisfaction that apparently Siegel felt comfortable with just the two of them as his bodyguards. Evidently they had done a good job of convincing him. The trip to Chicago would take 15 hours because of a stop in Cleveland. Then when business in the Windy City was complete, they would switch trains for the journey to St. Louis.

When the steel wheels beneath them jerked and the train finally moved, Siegel, who had a habit of ignoring someone talking to him as if they didn't exist, seemed to be in a chatty mood.

"Let's order some breakfast ladies," Siegel said. "We'll have them bring it here." Siegel pulled menus from a net pouch hanging on the wall. He had found out by now that both women were hearty eaters. Especially Zhanna who had sometimes gone without food for days during the war when supplies could not reach the forward positions.

Siegel ordered eggs Benedict, coffee and orange juice. Erika looked over the menu and ordered the biggest breakfast listed. Call a 'Texas Breakfast' it came with bacon and eggs, biscuits and gravy, a mountain of hash browns with flour tortillas for the refried beans, oh . . . and a fruit cup. It took two plates to serve a Texas Breakfast. Zhanna ordered the same.

"Eat up girls while I fill you in on what will happen over the next few days," said Siegel. "The airstrip in Las Vegas is right now used mainly by farmers for their crop dusters. The runways are not long enough for a commercial plane to land. Saul and Nico, who are already in the air, will land in Salt Lake City and board a small chartered plane to take them the rest of the way. After we get done with business in Chicago and St. Louis, we'll fly to Los Angeles then drive to Vegas."

"Anything special we need to know as your bodyguards about these meetings in Chicago and St. Louis?" Zhanna asked before she shoveled a mouthful of biscuits and gravy in her mouth.

Siegel shook his head. "Everything should go smoothly. These are investors who are counting on me to succeed. If they have muscle in the room with them, then I'll bring you into the room with me. If they have their guards wait outside, like last night at Bruno's, that's where you'll be. It will all depend on them. Because you're females it takes people time to adjust to you, but word spreads quickly in La Cosa Nostra. Many already know about you saving my life, and about you backing down those low-level clowns at the Roma on Monday night. You should start getting the respect you deserve. Just remember to stay calm and don't overreact to words that are spoken. I'll let you know if I need your help, understand?"

Both Erika and Zhanna nodded.

Siegel looked at Erika. "I've been meaning to ask you, Erika, since you are a former Nazi, what do you think of Jews."

"I know you are Jewish, Mr. Siegel. I have never had any hard feelings for your people and never understood my government's attitude. Yes, I was a member of the Nazi Party, but I wouldn't be working for you if I shared the feelings of the Party."

Siegel studied her for a moment and moved on. "When people are around, I want both of you to keep referring to me as Mr. Siegel, just like Saul and Nico do. But when we're alone, like now, you can call me 'Ben.'"

Bugsy Siegel would call on his Valkyrie bodyguards much sooner than he had expected. In fact, an incident happened just shortly after they stepped off the train at Chicago's Dearborn Station.

◊ ◊ ◊

Trouble seemed never far from Bugsy Siegel. At the meeting with the heads of the Chicago families and some of their top lieutenants, Bugsy kept staring at one of the mid-level management men. The man drawing Siegel's attention was Rocco Fishchetti, one of Al Capone's cousins.

From Erika's and Zhanna's standpoint, the meeting was boring but thankfully not long. Siegel's train had not arrived until midnight so everyone there seemed content to stay on business and avoid sidebars. The subject was kept almost entirely to the progress of the Flamingo hotel in Las Vegas, an enterprise many in the room invested in heavily. When the men stood up at 2 a.m., signaling the meeting was over, handshakes ended the night.

On the way out, as the men disbursed to their cars, Siegel caught up with Rocco Fishchetti. Erika and Zhanna were on his heels.

"Rocco, how ya doing?" Siegel asked.

"Oh, Ben, it was good to see you again. I'm doin' okay."

"You owe me four G's you sonuvabitch and I want my money."

"What are you talking about, Ben?"

"You need to work on your memory, Rocco. There was a little poker game the last time I was in Chicago. You were short and I fronted you four G's. Remember now?"

Fishchetti hem-hawed for a moment, then said, "It completely slipped my mind, Ben. You know I'm good for it."

"The fact that you owe me four G's slipped your mind? That's the type of memory loss that can get you dead, Rocco. My car's right here. Get in."

"What a minute, Ben. I'm not getting in any car." Suddenly he felt a gun barrel behind his ear and heard a trigger click.

"Get in the car, asshole," Erika said as she grabbed his collar and held her Beretta to his head.

"Ladies, I'll drive," said Siegel. "You two keep Rocco company in the back seat."

Rocco still tried to talk his way out of getting in the car but when Zhanna pulled a dagger and held it to his belly he knew the debate was over. As he bent over to get in the back seat, Erika put her shoe on his butt and kicked him into the backseat. Zhanna went around to the other side so Rocco was pinned in the middle.

"I'm staying at the Imperial Hotel, Rocco," Siegel said as he drove away. "I leave the hotel at seven o'clock this morning. That gives you about five hours to come up with my money. I expect it to be in the hotel desk safe when I check out. Understand?"

"I can't raise it that fast, Ben. Give me a couple of days. I'll wire the money to you in Las Vegas."

"Ladies," Siegel said.

Erika took a hold of Rocco's right thumb and dislocated it. The scream came just a second before Zhanna used the dagger to slice through Rocco's pant leg and penetrate the skin.

Siegel slammed on the breaks. "Now get the fuck out of my car you rat bastard!"

"I need a doctor, Ben!"

"If my money isn't at the hotel desk when I check out, you'll need an undertaker, not a doctor, Rocco."

Zhanna opened her car door, dragged the injured man out into the middle of the street and kicked him hard in the ribs a couple of times for good measure.

As they drove away, Siegel asked, "Is there much blood on the seat?"

"A little bit," Erika said.

"Zhanna, blood is messy. Remember where you are the next time. I don't really give a shit about this car because it's a rental, but we still have to clean it up because blood is evidence. If you're in a car, just break bones like Erika. It saves on cleaning time."

Chapter 15

To Los Angeles and Las Vegas
Thursday, 31 October 1946

Not surprisingly, Rocco Fishchetti had managed to find $4000, and it was waiting in an envelope in the hotel safe when Bugsy and the women checked out. The seven-hour train ride to St. Louis was uneventful, as was the brief meeting with local mobsters investing in Siegel's Flamingo Hotel. As he had told the Chicago mob, Bugsy talked about a grand opening around Christmas.

The trio boarded a United Airlines DC-3 at four in the afternoon. With no alternate stops, the plane touched down at the Los Angeles airport at two o'clock the next morning.

The taxi delivered them to a lavish, seven-bedroom Beverly Hills estate owned by Siegel's mistress, the actress Virginia Hill. Luckily, Erika and Zhanna had grabbed some sleep on the plane because Hill, despite the hour, had waiting for Siegel a private cocktail party. Her butler prepared the drinks; the maid delivered them along with assorted canapés.

Hill stared at the two women. "Where are Nico and Saul?" she asked Bugsy.

"They're in Vegas getting things in order."

"Where did you find those two?" Hill asked of Erika and Zhanna when they were out of earshot. "The blonde looks like a middleweight boxer and the other one a Gypsy knife thrower."

Bugsy laughed. "You don't know how close you came, Baby. They both fought in the war; the blonde for the Germans and the other one for the Reds. The blonde, Erika, was working as a floorwalker at the Nacional until one night she and Zhanna saved my life. If it wasn't for them, I might not be here with you tonight, Darling. Now whadda ya say we skip out of here and put that big bedroom of yours to use?"

[Washington. D.C. — late that afternoon]
"Leroy, it's Erika. Zhanna and I are in Las Vegas."

"What happened? I haven't heard from you since before you left New York. I instructed you to check in from each stop."

"We arrived in Chicago and St. Louis in the middle of the night, Siegel had brief meetings then we had a few hours in a hotel and that has been it. Zhanna and I have had no time to ourselves. There was no safe way to contact you."

"I assume it's safe to talk now."

"Yes," Erika answered. *"Siegel's laid up with some dancer trying to get a job at the casino and he gave us a couple of hours off. I'm calling from a pay phone outside a gas station down the road from the hotel."*

"Fill me in."

"From what I heard at the meetings in Chicago and St. Louis, I think some of the Dons are disgruntled with Siegel and his Flamingo Hotel. He's promising them a grand opening on December 26th, but I saw the place today. Half the rooms aren't ready, the bar isn't finished. The stage, dining rooms and kitchen all need a lot more work. He's got his work cut out for him if he wants to open by Christmas."

"Siegel's made his bed with the Dons so he has to sleep with them. That's not our concern. We received intel a couple of days ago that Lucky Luciano has called for a big conference in Havana that will also take place around Christmas. As we speak, Luciano and Lansky are trying to ensure that all the big names in La Cosa Nostra will be there. We have to make sure you and Zhanna are there for that."

"How are we going to do that if Siegel is planning on opening the Flamingo a few days later? With all the problems he's got, he'll have to be here, not in Cuba, and he'll want Zhanna and me with him."

"Erika, do you think you're the only one who does any work around here?" We've got moles in the New York mob monitoring this situation. The communists are in Cuba, not hiding behind the cactus in Nevada. If this Havana conference becomes a reality, that conference is going to be a lot more important to our mission objectives than having you and Zhanna out there in the desert chasing tumbleweeds. If the meeting in Havana takes place, you and Zhanna will be there. Find a way."

Chapter 16

Bayamo, Cuba
Monday, 04 November 1946

The small Russian outpost in Cuba had set up shop not in Havana, but in the town of Bayamo in western Cuba, about as far away from the capital as one could get and still be on the island.

The reasons for this were many, starting with the Monroe Doctrine of 1823 and expanding from there when the Americans decided after the Second World War that the communists were now the biggest threat to the United States.

However, the Americans could not keep a communist presence out of Cuba entirely since the Cuban government had legalized the party and had allowed it to be active since before the war.

But the Russians knew the Americans could make life hard for them and for Cuba, so instead of opening a full-fledged embassy in Havana, the Russians kept a low profile, working out of a hotel in Bayamo.

As he did every day, Soviet colonel Yegor Kuznetsov sat at his desk enjoying his cup of Cuban coffee before beginning that day's work; a knock on the door diverted his attention from the coffee. Desk intercoms were being installed but were not yet functional. Kuznetsov knew it was Lieutenant Egerow, his aide.

"What is it, Egerow?" Kuznetsov shouted at the door, irked that his peaceful time of the day shared with his coffee was being disturbed.

"Major Volkov is here, Colonel. He insists it is urgent."

The colonel could hear only half of what was said through the thick wooden door.

"Open the door, idiot!"

The lieutenant gingerly opened the door and repeated the information. Kuznetsov sighed. "Send him in then get out!"

Major Kir Volkov was the Cuban contingent's chief of intelligence. Volkov, a member of the Soviet NKVD, came in and sat down without Kuznetsov's permission. The NKVD was the Soviets' version of the

British MI-6 or the American CIA, and, if an analogy were to be made to the now defunct Third Reich, the NKVD served as the secret police, much like the Gestapo.

The arrogant bastard, Kuznetsov thought. *The NKVD thought they ran everything and should be kowtowed too.*

"What is it, Major?" Kuznetsov asked curtly. "I have a lot of work to do."

"I can see that, Comrade Colonel." Volkov glanced at Kuznetsov's coffee and smirked.

"Let's not waste time, Volkov. You're here for a reason. What is it?"

Volkov tossed a folder across the desk. Kuznetsov opened it. Inside were photographs of two women walking out of a hotel.

"Are you going to tell me who these people are or are we going to play charades?"

"Look closely at the woman with the black hair," Volkov said.

Kuznetsov looked impatiently at the NKVD major then pulled a magnifying glass from a desk drawer. After looking closely for a moment with the glass, the colonel paled.

"Is that . . .?

Volkov interrupted him. "Yes, that's her—Zhanna Rogova. Have you ever met her?"

"No," Kuznetsov answered. "I've only seen the *Wanted* posters."

"The photo was taken outside the Hotel Nacional in Havana one week ago," Volkov added. "The man in the center is the American gangster Benjamin 'Bugsy' Siegel. The other two men are just common leg breakers—the type most of these American gangster characters like to surround themselves with. The other woman is apparently also working for Siegel as his personal protection."

"Who's the other woman—the blonde?"

"I don't know yet, but I'll find out. You can rely on the NKVD to always find out."

Chapter 17

A cabana on the Cuban beach west of Havana
Wednesday, 06 November 1946

Meyer Lansky sat in Lucky Luciano's beachfront cabana sipping a Cuba Libre, a popular island cocktail made from Cuban rum, usually Bacardi, and Coca-Cola.

"Looks like everything is in place, Lucky. The top members of the New York and Chicago families can be here in December. I haven't heard back yet from the all the Dons in St. Louis and Kansas City but they'll be here. The St. Louis and KC Dons are paranoid about New York and Chicago. They'll be here just to keep tabs on anything that could affect them. I've set the start date for December 20th and made sure the hotel manager keeps all the best suites open for that weekend."

"What about Joe Bonanno?" Luciano asked.

"He'll be invited. Whether he comes or not, I don't know."

"That's a good move, Meyer. That keeps the pressure on him to keep the peace."

"What will we do about our Russian associates? They're bound to find out about the conference."

"We'll include them," Luciano advised. "But never in the meetings with the families. Set up separate times to meet with them."

Meyer nodded and sipped his drink. "The Russians have only a couple of men who speak English. Most of the Russians they sent here who speak a second language speak Spanish. We'll need our own translators to make sure what they are telling us is accurately translated. I don't trust any Russian interpreters."

"Good point," said Luciano. "Any ideas? What about that guy who works for Anastasia. You know the guy I'm talking about. The guy who speaks with the Russian accent."

"That's a Bulgarian accent, Lucky. Anastasia's guy speaks Bulgarian, not Russian."

Both men paused and took a drink.

Lánsky continued. "Those two female bodyguards Ben recently picked up speak Russian. One is from Russia. The other is German but supposedly speaks fluent Russian."

"How do you know that?"

"Ben told me when he came to me for clearance to hire them."

Luciano thought for a moment. "Okay. Make sure those broads are here for the meetings."

"Ben might object. He's out in Las Vegas trying to open the new hotel and casino."

"I don't give a fuck what Siegel objects to. He can get more bodyguards from Anastasia. In fact, send Anastasia out there to Nevada to relay the news personally. I've already been contacted by some members of the various families who think Siegel is skimming off some of the investors' money. If his cockamamie Las Vegas idea doesn't work out, Siegel will have a lot more to worry about than a couple of dames he probably keeps around just to screw." He looked at Lansky's drink. "Looks like your drink is getting low, Meyer."

From necessity, Luciano had picked up some rudimentary Spanish to establish some basic communication with his housekeeper who spoke no English. He pointed to the drinks and said, "Carmen, dos más, por favor."

A stooped, elderly woman who looked like she had worked much too hard in her life nodded and left to fetch the drinks.

So now, although she did not know it yet, Erika's problem on how to get herself and Zhanna to Cuba for the mob conference had been settled without her lifting a finger, thanks to Lucky Luciano.

◊ ◊ ◊

Later that day, after Meyer Lansky had left to return to Havana, Carmen swept the cabana and fixed dinner for Luciano. Her work finished for the day, she began her grueling seven-mile walk home to her village of Mariel. She stopped at the only phone in the village, a phone booth outside the post office, and called collect to Washington, D.C. Using the code phrase "a new tropical storm is due" got the collect call accepted and she was immediately patched through the CIA switchboard and to her D.C. handler—a Major Sheila Reid who also served as Leroy Carr's executive assistant.

In perfect English, Carmen relayed to Major Reid what she had overheard that day.

Chapter 18

Las Vegas
Friday, 08 November 1946

The airplane carrying Albert Anastasia, also known as the "Mad Hatter" or "Lord High Executioner," touched down on the gravel airstrip in Las Vegas shortly before noon. The head of *Murder, Inc.* had a taxi waiting to take him and his three "associates" to the Flamingo Hotel. The taxi was compliments of Bugsy Siegel. The three men with Anastasia were in reality bodyguards handpicked by Anastasia himself from his stable of Murder, Inc. hit men. These three were among his best, and all had numerous killings to add to their other dubious credits.

Siegel was waiting outside for Anastasia when the taxi pulled up to the hotel.

"Albert, great to see you! Welcome to my little oasis in the desert. Sorry I had to send a taxi and not a limo. Our limo and driver won't be here until the opening in December."

The exterior of the Flamingo was nearly finished. The entire façade was a bright pink and the neon Flamingo just above the entrance that greeted guests now flashed on and off.

Inside, Siegel had made considerable headway in just the few days since he arrived. The kitchen and bar were now functional. The stage was nearly complete. Yet Siegel's biggest problem was still only half of the rooms were finished and ready for guests. Most of the guest room problems concerned getting the bathroom plumbing installed. Needless to say, there remained a lot of work to do if Siegel were to make good on his promise to the Dons of a late December grand opening.

Siegel put his arm around Anastasia's shoulder. "You and your men are probably hungry. Let's go inside. I've got the chef, kitchen staff and some of the wait staff on duty just for you guys."

Bugsy led the way to a table where a huge bowl of enormous, iced-downed shrimp already sat waiting to be eaten. He waved over a waiter and the men gave the man their drink choices. Saul and Nico were there and sat down with Anastasia's men.

"I'll get right to the point, Ben," Anastasia said. "Where are those two broads that you claim are your bodyguards?"

"So that's why you're here," said Siegel. "I don't *claim* they are my bodyguards. They *are* my bodyguards. They're in their room. Why?"

"Bring them down; we need them here for lunch."

"Why?" Siegel repeated.

"Just get them the fuck down here," Anastasia said impatiently, then smiled to cover up. Siegel was an elite member of the mob so Anastasia had to treat him as such. "As a favor to me, Ben."

Siegel took a moment. He was a hard man to intimidate, even by a scary character like the much larger and built like a bulldog head of Murder's Inc., Albert Anastasia. It was more out of curiosity than pressure from Anastasia's bullying that convinced Siegel to say, "Nico, find Erika and Zhanna and ask them to come down."

When Nico left, Siegel asked Anastasia, "What's this all about, Albert?"

"I was sent here by Lucky and Meyer Lansky to talk to you about the conference in Havana next month. I'm sure you know about it."

"Yeah, I know about it. I've already told Meyer I can't be there because I'll be opening this place about the same time."

"Lucky is going to meet with some of the Russians who have backed us with some of the New York union problems. The commies won't be included in the meetings with the Dons. Luciano and Lansky will meet with the Ivans separately. We'll need translators and Lansky told Lucky that both of those female bodyguards of yours speak Russian. Is that right?"

"Yeah, that's right, but I can't spare them right now—I'm close to opening this place. There has to be other immigrants on the payroll who speak Russian, especially among the New York Longshoreman workers."

"The decision has been made by Luciano himself, Ben. He asked me to loan you a couple of my men to replace the women while they are away. Luciano said he'd pick up the tab for my men's salaries. That's a good deal for you, Ben. And in the end, we can sit here and yammer away all day and it won't change anything. The Cappo di tutti cappa has made his decision."

After hearing that the "Boss of all Bosses" had made up his mind, Siegel knew there was no sense arguing any further.

Finally, Erika and Zhanna were seen walking down the stairs behind Nico.

"I'll hand it to you, Ben," Anastasia commented after seeing the women. "Most of the guys in the family think these women are a couple more of your cumare (Italian slang for 'mistress'). "But they actually look like bodyguards."

"I'd advise you to tell your men not to call them a cumare to their faces," Siegel said. "Somebody's likely to get hurt."

Anastasia thought Siegel was joking and started to laugh. He saw Siegel was serious and said, "So you're telling me they are a couple of bad-ass broads."

"The blonde was a Nazi spy during the war and shoots a handgun as good or better than any guy you have in your crew. You might remember her. You sat in on her hiring interview as a floor girl."

Siegel continued, "The dark haired woman is Russian and was a sniper and later an assassin."

"A Russian assassin and a Nazi spy? I don't know whether to be impressed or to laugh my ass off."

Erika and Zhanna finally arrived at the table and sat down. Without emotions of any kind showing on their faces, they looked around at Anastasia and his henchmen who stared back at them. This went on for several minutes. Finally, Erika broke the stare-down. "I know who you are," she said to Anastasia. "You were among the men who hired me as a casino floor girl at the Nacional. I've also read about you in the papers."

"All good stuff I hope," grinned the head of Murder, Inc.

"I won't go that far," Erika retorted.

Anastasia laughed loudly. "I like this gal, Ben."

Erika said, "Since Zhanna and I were called down here, I assume you have business that affects us. Are we going to hear it? Or will we sit here all afternoon with your three goons staring blankly at us like they are dummies in the waxworks?"

One of Anastasia's men—the one seated beside Zhanna—cursed then stood up. Zhanna rose quickly and pressed her handgun to his left ear.

"Mr. Anastasia," Erika said, "I'd hate to see my friend decorate your expensive suit with this gentleman's brains. If I'm not mistaken, your suit is an Anderson & Sheppard, is it not? It would take a lot of dry cleaning. By the way, I admire your taste. You look very dapper."

Siegel ordered Zhanna to put down the gun. Anastasia told his man to sit down. Anastasia remained pokerfaced, but inside he had formed an immediate admiration for the women. *What I couldn't do with a couple of dames like these two,* he thought to himself. He decided right then that when their translator job for Lucky was finished, he would do whatever it took to take the women away from Bugsy Siegel.

"Well," said Bugsy, "not exactly the way I thought the introductions would go, but now that we all are friends, let's eat. Albert, I know you and your men must be starving." He summoned a waiter and ordered steaks all around.

During lunch there was a brief amount of small talk, almost all of which came from Bugsy. At last, Siegel told Erika and Zhanna what they already knew. Leroy Carr had relayed the information to them through Al Hodge two days ago—after the phone call from Carmen.

"This translator crap won't last long," Bugsy assured the women. "Then you'll be back here with me."

A slight smirk could be detected on Albert Anastasia's face.

Chapter 19

Hotel Nacional, Havana
Sunday, 01 December 1946

Lucky Luciano had ordered his Russian-to-English translators to be back in Cuba by the first of December. He wanted time to go over things with them before the meetings with the Soviets began later that month.

So, after three boring weeks in Las Vegas spending most of their time following around construction crews working on Siegel's *Flamingo* to ensure none of them included FBI men planting bugs, Erika and Zhanna were now once again checked into a suite at the Hotel Nacional.

Their first order of business was a clandestine meeting with Al Hodge who had remained in Havana in their absence. Since Erika was no longer a floor walker, the old ruse of her visiting Hodge's room for paid sex was no longer viable. They were forced to return to secret meetings outside the hotel.

Erika and Zhanna stood alone at a taxi stand in Old Havana when a Coco taxi pulled up and stopped. Coco taxis were commonly seen in Havana. In these three-wheeled vehicles, the driver sat exposed to the elements in the front. The maximum of two passengers sat in the back, covered by a canopy. The small motors wouldn't power the vehicle much faster than a bicycle, but the Coco taxis would get you there sooner or later. Erika confirmed the taxi number and she and Zhanna got in the back. The driver was Al Hodge who wore a cabbie hat, makeup that made him look more Latin, and a pasted-on mustache.

Erika and Zhanna settled in as Hodge cut back out into traffic. A truck honked; the driver unhappy at being forced to apply his brakes. The driver delivered what was surely a vulgarity-laced tirade as he passed. Hodge didn't understand the Spanish, but he gave the truck driver the one-finger salute anyway. The women laughed. Here was a top figure in the CIA flipping off a truck driver.

"You look cute, Al," Erika said.

Zhanna also got in her critique of Hodge's disguise. "He looks like a circus clown. Just give him a red wig and some big orange shoes."

"I'll take Erika's review if it's all the same to you, Zhanna. So what's up, ladies?"

"Nothing," Erika answered. "We flew in from Miami and landed around noon. After getting checked in at the hotel, we met briefly with Meyer Lansky then we headed down here to meet you. That's about it. One good thing is, since Siegel is not here, we are basically unsupervised. Lansky told us to check in with him once a day. Besides that, we can do what we want until Luciano decides to call us in for these get-togethers we were told he wants to have with us before the meetings with the Soviets."

Hodge nodded. "We couldn't ask for a better set up. Just the fact the mob needs you as translators, confirms our suspicions that the communists are involved with the New York Mafia in some fashion."

"What about Zhanna?" Erika asked. "She's on the Soviets Top Wanted list, and they know about me after the last mission to rescue Hedy Lamarr in Poland. We have to be concerned with our covers holding up."

"Leroy and I talked that over," Hodge said as he turned left on the Padre Varela. "It's a concern for sure, but one where we have a couple of things working in our favor. For the Russians, this Cuban outpost is considered one of the lowest places to be assigned. They don't send their top people here so we're banking on your covers holding up. Regardless, we have no choice but to give this translator assignment a try. We lucked into this. You'll be privy to all the negotiations between the Mafia and the Soviets. That's an intelligence bonanza we can't just walk away from. If at any time you think your covers are blown get to a safe place and contact me. We'll fly you out of here immediately."

Chapter 20

Bayamo, Cuba
Tuesday, 03 December 1946

Unfortunately for the Americans, they were unaware that Lucky Luciano's housekeeper, Carmen, worked both sides of the fence. She also collected money from the Russians for any intelligence she could relay from Luciano's cabana.

That same day she called Washington she dropped another peso in the telephone's coin slot and gave the operator a telephone number in Bayamo. Carmen didn't speak Russian, but the Russians always had on hand a translator for when any of their Cuban moles called.

Now, the Soviets knew that Bugsy Siegel's female bodyguards would be working as translators during the meetings to be held with the American gangsters later in the month. They also knew one of these women was Zhanna Rogova—currently listed number one on the NKVD Most Wanted list because of her flip to the Americans.

"Comrade Colonel, we now have the identity of the second woman," Major Volkov, the head of the NKVD in Cuba, said as he sat down in front of Colonel Kuznetsov's desk. A portrait of Marshal Stalin hung on the wall just above Kuznetsov's head. A Russian flag stood limp on a standard just to the side of Stalin's portrait.

"Is this the blonde you are talking about?" Kuznetsov asked for clarity as he scanned the photographs Volkov had sent him earlier. "The one seen here with Rogova in the photographs from outside the Hotel Nacional?"

"That's correct. Her name is Erika Lehmann. She's German. During the war her codename was *Lorelei* and she was considered the top spy for the German Abwehr. Obviously both Rogova and Lehmann are now working for the Americans. They teamed up for a mission backed by the CIA this past spring in Poland. All the details are in this folder." Volkov slid it across the desk.

"What are your plans, Major? I want anything you're planning to be cleared by Moscow."

"Obviously, our mission is simple. We want to capture or eliminate Rogova. We are not concerned about Rogova's German partner unless she gets in the way. All this is already approved by General Polzin in Moscow."

"I will check on that," said Kuznetsov. "As you know, we are in a politically sensitive state of affairs here in Cuba."

"Feel free to check with General Polzin," Volkov said impatiently. Polzin was the head of the NKVD and served as that organization's liaison with the Politburo. Polzin even had access to Stalin when needed.

"Very well," said Kuznetsov. "Tell me more about your plan."

"Grusha is on her way here. As you might know, she has an aversion to flying so she's currently at sea aboard a commercial ocean liner. We thought that more discreet than bringing her here on one of our naval ships. She is scheduled to arrive on Saturday."

"Grusha! Is having her involved in this really necessary? She's impossible to work with and can never be kept under control."

(Although her last name was Mustafina, a surname wasn't necessary to the higher-ups in the Soviet military or Politburo. Her first name alone identified her.)

"But she gets the job done," Volkov said. "The NKVD men who have been assigned to me here in Cuba are not among our most highly trained and cannot deal with Zhanna Rogova by themselves," Volkov admitted honestly. "The truth is, we're going to need a creature like Grusha."

Chapter 21

Hotel Nacional, Havana
Thursday, 05 December 1946

Lucky Luciano wasn't keen on the idea of people knowing the location of the cabana west of Havana where he was laying low. So, instead of having the female interpreters brought to his obscure bungalow, his driver delivered him to the Hotel Nacional. The hotel was not a place where Luciano couldn't be seen; it was simply a place where, for the time being, he shouldn't be seen too often. For Luciano, this meeting with the Russian interpreters was one of those times that warranted a trip to the hotel over a meeting at his cabana with two women he didn't know.

Luciano told Meyer Lansky that he would be at the hotel around noon, so Lansky ordered Erika and Zhanna to report to his private conference room at 11:00 a.m. Lansky didn't want Luciano to have to wait in case he arrived early. At noon, Luciano still had not arrived. Finally, Lansky led Luciano into the room nearly an hour after his scheduled arrival. When Luciano entered, Erika and Zhanna stood up, keeping form with proper Mafia etiquette for the Boss of all Bosses.

Charles Luciano had earned his nickname "Lucky" because of his numerous escapes from assassination attempts since the late 20s and throughout the 30s. Unlike Ben Siegel who hated the nickname "Bugsy", for Luciano the nickname "Lucky" was one he embraced because he actually thought the name brought him luck. Because of this, he allowed people to address him as such. Yet a name wasn't necessary for people to know who he was. Lucky Luciano was a man whose photograph had been pasted in numerous newspapers and magazines over the years. His facial scars and lazy right eye made him easily recognizable.

Lansky made the introductions. He pointed first to Erika. "Lucky, you have already met Erika. You were with us the day we interviewed her for a job as a floor girl. This other one is Zhanna."

There were no handshakes.

"Take a seat," Luciano said. "Meyer tells me you both speak Russian. How did you learn that language?" Lansky had briefed Luciano but the Don wanted to hear it from the women.

"I spent time in Russia toward the end of the war and after the war ended," Erika said.

Luciano looked at Zhanna.

"I am Russian. I was born in Leningrad."

"I talked to Ben Siegel on the phone yesterday. He wasn't happy about losing you, even if just for a few weeks. He says you two are as good or better than any bodyguards he has ever had. I'd like to know how two women can become such good bodyguards."

"I was a sniper and executioner for the Red Army during the war," said Zhanna. "I had years to perfect my craft."

Erika went next. "I was a spy for my homeland of Germany during the war and had undergone much training in hand-to-hand fighting and marksmanship with a variety of weapons."

"So you end up going from a floor girl to working for Ben," Luciano said to Erika. "That's a big career turnaround." So far Luciano had avoided using any profanity—unusual for a mobster Erika noted.

"Zhanna and I both got into some trouble in our countries. We came to Cuba for a fresh start."

"Russia and Germany were blood enemies during the war. How did you two meet?"

"I worked as a German-to-Russian translator for the Red Army during the last few months of the war after I was forced to leave Germany," Erika explained. "I had disobeyed some minor orders from my German supervisors, which was not acceptable in the Third Reich. Such things got you shot or sent to a concentration camp. With the Soviets, I mostly translated interrogations of captured German soldiers. One time I was assigned to the Red Army unit that Zhanna was also assigned to." Erika's fabrication wasn't remotely related to the way she met Zhanna, which wasn't until after the war, but it kept things simple. Erika knew the best cover stories were the simplest ones.

"Okay," Luciano said as if he had already grown bored. "So we can gets our ducks in a row, I want to meet with you two a couple more times after we decide on which days we'll be meeting with the commies. Make sure you check in with Meyer everyday as he told you. He'll let you know when our next meeting will be."

Luciano abruptly stood up, shook Meyer Lansky's hand and walked out of the room.

Chapter 22

Atlantic Ocean, 300 nautical miles east of the West Indies
Friday, 06 December 1946

This had been another long voyage for Roy Burke. Even though his job as an international salesman for John Deere required he make two Atlantic crossings a year, he had never grown used to the long ship rides. He had placed a request to his boss that he be allowed to fly. Pan-American Airlines now offered regular trans-Atlantic flights, but the company could save money with a third-class cabin on an ocean liner, so that was the end of that discussion and now he was once again at sea, this time on the *Aquitania* sailing out of South Hampton.

Burke still had three days before he would arrive home. The *Aquitania* would dock tomorrow in Havana then proceed to the Bahamas for another brief stop before ending her voyage in Miami where Burke would disembark. After a late night arrival in Miami, Burke would have to spend a night before boarding a train for Moline, Illinois—the company's headquarters and his home.

Still unmarried at 33 years old, Burke had no one special to return to yet it was always nice to get home.

On this night of the voyage, Burke stood against the port rail sipping Scotch and watching the hypnotizing sea breakers, their tips asparkle from the full moon. It was late, almost the witching hour. The cold on deck meant few of his fellow travels were topside. Passengers not already in their staterooms were below deck celebrating in the huge Palm Lounge or one of the ship's other watering holes. He pulled the collar of his great coat tight to his neck to ward off the cold sea breeze.

To his right, Burke noticed a woman at the rail. In front of her was an easel and canvas. He was intrigued so he walked her way, the deck's thin layer of frozen sea mist crackling as it broke under Burke's shoes. He stopped and stood beside her, but slightly behind so he could view the painting. This made it impossible for him to see her face. He glanced at the painting. It looked to be about half completed, but the full moon was there in all its glory. Burke was impressed.

"Very nice," said Burke. "The painting I mean. You're lucky to have clear skies."

"I prefer storms," she said. She spoke English but with a noticeable Russian accent.

"Really?" Burke responded. "Why is that?"

"Storms are more interesting."

Burke still had not seen her face, but from her voice, he thought she might be around his age.

"From your accent, I assume you are from Russia."

"That would be correct, and you are an American from your Midwest."

"Wow! How can you tell I'm from the Midwest?"

She didn't respond but continued her painting.

"May I buy you a drink?" Burke offered.

"Unless you enjoy swimming, if I were you I'd turn and walk away."

Burke was flabbergasted and didn't know how to respond. He walked away without ever seeing the woman's face.

Chapter 23

Bayamo, Cuba
Sunday, 08 December 1946

Yesterday, the *Aquitania* docked in Havana just after two o'clock in the afternoon. Two of Major Volkov's NKVD men, a lieutenant and a sergeant were waiting to drive Grusha directly to Bayamo—a bumpy ten-hour drive. The sergeant did all the driving.

This put her in Bayamo at midnight. The NKVD men dropped her at a small, poorly up kept hotel near downtown.

One of the NKVD men told Grusha there was a room already reserved for her and she only had to ask for the key at the desk. Then he said they would return at eight o'clock the next morning to take her to her first briefing. He handed over two files for her to study.

"I know you probably won't have time to read the entire files tonight, since you'll need your rest," the man said. "However, Major Volkov requests that you at least glance them over before tomorrow. This way you won't attend the meeting tomorrow morning totally unprepared."

Grusha shot him a dark, icy look that made him back up. "I am never unprepared."

[8:00 a.m. That morning]
When Grusha was escorted in to Colonel Kuznetsov's office at precisely eight o'clock by the same two men who had driven her from Havana, Kuznetsov and Volkov were already waiting.

"Thank you Comrade Lieutenant," said Kuznetsov. "You and the sergeant may leave us now." The lieutenant nodded and both men retreated out the door, closing it behind them.

A tall woman, nearly six feet, sat down in a chair opposite Kuznetsov's desk without asking or extending any polite protocol. Grusha Mustafina was an oddity in that she was not assigned to the Red Army or the NKVD, so neither Kuznetsov nor Volkov had any type of real control over her. Grusha answered only to the Politburo in

Moscow. This placed both the Red Army colonel and the NKVD major in the room in a dicey situation.

Grusha was not only tall but sturdily built as well. If that was not enough to single her out, her face assured the job. Her mother was a member of the Yupik tribe of Eskimos that lived in the Russian arctic. Her father was a Moldavian with Finnish features. So Grusha's mother's gifts to her were her black hair, black eyes and dark complexion. From her father, she had taken his Nordic Caucasian features of a square-cut face and jaw.

Grusha's appearance conveyed an intimidating and standoffish trait to most, topped off by a jagged facial scar that started from her left eyebrow and preceded backward, ending at a left ear with a missing lobe.

"Nice to see you again, Colonel," Grusha smiled. She knew her last collaboration with Kuznetsov in Romania did not go well, especially for him.

"Grusha, yes, of course, it is good to see you again," Kuznetsov lied. "I have to apologize for billeting you in that rundown hotel. There aren't any hotels like the Savoy or Ritz here in this town. I have some of my staff looking for nicer accommodations. Perhaps we can rent you a bungalow."

"The hotel is fine," Grusha responded. "I will stay there. Those types of places are less conspicuous."

"Very well, if that is your choice," said Kuznetsov. He wasn't about to argue, he just wanted this apparition out of his office. "Have you met Major Volkov of the NKVD?"

Grusha looked at Volkov and addressed him. "We have never worked together but I have seen you somewhere."

"We talked briefly at a Kremlin cocktail party about a year ago," Volkov replied.

Grusha turned back to Kuznetsov. "I have read the two files given me last night. Am I to believe Zhanna Rogova is in Cuba?" Everyone in Russia had heard stories of Zhanna Rogova, a hero of the war against the German invaders.

"Yes, she is in Cuba as we speak," Volkov interjected. "Staying at the Hotel Nacional in Havana with the other woman we gave you a file on."

"I read her file. This Nazi intrigues me."

"She now works for the American CIA as does Rogova."

"Yes, I read that," Grusha smirked impatiently. "Let's not be redundant. Tell me something I don't know; most importantly, what is my mission?" Grusha had not been briefed in Moscow. Her sole orders were to report to Kuznetsov in Cuba.

Volkov did the talking. "You are to capture or eliminate Zhanna Rogova. If her German comrade gets in the way, the same applies to her."

Grusha's dark eyes brightened. This was a dream come true assignment. Even though she had established her reputation in Russia, she had never been able to escape the shadow of Zhanna Rogova. Bringing the great Rogova down would cement Grusha's sole claim of being the best.

"What can you tell me about their current activities?" Grusha asked. "Why are they here in Cuba?"

"We will hold a series of meetings later this month with some Americans who control gambling here in Cuba."

"Americans who control gambling? That sounds like the American gangsters in the motion pictures."

"That's exactly who they are, only these men are not actors; they are the real thing. In any case, back to what's important. Zhanna and this German both speak Russian and English. They are here to serve as interpreters for the American gangsters at these meetings."

"Interpreters, you say?"

"Yes," answered Volkov. "Somehow they have infiltrated the American Mafia ranks."

Grusha paused briefly. It took her less than a minute to formulate a rough draft of a plan. For now, she kept it to herself.

Volkov broke the pause. "I have men at your disposal. Just let me know what you need. My orders from Moscow are to cooperate fully with your mission."

"The only thing I require from you now is a car and driver. Have him at my hotel tomorrow morning at six o'clock."

"I'm aware that you have an aversion to flying, but if you need to go to Havana, I can supply you an airplane and pilot." Kuznetsov offered. "The ten-hour drive becomes a 2½-hour flight."

Grusha shook her head. "The car and driver will do."

Chapter 24

Lucky Luciano's cabana west of Havana
Tuesday, 10 December 1946

Luciano's cabana could serve as a picture post card advertising to tourists: *Welcome to Cuba.* The thatched roof bungalow not fifty yards from the bay during high tide wouldn't be a place you'd want to hunker down during one of the island's hurricanes, but under blue skies, such as today, it was Xanadu.

Lucky Luciano had decided he would trust Bugsy's two female bodyguards and had them driven here from the hotel. Like with most of the people Luciano trusted, with Erika and Zhanna it was trust built around the crime boss holding all the chips. Luciano knew the women were being hunted—hiding from their respective countries because of treason and past crimes. This gave Luciano leverage to ensure their loyalty. Luciano was a man who always wanted leverage, and he knew how and when to use it.

The women were encouraged to bring bathing suits and enjoy a swim in the bay. When Luciano himself called their room at the Nacional, he noted that while the current temperature in NYC was 29°, here it was 88° and the bay waters off the Caribbean still comfortable.

Erika and Zhanna had taken their swim and now sat in wooden cabana chairs wrapped in towels. Carmen had just brought them each a Cuba Libre. They had yet to see Luciano.

"Do you have any smokes, Carmen?" Erika asked her.

"No entiendo, Senorita," the housekeeper replied. Then she apologized for not speaking English. "Lo siento."

Erika brought two fingers to her lips to simulate smoking.

Carmen now understood. "Ah, si, Senorita." She retreated into the bungalow and in a moment returned with a cherry-wood humidor containing both Cuban cigarettes and cigars. Both Erika and Zhanna chose a large black cigar, snipped the end with a guillotine from the humidor, and lit up with matches from the same box. Carmen left the humidor on a small table near them and disappeared back inside the bungalow. Erika turned to make sure Carmen was out of earshot.

"That's interesting," she said to Zhanna.

"What's interesting?"

"That housekeeper acts like she doesn't understand English, but she does."

Zhanna gave Erika a quizzical look. "How do you know that?"

"The eyes will always tell you if you're being understood. She understood when I first asked her in English about something to smoke."

"Luciano probably has her act like she doesn't speak English so she can tell him anything that's said by his gangster friends if he's out of the room."

"Maybe," said Erika. "Or maybe she works for us or the Russians. Just be careful what you say."

Luciano arrived; his driver bringing him back from wherever he had gone. He emerged from the car and walked directly toward Erika and Zhanna without going inside the bungalow.

"I see you took your swim," said Luciano. "How was it?" This was the first time Luciano had seen Zhanna's scar. He had plenty of ugly scars himself so he didn't bother to ask about it.

"Very nice," Erika answered and Zhanna nodded.

Carmen had heard the car drive up and came out of the bungalow.

Luciano told her, "Bourbon." Then he pointed to the women's drinks to signal her to bring two more.

"Carmen is a good housekeeper," said Luciano, "but she doesn't speak English which makes it a pain in the ass sometimes." Then he chuckled. "I think the only words she knows are 'bourbon' and 'Scotch' and for all I know those words might be the same in Spanish."

Erika and Zhanna smiled with him. Carmen delivered the drinks pronto then again went inside.

"So, what exactly can we do for you concerning these translations, Mr. Luciano?" Erika asked. "Zhanna and I assumed there is more to it than simply translating since we are having this meeting."

"I want you to get to know these Russian characters—to get on friendly terms with them. They will also have their own translators. Concentrate on them. A translator will know things. Go out for something to eat with them, or even better go out drinking with them.

74

The Russkies are famous for running their mouths and being indiscreet after they get loaded."

Zhanna finally contributed to the conversation. "When do the meetings start, and where will they be held? This we will need to know so we can have a plan ready."

"They start this weekend, on Saturday," Luciano answered. "As far as where, we don't know exactly how many meetings will take place— probably five or six—but we will pick half of the meeting places and the Russkies the other half. Our picks will be the Nacional. No one knows where the Ivans will decide to meet when it's their pick."

Luciano turned up his bourbon and added. "I want the two of you to decide on an alias last name. Meyer did some checking and he told me your first names are pretty common in your countries, so we'll just use a phony last name. Erika is already known by my men at the Nacional as 'Erika' and if we change your first name we're liable to have some dumb sonuvabitch call you 'Erika' when the Russians are around the hotel. And many of my guys now know Zhanna since you have been staying at the hotel. So let's keep your first names. I wouldn't want the Russians or Americans to know about you two because I know you'll do a good job for me."

It was a veiled threat Luciano knew both Erika and Zhanna understood.

Chapter 25

Havana
Same day—10 December 1946

Luciano had his driver take Erika and Zhanna back to the Hotel Nacional later that afternoon. Erika could not get in touch with Al Hodge, so from a pay phone a few blocks from the hotel she dialed Washington. Sheila Reid put Erika's call through to Leroy Carr immediately.

"Hello, Erika," said Carr. "How are things going down there under the palm trees? I checked the weather in Cuba yesterday and the temperature was in the upper eighties. Right now it's in the twenties here in Washington."

Erika ignored the chit chat. *"Leroy, the meetings with the Russians begin this Saturday, the 14th."*

"That makes sense," Carr replied. "We've found out the mobster convention starts on the 20th. Luciano probably wants to get the meetings with the Russians out of the way before the Mafia pow wow starts. Where will the meetings with the Russians be held? Have they told you that yet?"

"Each side gets to pick alternate meeting places. According to Luciano, he doesn't know where the Russians will choose to hold their meeting when it's their turn to pick the location. Luciano and Lansky will have the meetings at the Nacional. Pretty bold on their part, don't you think? They have to suspect that the CIA is watching the hotel."

"They probably don't care. They know the laws. Just being seen in the company of communists is not a crime, even in the States. The only thing we could get on them that could hurt them is if we could prove that they were hatching some plot that could harm the United States, but I imagine these meetings just concern their operations in Cuba. We have no jurisdiction there and they know it. The only thing we can do is gather information. Anything we do has to be clandestine. That's why you and Zhanna are there."

"Zhanna and I met Luciano today at his hideaway. I'm sure you know where that is."

"That's the cabana on the coast west of Havana, right?"

"That's right. By the way, I couldn't get in touch with Al today."

"Al's here in Washington. I needed him for a few days. I would have told you, but I can't contact you at the hotel—too risky. I'll make sure he's back down there by Saturday. Do you foresee a need for backup?"

"Sending down three or four men with Al might be a good idea in case our covers are blown. Luciano is going to have Zhanna and me use phony last names, but that's not much to protect us—not with Zhanna's reputation with the Russians."

"Okay. I'll send down some good men with Al. Anything else to report?"

"Luciano wants Zhanna and me to try and get close to the Russian's interpreters. Take them out drinking and see if they spill anything of interest—that sort of thing."

"Good thinking on his part."

"One more thing, Leroy. Luciano has working for him a Cuban housekeeper who understands English but pretends she doesn't."

"That's Carmen, she works for us."

"Did you recruit her and plant her there?"

"No, she's been the housekeeper at that cabana for years. When Lucky Luciano rented it and she found out who he was, she contacted us out of the blue."

"So you pay her for information?"

"Yes, why do you ask? Do you think she's selling the same information to the Russians?"

Erika thought for a moment. *"I don't know. We have to hope not or Zhanna and I go into these meetings with our covers already blown."*

Part 3

"Right now our efforts in Cuba are reduced to games of cat and mouse between American agents and ours. If we fail, we hand over another opportunity to the Americans."

— Nikita Khrushchev
Soviet Politburo member, 1946

Chapter 26

Hotel Nacional, Havana
Saturday, 14 December 1946

This first meeting would not take place in Meyer Lansky's private conference room which was too small. As things turned out, twelve people would attend these meetings. For the Americans three men would attend: Lucky Luciano, Meyer Lansky, and Albert Anastasia, plus their two female interpreters. The Soviets also had two interpreters.

After drinks and hors 'd oeuvres were delivered, Luciano signaled Erika to start.

"Welcome to the Hotel Nacional to our Russian comrades," she said in Russian. "I've been asked to tell you that we want you to take full advantage of all that the Hotel Nacional has to offer. Food, drink, and gambling are complementary to our allies during the war who join us here today. If any of you wish to spend the night, your suite is also complimentary, of course.

"Now please allow me to make introductions. We have with us today Mr. Charles Luciano, Mr. Meyer Lansky, and Mr. Albert Anastasia." Each man nodded when he heard his name called. "Miss Zhanna Ivanova and I will serve as interpreters for them. My name is Erika Jung."

Zhanna stood and said, "добро пожаловать." (welcome). Her famous neck scar was covered by a light green silk scarf.

Among the two Soviet interpreters there was a man and a woman. When Erika finished and sat down, the man stood. He introduced the five-man Russian contingent; among them were Colonel Kuznetsov and Major Volkov. Although introduced with their rank if they were military, none of the Russians were in uniform; all wore suits to be less conspicuous at the hotel. The interpreter finished with, "My name is Sergei Datsyuk, and my comrade interpreter here is Olga Kabaeva." The woman stood briefly. She wore the common, drab gray dress that covered all but her ankles—a dress seen often on Russian working women. She quickly returned to her seat. Zhanna had carefully scanned the Russian names and faces and did not remember meeting any of them during the war. This was a relief. If she had not met them; they had not met her.

Several items were discussed over the next two hours with sometimes lengthy pauses while each side's interpreters translated the conversation to their group. The first order of business agreed upon was that the Americans would guarantee the safety of the Russians during any meetings at the Nacional. In turn, it would fall on the Russians to ensure the Americans safety at meetings held at venues of their choice. (Of course, with neither side trusting the other, both sides would have their own bodyguards at every meeting. Right now, those men were either standing vigil outside the conference room door, or patrolling the nearby hallways. All the Soviet bodyguards were members of the military. The American guards were men from Anastasia's Murder Inc.).

The last order of business discussed was the time, date, and location of the next meeting. The Russians told them the next meeting would be held in Bayamo on Monday, two days from now. The meeting would begin at two o'clock in the afternoon.

When the meeting was adjourned, the highest-ranking Russian— the colonel, Kuznetsov—told Lansky that they would accept his offer of rooms for the night and a taste of American nightlife. This gave Erika and Zhanna the perfect opportunity to approach the Russian interpreters.

"Well, it looks like you will be spending the night," Erika said to Sergei, who seemed to be in charge over the woman. "Why don't you allow Zhanna and me to show you around the hotel?"

"I do not mean to offend . . . your name is Erika, correct?" He spoke fluent English but with a heavy Russian accent.

"Yes, that's my name," Erika answered.

"Erika, again, I do not want to offend you or your comrades, but Comrade Kabaeva and I are not interested in your decadent capitalistic lifestyle."

Olga Kabaeva, the female Russian interpreter, interrupted. She also spoke fluently but like her counterpart with a very noticeable Russian accent. She was a tall woman; Erika guessed 5'11" if not six-feet. Olga had black hair like Zhanna, and Erika noticed a scar on the side of her eye and temple area that disappeared under her hair. "Sergei, don't be ridiculous," Olga said. "We must not refuse our American friends their kind offer. It sounds like fun. There is nothing wrong with having a bit of fun."

Sergei looked at her and immediately changed directions. "Of course."

Olga looked at Erika and Zhanna and smiled. "Thank you for your kindness."

Chapter 27

Hotel Nacional, Havana
That evening—Saturday, 14 December 1946

It was agreed among the translators that they would meet in the hotel lobby at six o'clock. Instead of changing into cocktail gowns—attire more suitable for a casino—Erika decided she and Zhanna should remain in their business attire as to not make Olga feel even more out of place in her drab dress. Olga was already waiting when Erika and Zhanna came down.

"Where is Sergei?" Zhanna asked.

"He is tired and not feeling well," Olga explained. "He thought it best if he retired for the evening."

"Nothing serious, I hope," said Erika.

"I'm sure he will be fine." (Grusha ordered Sergei to stay behind. She wanted to meet her marks without being encumbered by Sergei's dour personality).

All three women were full after eating liberally from the cornucopia of fresh fruit and hors 'd oeuvres offered during the meeting, so it was mutually decided that dinner was not necessary.

Erika and Zhanna walked Olga around the hotel, ending in the casino.

"Amazing," Olga expressed. "I have never seen a place like this." It was a lie. She had been inside the casinos of Monte Carlo and the French Riviera during a previous mission hunting a Frenchman who held information on a new system of detecting ocean mines. She found him, tortured the necessary information out of him, and then disposed of the body.

As Erika and Zhanna led Olga through the casino, Zhanna asked, "Olga, where are you from in Russia?"

"Moscow, and you?"

"Leningrad," Zhanna answered. "Where did you learn English?"

"It's a funny story, really. As a teenager I loved movies, and since most of the better ones were from Hollywood, they are the ones I watched much of the time. But I hated being forced to read subtitles;

84

you lose so much of the visual part of the movie so I enrolled in English classes so I could watch American movies without being forced to read the subtitles. Then when I was out of school, I spent nearly a year in South Africa with an uncle and his family. That's where I really perfected it. I was in South Africa in 1941 when the Hun invaded my country—no offense intended Erika."

"None taken," Erika replied.

"After the invasion I returned home and joined the Red Army. My service was not very exciting. I spent the war in Moscow working as a secretary. I translated communiqués from the British and Americans." Her story was all true up until the secretary part. Grusha spent the war working as a sniper or interrogating captured German prisoners. Most of these interrogations involved torture.

Grusha was now 33 years old—two years older than Zhanna and four years older than Erika.

Erika went to one of the teller cages and withdrew some complimentary chips, her name being on a list sent down earlier from Meyer Lansky's office.

They lost money playing roulette then moved to the blackjack tables where they won most of it back. Erika had to teach Grusha how to play but she was a quick study. After gambling for about two hours, they decided to take a break from the tables and get a drink in the casino bar. They found a table and sat down.

"That was fun," Olga said. "I'll have to watch myself so that I don't turn into one of Sergei's decadent capitalists."

All three women laughed, including Zhanna although she didn't find it particularly funny. Regardless, Olga turned out to be a humorous and fun companion for the evening.

"Yes," Erika replied. "We didn't win any money, but we had fun and just about broke even. That's a victory in itself in a casino."

Zhanna and Olga ordered straight vodka. Erika ordered a Margarita with a shot of tequila on the side.

"What is that drink?" Olga asked Erika.

"It's a Spanish drink made from tequila and limes, but they never put enough tequila in them so I always order an extra shot to add to it.

Erika took a drink to allow room to add the extra tequila then she poured the shot into the drink and stirred it up with a swizzle stick.

Olga turned up her vodka, finished it then said, "I'll try one of those Margaritas."

The three women spent another hour together in the bar before deciding to retire.

"It's a long trip back to Bayamo tomorrow—a ten-hour drive."

"You drove here?" Erika asked. "I assumed your group would fly."

"Everyone else flew. I have a problem flying. I've been on an airplane only once and swore it would be my last. My heart started racing; I was perspiring, and I thought I'd go out of my mind.

"But our meeting Monday is in Bayamo. I'll be much fresher. It will be my turn to show you two around. I'm afraid Bayamo doesn't have nearly as much to offer as Havana when it comes to nightlife, but there are several cantinas there that serve excellent Cuban food. I'll ask my superiors for a voucher so I can host you to a dinner."

"That won't be necessary, Olga," Erika said. "We can buy our own."

"No, I insist."

"Very well, but Zhanna and I will buy the drinks,"

Olga smiled. "Agreed."

They all exchanged warm handshakes before departing to their respective rooms.

Chapter 28

Bayamo, Cuba
Next day—Sunday, 15 December 1946

All the Russians except for Grusha had flown back from Havana so they had to wait several hours until her return by car to Bayamo.

Finally, at six o'clock that evening she sat down with Colonel Kuznetsov and NKVD Major Volkov.

Volkov started the meeting with a rebuke. "Grusha, you need to put this hesitancy of flying out of your mind. It's already becoming a hardship for all of us. The Colonel and I have been back in Bayamo since before lunch."

"A hardship to you is of little concern to me. My being driven instead of flying will not interfere with me accomplishing my mission and that is all that should concern you. I don't want to hear any more of your whining. You sound like an old woman, Volkov."

Volkov turned crimson. He was unaccustomed to being talked to in such a way.

"Let's not argue," said Kuznetsov. "Grusha, you went out for an evening with Zhanna Rogova and the German woman. What do you have to report?"

"The German—Erika—does nearly all the talking. It's apparent that she's in charge."

"What conclusions do you draw from this?" Volkov asked.

"It means I will probably have to eliminate her before I can get to Zhanna."

"It doesn't matter what you do with the German," Volkov added, "but I don't have to remind you that our first priority is to capture Zhanna Rogova, and only if capture is not possible the next step is elimination."

"And in the end, that decision is up to me," Grusha stated firmly.

Kuznetsov piped in, "What impressions did you get of Zhanna?"

"It was an honor to meet her," Grusha replied. "It will be a bigger honor to kill her."

"You mean capture her or kill her," Kuznetsov corrected her.

"Of course, capture or kill her," Grusha responded.

[From a telephone booth in Havana—same day]

"Hello, Leroy," said Erika. After yesterday's meeting, and before they met 'Olga' for the evening, Erika had called Carr's office in D.C. and given him all the names from the Russian contingent. It was Sunday so she had called his home. "Any intel on the names I sent you yesterday?"

Carr had the files ready,

"Kuznetsov—the colonel—is the head of the Soviet outpost in Cuba. He works out of Bayamo. That's a medium-sized town on the other side of the island, about as far away from Havana as you can get and still be in Cuba."

"That's where the next meeting on Monday will be held," Erika interjected.

"Good, you can look the place over and get a feel for it. As far as the rest of the names you sent in, Major Volkov is really the only one of interest. He's the top dog of the NKVD in Cuba. I knew the Russians would have someone from their secret police at the meetings who would report faithfully back to Moscow. That's Volkov."

"Who are the rest?"

A couple of officers on Kuznetsov's staff and a lower-level diplomat. The interpreter, Sergei Datsyuk, was at one time an interpreter at the Soviet's British Embassy. We have nothing on the other interpreter, the secretary whose name you sent—Olga Kabaeva. But if she was a low level secretary it's not unusual that we don't have a file on her. So far, we have no reason to believe your covers are not intact."

[later that night]

As she did every night before she retired, Erika took out a photo and gazed at it for a long time. The photo showed her with her dead husband Kai and their small daughter Ada from happy times gone by. In the suite's other bedroom, Zhanna could hear the faint weeping. The sound was very uncharacteristic coming from the tough German

Abwehr spy that she had grown to know. Zhanna Rogova didn't understand grief over loved ones because she had never had a loved one in her life. She ignored it, turned her head away, and went to sleep.

Chapter 29

Bayamo, Cuba
Monday, 16 December 1946

The New York City Dons were not about to drive ten hours over the twisting and bumpy roads from Havana to Bayamo. A chartered Lockheed A-20 Hudson sat waiting for them at nine o'clock in the morning. The Hudson cruised at 220 miles per hour so the flight to Bayamo would take 2½ hours. Still, this was enough of an inconvenience to irritate Albert Anastasia.

"Why can't all the meetings with these Ivans be held in Havana?" Anastasia asked Lucky as they boarded the plane. "Why do we have to fly to Shit Water, Cuba?"

"That was the agreement, Albert. We pick a location; then they pick one," Luciano answered.

Anastasia shook his head and mumbled some vulgarity.

Once all were on board, the co-pilot closed the door as the pilot fired up the engines one at a time starting on the starboard side. A dark cloud of black smoke belched from the engine, but only for a moment then the engine ran smoothly and cleanly. The same procedure followed with the port side engine. The pilot spent a few minutes letting the engines warm, gunning the revolutions several times while he and his co-pilot checked gauges and went through their pre-flight check list.

On board were nine passengers: Lucky Luciano, Meyer Lansky, Anastasia, four bodyguards from Anastasia's stable of thugs, and the two interpreters—Erika and Zhanna. The Hudson would transport 18 passengers so that left plenty of room to spread out. The three Dons sat in front and the bodyguards in the middle. Erika and Zhanna sat in the rear seats where they could talk discreetly.

After the Hudson became airborne and had leveled off at eight thousand feet, Erika turned to Zhanna and spoke softly in Russian, "It's unlikely that anyone can hear us over the engines, but let's speak in Russian."

Zhanna nodded.

"Hopefully the gangsters and the Russians will get down to more detail at this meeting—something worth reporting back to Leroy. The first meeting was a meet-and-greet and that was about it. The only thing good that came of it was establishing a relationship with the secretary—Olga."

"She doesn't look like a secretary to me," Zhanna said. "She reminds me more of the strong lady in a carnival freak show."

Erika couldn't help but laugh. "At any rate, Carr ran her through the files and came up with nothing."

"Which means nothing if her real name is not Olga Kabaeva," Zhanna argued.

"All of what you say is true," Erika countered, "giving us even more reason to get to know her. Don't give her any indication that you have suspicions about her. If she's not whom she says she is it's our job to find out. Just stay wary."

◊ ◊ ◊

The brick runways of the Bayamo airfield were still slick from overnight drizzle, and under cloudy skies the Hudson skidded down at just before noon. Waiting to greet them when they descended the airplane's ladder were the two interpreters—Sergei and Olga—and one of the diplomats who had attended the first meeting in Havana. The diplomat welcomed them in Russian and Zhanna translated. Sergei translated Lucky Luciano's return greeting.

A fleet of five cars were waiting and the Americans were driven directly to the site of the meeting. The city was not the backwater that the American mobsters had been expecting. Bayamo was a city with a population of 175,000 and served as the capital of the Gramma Province in eastern Cuba. Several tall buildings could be viewed out of the cars' windows.

As the Americans had done in Havana, time was not wasted taking everyone to lunch. Food and drink were brought in to the conference room of an office building where one entire floor had been leased by the Russians. It certainly wasn't as glittery a venue as the Hotel Nacional, but it served its purpose.

The meeting began as soon as everyone found a seat.

After brief pleasantries were exchanged, the meeting got down to business. Unlike the first meeting in Havana where most of the time was devoted to feeling each other out, serious business was discussed this time.

The Soviet-controlled poppy fields of Turkey, Georgia, and Armenia led to some heated discussion before a compromise was reached. Part of the compromise entailed a cheaper price for the mob on the raw opium in exchange for more Soviet agents being hired into the NYC Longshoreman union where they could monitor the type of cargo loaded on ships and its destination.

This second meeting lasted nearly four hours—twice as long as the first meeting at the Nacional. When adjourned, Colonel Kuznetsov told the Americans. "I have rooms reserved for all of you at the Hotel Gramma, our finest hotel. If you are not flying back to Havana tonight, I hope you'll take advantage of our hospitality. Bayamo doesn't have all to offer of Havana, but there are some fine Cuban restaurants in this city."

Lucky Luciano responded to the invitation. "We'll spend the night and fly back to Havana early tomorrow morning."

Chapter 30

Bayamo, Cuba
That evening—Monday, 16 December 1946

The Hotel Gramma certainly wouldn't be mistaken for the Nacional, but Erika and Zhanna's room was efficient and clean. Earlier, when the meeting adjourned, Olga reminded them of her promise to buy dinner. Erika and Zhanna returned to their hotel and Erika had time to take a walk and make her phone call to Leroy Carr from a telephone booth. She filled him in on what was discussed at the meeting.

At 7:00, Erika and Zhanna stood in front of the hotel when Olga drove up in a black, ten-year-old Plymouth.

"Shall we speak Russian or English?" Erika asked after she and Zhanna were inside the car. Erika sat in the front beside Olga, Zhanna in the backseat.

"I think English would be best," Olga replied. "The locals are accustomed to hearing Russian because of the sizable Soviet delegation here, but if any locals speak anything other than Spanish it's much more likely it will be English rather than Russian." Instead of her drab office dress, Olga wore a conservative woman's business suit with a necktie. It was an outfit one might see Marlene Dietrich wear in a movie, and it looked smart on her. Erika and Zhanna both wore modest skirts and blouses.

"Is this your car?" Zhanna asked as Olga pulled out into traffic.

"No, it's one of the delegation cars. They have newer ones like the cars that picked you up at the airport, but being a secretary and low on the list of importance, this is what they gave me for tonight."

'So, where are we going?" Erika asked.

"*César's,*" Olga answered. "Most people think it's the best restaurant in Bayamo. I've eaten there and would have to agree. There are cattle ranches and farms all around Bayamo, and we're only twenty-five miles from the sea so everything is fresh. After that, perhaps we can stop in at a club."

Olga was right about the food at César's. The bill of fare was traditional Cuban cuisine which was a mixture of Spanish, aboriginal,

African, and Caribbean influences. Erika had a large swordfish steak deliciously prepared in a wine sauce with pecans. Zhanna and Olga each ordered a beef steak smothered in mild Cuban chilies and onions. A carafe of red wine and one of white was ordered.

Half way into dinner Zhanna asked Olga, "How did you get that scar?" referring to the scar on Olga's temple. The scar was given to her by one of her early marks. The man caught the side of her head with a dagger just before Grusha snapped his neck. Her missing earlobe could not be seen under her hair.

"Stupid clumsiness, I'm afraid," Olga answered. "I fell and hit my head very hard on a jagged piece of metal."

Olga asked a question she already knew the true answers to, but was curious about what Erika and Zhanna would say as a cover. "So what did you two do during the war?"

"My family moved to the States shortly before the war broke out," Erika said.

"I was in Finland when the Germans invaded Poland in '39," Zhanna said. "Before they invaded the Soviet Union in '41 I had managed to make it onto a freighter and spent the war in Edinburgh."

When dessert of Guava helmets in syrup was finished, Olga said, "There is a club I'd like to take you to. It won't compare to the clubs in Havana, I'm afraid, but it can be fun."

"We'd love to see it," Erika replied.

After a twenty-minute drive, Olga pulled the Plymouth into the gravel parking lot of a building near a set of railroad tracks. In fact, the English translation of the name on a small sign above the door was *Other Side of the Tracks.* The doorman, looking like a prototype of Neanderthal man, apparently recognized Olga. He opened the door to let them enter without comment.

The seamy look of the outside was not arrested by the inside decor. Bathed in red light was one large smoke-filled room crowded with pool tables and slot machines. The bar with a juke box and small dance area nearby took up a small area in a corner. No one was dancing because there were no female customers at the time. The clientele were men shouting and arguing about bets on pool games— the money in question resting on the rails. It was a question to Erika why Olga brought them here but she made no comment. When the three women entered, the shouting stopped for a moment while the men looked over the women.

"Perhaps it was a mistake bringing us here. The other times I've been here have always been with men from the delegation."

"It will be fine," Erika assured her, "but I better call our bosses and let them know we'll be out late. We told them we were just going out for dinner."

Olga nodded and Erika found a pay phone near the bar while Olga stayed with Zhanna and looked around for a pool table. "I'm pretty good at pool," Olga said. "Maybe we can win some money. I usually do. Half of the men in here are drunk, which interferes with their ability to play."

"How often do you come here?" Zhanna asked.

"Not that often, but when I do, like I said, it is always with male comrades who keep the wolves at bay. Maybe I should have picked a different place. I'm a bit nervous that it's just us women, are you?"

"No," Zhanna said assertively.

As Zhanna passed a man staring at her she said, "What are you looking at, ass-hole?" He didn't understand the English so there was little reaction. Just after this, Erika returned to join them.

Olga knew the bartender spoke some English so she approached him. "My friends and I would like to get in on a game of pool with some of the betting men, can you help us?"

The bartender looked around the room and nodded. "Ask those two men at table nine (each table had a number above the light over the table).

Olga nodded, ordered and paid for three cervezas then led Erika and Zhanna to table nine.

Chapter 31

Bayamo
Same night—Monday, 16 December 1946

The names of the two men at pool table nine were Roque and Chico. Roque spoke rudimentary English and could usually decipher most of what was being said if the English speaker spoke slowly.

Olga introduced Erika and Zhanna and asked if they could join the game.

"We play for dinero," Roque warned them.

"So do we," Olga replied.

Roque said something in Spanish to Chico and both men laughed. Roque looked at the women and shrugged. Each of them walked to a pool rack to choose a cue stick.

Olga had been right, she was pretty good at pool and the first few games of 8-ball were close, with the men winning in the end.

More money was laid on table rails and a new game began. Erika was not that experienced with the game but she hit a couple of lucky shots and Olga came to the table with only the 2-ball and 8-ball to sink for the win. She dropped the 2-ball into a side pocket. She chalked her cue and lined up the 8-ball. She declared, "Corner pocket," and used her cue stick to point toward the pocket. She dropped the 8-ball for the win.

"Wait a minute!" Roque declared. "You forfeit. You didn't declare the 8-ball."

"I did declare it," said Olga. "I said 'corner pocket' and pointed to it."

"Chico and I don't think so." Roque began picking up the money from the rail.

"Hey, Roque!" Erika exclaimed. "Olga did declare it but I'll tell you what. If you can gather that money and still have a hand when you're done, you can have it."

"Let them have it, Erika," said Olga. "Let's not have a confrontation."

Zhanna had heard the English and was aware they were being cheated.

Roque laughed and continued to gather the bills from the rail.

Zhanna produced a dagger from a sheath under her skirt and plunged it through Roque's hand—crucifying his hand and the money he had collected to the pool table rail. He screamed in agony. Zhanna calmly pulled out the dagger and gathered the blood-soaked bills.

Chico drew a gun—an old revolver that looked like it might fall apart if fired. He grabbed Olga by the hair and held her in front of him, then pointed his gun toward Erika and Zhanna. Olga looked terrified. With Chico holding her hair pulled back, both Erika and Zhanna saw the extent of her scar and the missing earlobe.

Erika quickly pulled her Beretta from a holster at the back of her skirt and grabbed Roque, creating a faceoff. Roque tried to reach behind him and stick his knife into Erika. She dodged his hand and shot Roque in the temple, spraying blood on her face and blouse. His body dropped to the floor.

"Put the gun down and let Olga go, Chico, or end up like your friend," Erika threatened. Chico had not understood the English but what he had just seen convinced him to release Olga. He dropped his gun on the pool table, and raised his hands. Zhanna promptly shot him between the eyes with her Smith & Wesson.

The rest of the scoundrels inside the bar sat catatonic watching the events at table nine unfold but they quickly came to their senses and began pulling out knives or handguns.

The telephone call Erika had made earlier was to Albert Anastasia. It was just then that Murder, Inc. walked into the *Other Side of the Tracks.*

◊ ◊ ◊

The Neanderthal doorman was already dead, strangled from behind by one of Anastasia's four men. When Murder Inc. entered the pool hall, Anastasia and two of his men carried Thompson machine guns, the other two sawed-off shotguns.

The Cubans inside the pool hall, almost all of whom held some type of weapon directed at Erika and Zhanna, stopped and looked at Anastasia.

Anastasia spotted Erika and Zhanna then redirected his attention to the men.

"These women are part of Lucky Luciano's crew from New York and members of the Mangano family," Anastasia announced loudly with the look of a wolf in his eyes. "I know even you stupid back-water Cuban shits have heard of Lucky Luciano. Nobody fucks with anyone on our crew."

Anastasia and his men opened up. The cacophony of the Thompsons inside a closed building and the deadly spray of bullets sent men diving for cover. Some found it; some did not and were hit. The men with shotguns blew out the bar mirror and shattered nearly all of the liquor bottles. The bartender was hit in the arm by some shotgun pellets but managed to dive behind the thick and heavy wooden bar.

Erika and Zhanna did some more shooting of their own then Erika grabbed the terrified Olga and ran her out of the pool hall.

"What about my car?" said Olga, trying to regain her composure as Erika shoved her into one of Anastasia's vehicles. "I'll get in trouble if I don't return it."

"Forget about it," Erika responded.

A couple of Anastasia's men used Molotov cocktails to torch the club. The men of Murder Inc. walked calmly out of the club, joking and laughing as the *Other Side of the Tracks* went up in flames.

Chapter 32

Bayamo
Next day—Tuesday, 17 December 1846

Inside the office of Colonel Kuznetsov, Grusha paid little attention to the rants and complaints of Kuznetsov and Volkov. She looked more bored than concerned over the dressing down.

"Last night was supposed to be a simple operation to prove to the CIA women that you are no threat," Kuznetsov thundered.

"And it worked," Grusha countered calmly. "They saw me as a scared mouse."

The NKVD major piped in. "Yes, and I lose two of my best informants," Volkov said, referring to Roque and Chico. Then the New York gangsters show up and kill or wound half the people in the place then burn it to the ground."

"That I wasn't expecting," Grusha admitted with a wry smile.

"I should think not."

"The bartender who cooperated by guiding you and your women friends to the table with Roque and Chico was one of the lucky ones who made it out alive," Kuznetsov added. "The man has friends among the Cubans in local government. We haven't heard the last of this, Grusha."

Grusha had heard enough. "Enough of your lecturing. I'll remind you that I report only to General Polzin in Moscow who happens to also be your NKVD boss, Comrade Volkov. The collateral damage last night was acceptable. I now have a better understanding of whom I'm dealing with, especially in the case of the German, Erika."

"Explain," Kuznetsov said.

"I knew Zhanna Rogova was a cold-blooded killer. I did not know the Nazi was the same." Then with a tone of admiration in her voice, she added. "The Americans have found themselves quite the pair."

"So when can we expect this to be over?" asked Volkov.

"I'll end things at our next meeting in Bayamo."

◊ ◊ ◊

[Washington, D.C.—later that day]

Erika and Zhanna and the rest of the mob were now back in Havana. Leroy Carr wasted no time in getting Erika on the telephone.

"What in the hell is going on down there, Erika? Al got a report that you and Zhanna and Murder Inc. destroyed a Bayamo pool hall with several people being killed!"

"It's regrettable, Leroy, but it couldn't be helped."

"What do you mean by that?"

"The mission, and Zhanna and me, were in danger. I knew it was a setup the minute we walked in the place. It was a rat's den full of thieves and thugs. We were the only women in there and I knew that meant trouble with that clientele. I had to call Anastasia."

"Why didn't you call Al? He and his men were in Manzanillo, that's a half-hour away."

"That's too far, Leroy. I needed backup that could be there sooner than that."

"So you called Albert Anastasia?"

"Yes, I did."

"You should have known how that would turn out, Erika."

"I knew, but as I said, Al and his team were too far away."

There was a pause and then Carr asked, "What made you think it was a setup as soon as you walked in the place?"

"I think it was a set-up by the Russians. Zhanna and I have grown to know one of the Russian translators, Olga. A sleazy pool hall doesn't seem like a place she would go, even though she said she'd been there before with some of the Russian men."

"Well," Carr said, "at least the mob will take any flak from what happened last night. We're in the clear. At least I don't have to go before the Secretary of State and make excuses why this happened. We need to keep our heads down until we're officially approved by Congress."

"When will that be?" Erika asked.

"We're on the docket for the first session in '47—in a few months."

Carr returned to the business at hand. "So you think this Olga set you up?"

"I'm not sure. She might be a pawn who was ordered to take us there and forced to lie that she'd been there before. It might have been an NKVD operation. Maybe Zhanna's and my covers aren't as secure as we think. If they know we're CIA, last night would make sense."

"When are the next meetings with the Russians scheduled to be held?"

"They're coming to Havana tomorrow then the last meeting will be in Bayamo the next day—Thursday the 19th."

"Makes sense," said Carr. "That way Luciano and Lansky will be done with the Russians before the mob conference convenes on Friday."

[Havana—that evening]

Zhanna had been on the hotel room phone for forty minutes trying to get a called through to Puerto Barrios, Guatemala. There lived an old colleague she was on friendly terms with from her days in SMERSCH, the Soviet organization that eliminated spies. Although SMERSCH was no more, Zhanna knew the man still had contacts in the NKVD.

Finally, the call got through to the man's ranch. After another wait, the housekeeper at last got the man to the telephone.

"Yes," he answered irritably, as if he had been called away from important business.

"Demetri, this is Zhanna."

"Zhanna!"

"Yes, it's me. I need your help, Demetri."

"My housekeeper told me the operator said the call was from Cuba. Why are you there?"

"I can't tell you that."

"Why do you need my help?"

"I need you to use your contacts and make some inquiries about a Russian-to-English translator. She goes by the name Olga Kabaeva."

"Never heard of her."

"She's tall—almost six-feet I'd say—dark hair and eyes and a facial scar on her temple. She's missing an earlobe."

There was silence from Guatemala.

"Demetri, are you there?"

"Yes, I'm here. I won't need to call my contacts. The woman is no translator. Her name is Grusha. She's never referred to as anything but Grusha so I don't know a last name."

"Who is she?" Zhanna asked.

"When you disappeared, Grusha took over your role as our country's number one assassin. If you have any dealings with her, watch your back, old friend. Grusha has earned her reputation well."

About ten minutes after Zhanna hung up the phone, Erika returned from a swim in the hotel pool.

"I've got a bit of news for you," Zhanna told her.

Chapter 33

Havana
Wednesday, 18 December 1946

The Soviet contingent was scheduled to arrive at the Hotel Nacional in one hour. Erika and Zhanna stood in front of mirrors in their hotel room applying finishing touches to their makeup, dressed in the conservative business suits they had worn at the previous meetings.

They had talked into the wee hours last night. Grusha could be here for only one purpose: to capture or kill Zhanna, something the Russians held high on their list since Zhanna defected to the USA last spring. Both women reasoned that Erika might also be somewhere in Grusha's plan since she had betrayed the Russians both during and after the war. However, the Soviets would not put an operation like this underway just because of Erika who was just doing her job as a German to fight the Bolsheviks.

The main focus had to be Zhanna.

"I knew these covers as gangster bodyguards wouldn't hold up," said Erika. "All they did was open us up. We became much too conspicuous."

"Too late for that now," Zhanna rejoined.

"Do you think she'll make a move today in Havana?" Erika asked.

"That would be unwise on her part. She'll wait until the last meeting tomorrow in Bayamo—her turf. It will be easier in Bayamo to separate me from the American gangsters, which she will want to do after the other night."

"At least Al Hodge and his team are close by now in Havana," Erika said. "And tomorrow they will be stationed much closer to Bayamo. Carr found a ranch owned by a Cuban-American who served as a Marine during the war. His ranch is only five miles outside Bayamo. Hodge and his men will be there if we need them."

◊ ◊ ◊

When the Russians arrived at the Nacional, Erika and Zhanna gave Olga a hug which she returned enthusiastically. However, time was not given for chit-chat as the Russians demanded the meeting start immediately. The Russians brought the same five men as had attended the previous meetings (plus their two translators). The mobsters were represented by the normal triumvirate of Luciano, Lansky and Anastasia. To keep the Russians on their toes, Lansky moved the location of the meeting from the conference room they used for the first meeting to the hotel's private Salon de la Historia.

The Russians wasted no time, starting out with their demands concerning the pile of burnt ruble that two nights ago had been the *Other Side of the Tracks* pool hall.

"You will pay for the building," Kuznetsov demanded. "As far as for those killed, it is too early to tell you what will happen there. The bartender who owned the place has friends in the local government and police department. He can cause considerable trouble."

Erika translated Kuznetsov's words.

"We'll pay for nothing," said Lucky Luciano as if Erika and Zhanna were not in the room, he added. "Two members of my crew were attacked first. That's what caused all this. You can go screw yourselves. Rebuild the place yourself."

Olga translated word for word.

Luciano added, "But don't think you can go back on our deal we've already made for reduced opium prices. If you do there won't be one commie left in any of the New York trade unions. Unfortunate accidents can happen quickly."

The meeting began on such a bad note, very little other business was discussed and the gathering was over in less than an hour.

"Like at the first meeting," Luciano said as the Russians were preparing to leave. "We hope you'll enjoy our hospitality here at the Nacional."

"No, we will return to Bayamo tonight," Kuznetsov answered curtly. "Our final meeting will be held tomorrow in Bayamo. Make sure you have on your agenda any final thoughts that need consideration. We will do the same."

After the Russians had stormed out of the room, Luciano said, "Those Russian fucks have a lot of nerve asking us to pay for that bar. They're lucky we don't burn down their office building while they're inside polishing their jackboots."

Meyer Lansky and Anastasia laughed.

Luciano looked at Erika and Zhanna. "Good work the other night, ladies. You two are now off Ben Siegel's crew and on Albert's. I think Albert's crew is more suited to your talents than watching the paint dry on the walls with Siegel out in Nevada. You'll stay as translators until after tomorrow's meeting then you'll join Albert and his crew when he returns to New York. Don't worry about Ben; I'll give him the news."

Albert Anastasia showed no emotion over the decision, but it was something he had lobbied Lucky for since he visited Bugsy in Las Vegas and first met the women. Cold-blooded females not reluctant to pull a trigger were rare. They could get closer to wary targets than men.

Chapter 34

Bayamo, Cuba
Thursday, 19 December 1946

The rubber tires of the Lockheed Hudson carrying Lucky Luciano, Meyer Lansky, Albert Anastasia and his four men, and the group's two female interpreters struck down on the Bayamo airfield brick runway at 12:30 p.m.

The weather forecast warned of a tropical storm headed this way that should make landfall that evening. Luckily, it was not predicted to turn into a hurricane but a Caribbean tropical storm was bad enough—close enough to convince anyone who had never experienced a hurricane that they were swept up in one. If the tropical storm did make an appearance there would be no flight out. The group would be forced to spend the night in Bayamo—something none of the American mobsters wanted. Lansky, especially, wanted to get back to Havana tonight in order to continue preparations for the Mafia conference that began tomorrow. Some of the top mobsters from New York, Philadelphia, Chicago, and Kansas City had already checked in at the Nacional. Lansky had asked Luciano to be excused from this last meeting with the Soviets, but Luciano denied his request.

The Russian cars were waiting but this time without the pomp of an official greeting by Kuznetsov, Volkov, and other Russian higher-ups. The only men standing with the cars were the drivers, who took them directly to the offices of the Soviet delegation in Cuba.

◊ ◊ ◊

"The Bayamo police are corrupt," Kuznetsov told the Americans shortly after the meeting got underway. "We have paid them to include in their reports that the incident that happened earlier this week at the pool hall here in Bayamo was a drug deal gone bad."

"Smart," Luciano responded. "It always helps to have cops on the payroll. If you knew how much we shell out to cops in New York you'd shit your pants, Kuznetsov."

"Nevertheless, we took care of the problem. Now it's time to finish our business. We have one final concern. We want our agents working the docks expanded to Philadelphia."

"That's not a problem," Luciano said, then countered with. "We want more influence in South America. It's our prediction that Columbia will soon become a major player in the cocaine trade. We want to control that."

"Columbia is a country in constant revolution," Volkov chirped in. "We cannot assure you that we can help you with this. It depends on who has power from one day to the next."

"You can help, and you will," Luciano said. "If democratic forces control the capital, there will always be the communist revolutionaries in the jungles. That's where the cocaine comes from."

"I will look into this and get back to you," Kuznetsov told Luciano. "Something this extensive will require the help of Moscow."

"Take your time," Luciano replied. "Just not too much time."

"So we don't end our time together on a bad note," Volkov said. "We will host a dinner for you tonight at César's. It's the best restaurant in Bayamo (the eatery Grusha took Erika and Zhanna to before the pool hall disaster). We guarantee your safety but feel free to bring your men if you wish. Dinner is scheduled at seven o'clock. Our cars will be at your hotel at 6:15 to pick you up for cocktail hour. Is this agreeable?"

Luciano nodded. "I'm hungry. I bet you are too, Meyer."

Meyer Lansky nodded.

"How about you, Albert? Are you hungry?"

"You bet," Anastasia said as he chewed on his cigar and stared down the Russians.

Chapter 35

Bayamo, Cuba
That evening, 19 December 1946

The cocktail hour ran long. By the time the Russians and American mobsters sat down for dinner at César's it was nearly 7:30 p.m.

At the long table were the key players: Kuznetsov, Volkov, and the other three members of the Soviet delegation who attended the previous meetings. Also, their interpreters, Olga and Sergei, were on hand. The only Americans at the table with Luciano, Lansky, and Anastasia were their two female interpreters. But unknown to other César's customers, the establishment was crowded with firepower. The Russians had their undercover bodyguards scattered here and there around the room. Anastasia's four Murder, Inc. men were dispersed around the room, as well. Al Hodge and his three well-armed CIA operatives sat at the bar dressed like tourists drinking Cuba Libres.

After the waiter took the dinner orders, Olga asked Zhanna, "I need to freshen up. It's been a long day. Zhanna, as one Russian to another, would you like to go with me?"

"Конечно," Zhanna said, meaning 'certainly'.

Olga and Zhanna rose and departed for the ladies room. Erika ignored them as they walked away.

Inside the ladies room, both women went about the business of checking their makeup and attire. Olga wore the Marlene Dietrich male attire as she had two nights ago. Zhanna had on a long dress.

As Zhanna leaned over the sink, suddenly she felt a strong arm around her neck and a pistol barrel pressed to her forehead.

"It is nice to meet you Zhanna Rogova," Grusha snarled. "My name is Grusha. I've been an admirer of yours for years. You will go with me now or your Nazi friend, Erika, and the American gangsters will all be killed. I know your comrade Anastasia has men in the restaurant, but I have several men ready to carry out those orders regardless of if they survive or not.

"So tell me, will you cooperate?"

Zhanna nodded.

Grusha kept her hold on Zhanna with her gun to her head and led her out through the kitchen, passing terrified cooks and waiters. A car with the engine running was waiting in the alley. Grusha shoved Zhanna inside the backseat of the car and got in beside her. The car quickly drove off through the first drops of rain from the predicted tropical storm; the wind that transported the storm from somewhere out in the Atlantic picked up its pace.

[Washington, D.C. — late that same night]

"So Zhanna's capture went according to plan?" Leroy Carr asked Erika.

"As far as I know, yes. We knew Grusha would have to make her move tonight—the last night of the meetings. They went to the ladies room and never came out. Do you still feel positive they will not simply execute her, Leroy?"

"Yes, I'm positive. If all the Russians wanted to do was kill her they could have done that with much less trouble. They know she's CIA. They'll take her back to Moscow for interrogation and torture to find out what they can before they kill her."

"Zhanna has been through torture before at the hands of the SS. It's unlikely torture will work."

"I might agree with you, Erika, but almost everyone eventually talks under torture. You have your assignment—do whatever it takes to follow Zhanna and find out what you can about the Soviets' current operations. You've supplied us with important information about the Russians ties with the American mob. Now go to work finding out about any similar influences in Europe. This Grusha creature refuses to fly. She won't let the prize catch of her life out of her sight, so they will return to Europe by ship. They'll have to make a stop somewhere for refueling and supplies before they get to Moscow. I have our top analysts working on that and I will supply you that information. We'll know as soon as we find out what ship they are sailing on. I have good men covering the docks."

"There is a big storm moving in here tonight, Leroy. It's already pouring rain."

"That can work to our advantage. It might delay them from getting Zhanna out of Cuba."

"Erika, you have your orders, after completing your mission, save Zhanna. Protocol would call on me to order you to eliminate Zhanna if you can't free her, but I know you would never kill one of your partners unless he or she betrayed you. That means you have to get her back."

"I understand, Leroy" Erika answered.

Both parties hung up the telephone simultaneously without a goodbye.

◊ ◊ ◊

The destination of the car containing Grusha and Zhanna was Santiago de Cuba, about a two hour drive away on the extreme southern coast. There, Zhanna would be held in a secret, heavily-guarded safehouse until she could be smuggled out of the country at the earliest opportunity. Yet Grusha's mind was already working at whirlwind speed.

The capture of the great Zhanna Rogova had been much too easy.

Chapter 36

Bayamo, Cuba
Next morning—Friday 20 December 1946

The tropical storm delivered a great deal of rain overnight but the winds were lesser than experienced with most Caribbean storms of this nature—at least in Cuba. Instead of hitting Cuba full-force, the storm decided to settle in over the Dominican Republic and Haiti just to the east.

Much to Meyer Lansky's relief, the Hudson carrying him and Lucky Luciano was cleared for takeoff for Havana early that morning amidst just a light rain.

Albert Anastasia and his crew remained behind in Bayamo to look for Zhanna. She was now on his crew, and Anastasia wouldn't suffer any high jinks by the Russians.

"You know her best, Erika. What do you think happened?" Anastasia asked. He and his men were all assembled in his Bayamo hotel room.

"Maybe some perverts forced Zhanna and Olga into a car," Erika sighed.

"Come on!" Anastasia shouted. "I've seen that broad at work. No perverts are going to pack her off. They'd be dead before they got her out to the alley. It's got to be the Russians!"

"Maybe," Erika responded. "So what can we do if it is the Russians? We can't go breaking down doors and shooting up places helter-skelter."

"Why not?" Anastasia smirked.

"Let's find Zhanna first then we'll bring out the firepower."

Anastasia looked at her. "Do you have any ideas?"

"I might have one."

"Then you're in charge of finding her. Don't let me down," the Mad Hatter added menacingly. "You've seen what I'll do even when you and Zhanna were still members of Bugsy's crew. Now Zhanna is with us. Nobody fucks with my crew and lives to talk about it. Capiche?"

Erika nodded. "Capiche. And thank you, Albert. I will find Zhanna."

◊ ◊ ◊

Erika had a decision to make. Work with Anastasia and his team of killers or do as she should, disappear from Anastasia and work with Al Hodge and his men from the CIA. The decision didn't take her long. Her greatest odds lie in staying with Murder, Inc, at least for now, but use Hodge for information.

[that evening—On a ranch outside Bayamo]
Erika stood next to Al Hodge, leaning on a rail. Two beautiful Andalusians and a snow white Appaloosa playfully snipped at each other as they trotted around the corral.

"So let me get this straight," said Hodge. "You want me to get Leroy's okay for you to work with Albert Anastasia, while using any information the CIA can forward to you and those gangsters."

"That's right, Al."

"Are you nuts?"

"It's the best way to complete the mission," said Erika. "I know you can see that."

Al Hodge had worked with Erika Lehmann for over three years. He was exhausted from dealing with her, but he was well aware of her sterling record of successful missions.

Hodge paused for a long moment. "I'll call Leroy," Al frowned, "but I hope he turns you down."

Erika good-naturedly kissed his cheek. He grimaced and pulled away.

Erika almost laughed and this time kissed him on the lips just for amusement.

"Don't do that Lehmann, you already grate on my nerves something fierce. I don't need any more of your bullshit."

Erika grinned. "Thanks, Al. I knew you'd see it my way."

"It's up to Leroy, not me," Hodge stressed.

"You'll convince him. I know you will."

Erika knew that above all, Al Hodge was a professional spook. He had been one since the early days of the war with Leroy Carr at the OSS. She turned and walked away from the corral.

"I have to get back to Bayamo, Al, before Anastasia becomes suspicious. I'll expect your phone call soon. You know my room number at the Nacional. When you call, just say 'Algiers' if Leroy has given his approval."

"And what if he doesn't approve?"

"That would be unfortunate for the mission's sake," Erika answered.

[two o'clock a.m.]
The telephone woke Erika. She picked up.

"Hello."

"Algiers."

The phone at the other end immediately clicked off.

Chapter 37

Bayamo, Cuba
Saturday, 21 December 1946

Al Hodge's men had the docks in Santiago de Cuba under surveillance. It was the only practical staging area in eastern Cuba for large, ocean-going ships.

Hodge heard the phone in his room at the ranch ring at four o'clock that morning.

"Yes, Hodge here."

"Sir, the women Grusha and Zhanna just boarded a Russian naval frigate accompanied by three men. It was dark, but I'm positive it was them. The bow number of the frigate is 491."

"Good work, Roger," Hodge said. "Is it still in port?"

"No sir, it sailed within minutes of the women coming aboard."

"Okay. You and your men report back to the ranch."

[ten minutes later—Washington, D.C.]
"Leroy, they have Zhanna on a Russian warship, a frigate that has already sailed."

Carr was sitting on the edge of his bed after the predawn phone call. His wife Kay rolled over and went back to sleep. Kay had long ago learned to live with middle of the night phone calls.

"What's the ship's number?" Carr asked.

"491," Hodge said from Cuba.

"Okay, Al. I'll put our people to work on it. Call Erika and tell her the latest. I'll call her when we find out where the frigate will refuel. She'll have to pick up the chase in Europe when we get that information. With Zhanna taken out of the country so quickly, it doesn't look like Erika will need Anastasia and his gang of cutthroats anymore. That's at least one positive thing to come out of this."

"You got that right, Leroy."

[that morning]
This time, it was the phone in Erika's hotel room that rang.

"Yes," Erika answered.

"Call me from a pay phone." It was Leroy Carr, who immediately hung up.

Erika walked a block down the street, entered a phone booth in front of a bakery, and closed the door. She dropped several coins into the slot.

"Yes, Leroy. It's me."

"I assume Al got in touch with you on the latest. They've already got Zhanna out of Cuba."

"Yes, this is my second trip to this phone booth this morning. Al gave me only the basics—that Zhanna was already out of the country."

"She was loaded onto a Russian frigate early this morning," Carr told her. *"Al's men got the ship's number and we accessed the Soviet maritime naval log they don't know we have. One of our agents photographed the pages from a copy inside the Soviets' Caracas embassy a few months back. It keeps track of the location of all Soviet naval vessels."*

"And?"

"Looks like you're going to Iceland, my dear. The ship refuels in Reykjavik. We'll fly you there tomorrow so you have plenty of time to set up shop before the frigate arrives in three days. Al will contact you. He'll fly you to Miami and you'll leave from there. It will get you to Iceland quicker this way. Al and three of his men will go with you."

"I'll be ready."

[two hours later]
Erika sat in the Hotel Nacional coffee shop with Albert Anastasia.

"How is the big meeting going?" Erika asked, referring to the assemblage of top mobsters in Havana for the conference.

Anastasia shrugged. "I don't pay much attention to that shit. There have been meetings before between this family and that family. Agreements are made then broken and things are back to where they started out. Anything you can tell me about Zhanna?"

"She's already been taken from Cuba, Albert. The Russians are taking her to Moscow."

"Then we take a bunch of those Russian fucks in Bayamo hostage and demand her back."

"That won't work. I will go to Europe and try to rescue her. The ship has to refuel before it gets to Helsinki, Finland."

"Where the fuck is that?"

It's where the ship will dock. From there, they'll have to transport her by land—probably by train. But like I said, they have to stop to refuel somewhere first. That's when I'll make my attempt."

"How will you know where this ship will refuel?"

"I'll find out somehow." (Erika didn't want to tell him about Iceland.)

"I'll send a couple of my guys with you."

"Because of their criminal records, none of your men have passports, Albert. That's not a big deal when it comes to getting into Cuba because the New York families are in bed with the Cuban government and these things are ignored. Overseas it's much different. Your men would never be let into a European country without a valid passport.

"This is the only way, Albert. When I get Zhanna back to the States, we look forward to being on your crew."

[one hour later—at sea aboard Soviet frigate 491]

Zhanna had been kept in the ship's brig since coming aboard. Suddenly the screws of the ship stopped and Grusha appeared at the cell door with a seaman whose duties included jailor if any one happened to be held in the brig.

"Unlock her door," Grusha ordered the Russian seaman.

"Come with me," she said to Zhanna.

Grusha led Zhanna to the deck where off the port bow a submarine bounced in the waves. The ships were 200 miles north of Haiti. The trip aboard Frigate 491 had been a short one.

"I have never seen a submarine like that," Zhanna commented. The large conning tower rose out of the deck much closer to the stern of the boat than it normally did with other submarines.

"It's Romanian," Grusha answered. "During the war they operated in the Black Sea. Onboard is a Russian crew. After the war, we confiscated any Romanian naval vessels that could be useful to us."

"Then I assume plans have changed," Zhanna said as she looked out at the submarine.

"Yes, the famous icon from the war, Zhanna Rogova, was captured much too easily. I'm disappointed that you must think me a fool. This was your mistake. You should have made your capture much harder," Grusha said harshly. "I adjusted the plan. I knew your CIA would be watching the docks at Santiago de Cuba so we loaded you on this ship. This is the ship your German friend and any CIA accomplices will think you are on. It will be a 'wild goose chase,' as the Americans say."

"So where are we going?" Zhanna asked.

Grusha laughed. "I'm surprised you'd ask such a humorous question, as if you thought I would tell you. Let me just say we are going to a place much closer than Moscow and one that is the safest place on earth where the Americans have no access."

A deck mounted crane lowered a rubber skiff down the port stern. Rifles were drawn by crewmembers and pointed at Zhanna. Grusha followed Zhanna down a rope ladder to the bobbing boat. The coxswain immediately fired up the engine and headed out toward the submarine.

Part 4

"Russian female snipers are among the best in the world. The Hun should beware."

— *General George S. Patton, 1944*

Chapter 38

To Iceland
Sunday—22 December 1946

Erika took off from Miami aboard an Air Force DC-3 at eight o'clock that morning. On board with her were Al Hodge and three CIA operatives. They would land in Reykjavik late that evening, in plenty of time to prepare for the Russian frigate's arrival on Tuesday.

[meanwhile]
Zhanna was not heading to Iceland. The submarine spent the journey submerged except during the required time it had to surface to replenish air and charge its batteries. Because of all the submerged time when the boat could sail at only five knots, this made the trip up the Eastern seaboard of the United States a slow and tedious one.

The next day, when the submarine finally came to the mouth of the Chesapeake Bay, it lay on the bottom until nightfall. When it surfaced in the dark waters the crabbing trawler was waiting. Zhanna and Grusha transferred to the crab boat. The submarine disappeared under the waves immediately. The trawler sailed through the Bay and up the Potomac River.

Reykjavik, Iceland
Monday, 23 December 1946

Al Hodge picked up his phone at the Hotel Borg in Reykjavik.
"Hodge here."
"Al it's Leroy."
"Yeah, Leroy. We're ready to go here in Iceland. When the frigate gets here we'll get aboard by posing as part of the dock refueling crew. We have the schematics of that ship and know where the brig is. That should be where they keep her. I think we can smuggle Zhanna off without too much brouhaha, although we might have to deal with that Grusha character. That will be Erika's job."

"Forget all that, Al. Get everyone on the plane ASAP and get back here to Washington. We've been double shuffled."

"What are you talking about, Leroy?"

"An hour ago, just before daybreak here in D.C., our men working surveillance outside the Soviet embassy saw Zhanna get shoved out of a car by a tall woman and taken in through the backdoor of the building."

Chapter 39

Washington, D.C.
Tuesday, 24 December 1946

The meeting in Leroy Carr's Pentagon office had already been going for an hour. Erika and Al Hodge were there.

"Smart move on their part taking Zhanna to the Russian embassy. That's technically Russian soil. Everyone in the consulate is protected with diplomatic immunity. Even Zhanna, who is Russian, is protected as long as she's on embassy property since we never declared she is working for us and we never filed any formal charges against her for her espionage mission against us in '45. But they won't let her off the property. They know we can't get to her there, but any of the others can come and go around Washington or anyplace else as they wish. Any type of breech by us of diplomatic immunity would violate all the international laws concerning the autonomy of embassies. If we go in there to retrieve Zhanna, the Soviets will have an excuse to immediately invade our embassy in Moscow. We keep a boat load of sensitive, top-secret documents there and we can't take any chances."

"How about getting a mole inside the embassy?" Erika ventured.

Carr shook his head. "Practically impossible. The Russians hire no American help. Even their embassy janitors and dishwashers are brought over from Russia. Let's meet here again this evening at seven. Maybe I can put together some plan of action by then. I need some time to think. You two also think about it."

[same time]
Grusha sat in the office of Minister Anatoly Trukhin. The office of consulate minister was second only to that of the ambassador.

"You're to be commended, Comrade Grusha. I'm sure there will be a commendation for you and perhaps even a promotion from Moscow."

"Thank you, Comrade Minister. I will begin the interrogation immediately."

"Not just yet," Trukhin said. "She is to receive good treatment for now, at least until I say differently. I will tell you when her interrogation can begin."

Grusha shot him a sinister look. "I don't like what I'm hearing, Comrade. Why should this traitor receive good treatment?"

"Because those are your orders and they have been agreed upon by General Polzin back in Moscow. From what I have been told, he is the only one you report to. General Polzin has appointed me as your supervisor while you are here in Washington. So now you answer to me. Is that clear?"

Grusha continued to look him over with a nasty expression. "I hope you know what you are doing. Zhanna Rogova is not one who should be dealt with like a regular prisoner. She is ruthless and cagey. If given too much freedom she will escape this building. I wrote in my report that in my opinion she allowed herself to be captured. We need to find out the reason why."

"She will not escape," Trukhin said, "because you will be her chaperone. If for some reason you fail and Rogova gets away then you know how this will affect you."

"Is that a threat?"

"Just go get Zhanna and bring her to my office."

"Gladly, but I will sit in on your conversation with her."

"Don't push this hard line too far, Grusha. I know your reputation as hard to deal with. I'm being courteous to you because of your recent success; however, my patience will take you only so far. You won't sit in on any meeting I have with the prisoner or anyone else unless I want you to be there. As it happens, this time I want you here. Now obey your orders and bring the prisoner to me."

◊ ◊ ◊

Grusha returned with Zhanna in ten minutes.

"Take those handcuffs off her immediately," Trukhin grumbled.

Grusha begrudgingly removed the handcuffs.

Trukhin quickly stood up, moved around his desk and put his arms around Zhanna. She returned the embrace. "Zhanna, my dear, I hope you've been well these past couple of years."

"It is very good to see you again Anatoly," said Zhanna.

He kissed her on both cheeks.

There wasn't much that could dumbfound Grusha, but this was one of those times. She stood frowning.

"I have ordered that you receive good treatment, Zhanna. Grusha here will ensure that. Tonight you will dine with me alone in my quarters."

Trukhin redirected his attention to Grusha. "You may leave us now. I know you must be tired, Grusha. You won't be needed until tomorrow morning. Get some rest."

Chapter 40

Washington, D.C.
Same day—24 December 1946

It was only the second Christmas Eve since the war ended; unlike during the war when the city was under blackout, the streets of Washington were bright with lights festooning curb trees, store windows, and eaves of homes. Leroy Carr made the evening meeting as brief as possible so everyone could get home to their loved ones.

"Our best option right now is to find someone the Soviets will agree to exchange for Zhanna."

"She's number one on their capture or kill list, Leroy," Al reminded. "They're not going to trade her for some half-baked mole. Who could we possibly offer them that would tempt them to give up Rogova?"

"I don't know yet, Al. It's our job to come up with someone."

"Maybe this situation isn't all bad, boys," Erika piped in.

"What do you mean?" Hodge asked.

"Zhanna is inside the Russian embassy. How long have you been trying to get someone inside?"

"As far as what you're saying, Erika," said Carr. "For Zhanna to do us any good in that regard we'll have to establish some way to communicate with her. Then we have to have a feasible exit strategy to get her out of there when the time comes. All of that is a big order. Plus, she'll most likely be spending most of her time shackled and guarded to the teeth in some basement cell. She might already be undergoing torture."

◊ ◊ ◊

[same time—Soviet Embassy]
The Embassy of the Union of Soviet Socialist Republics was located in a historic Washington, D.C., mansion on Sixteenth Street. The former private home, although large for its initial intended use, was much too small for the ambassador, his minister, the numerous chargé d'affairs

and large help staff. Every closet and every nook and cranny had to be put to efficient use.

A major obstacle was that there were not nearly enough bathrooms. The female cooks and typists all roomed together on the top floor. They all shared one common bathroom down the hall with three more rooms of maids and low-level female staff. This demanded resourceful bladder control techniques or possession of a handy bucket.

Land had been acquired for a new embassy with greatly expanded facilities. Work had started, but for now it was the former mansion on Sixteenth Street where there was not even enough room for wives of the higher officials. Even the Ambassador's wife remained in Moscow. Bringing the wives to America would have to wait until the new facility was ready.

The only officials with private quarters were the Ambassador and his Minister, Anatoly Trukhin. Trukhin's suite, which had served the previous owners as a guest bedroom, was small, but elegantly appointed with valuable paintings, furniture, and carpets. The posh furnishings had been acquired during the purchase from the former owner, an American millionaire oil lobbyist.

Unlike the city outside, there were few reminders of the Christmas season among the technically atheist Soviets. One of the maids, a Russian Orthodox, had placed a few decorations around her shared quarters but this was ignored by the higher-ups. They knew many Russians still held tight to their faith and it wasn't worth the trouble to concern themselves with a few icons placed in a maid's room.

Zhanna was brought to Trukhin's private quarters at exactly seven o'clock. She wore a shiny satin evening gown. That afternoon, Trukhin had a female courier take Zhanna's measurements and the dress was purchased from an exclusive D.C. department store.

Trukhin dismissed the guard who delivered Zhanna then he closed the door behind her. "You look lovely, my dear. I hope you like the dress."

"You know I've never been a woman who is much concerned with dresses, Anatoly, but it is nice. Thank you." Zhanna hated the high-heels that the courier also bought, but she held back any comment.

He led her to a small table where a make-shift bar had been set up that afternoon by the embassy butler.

"What are you drinking, my precious Zhanna?"

"Vodka."

Trukhin poured her a snifter and one for himself. They clinked glasses and both completely down the spirits in one gulp.

"I feel I must apologize for your quarters," Trukhin mentioned. Zhanna was still being held in a locked basement cell. "There is simply not enough room here in this building. We have maids and cooks sleeping four or five to a room. Believe me, where you are now is better. At least you have private toilet facilities, something none of the workers I just mentioned enjoy." He refilled her glass.

"I understand, Anatoly."

"If at any time you want to see me, just let a guard know. You can also take walks outside on the embassy property. Grusha will escort you and serve as your chaperone."

"How does Grusha feel about that?"

"Grusha must accept the fact that we all have superiors, including herself," Trukhin said firmly. "While Grusha is in Washington, I've been appointed to act as her supervisor. Moscow expects her to follow my orders."

"I'm sure she's happy about that—about being my chaperone, that is."

This caused Trukhin to laugh. "So, I see you know Grusha."

"I just recently met her."

"She knows you were the best, Zhanna. I think that's what Grusha yearns for—to be held in the same regard as you. But enough of this business talk. I'll have dinner brought up."

Zhanna removed her neck scarf, revealing her gruesome scar. "I don't need this, Anatoly. You have seen me as I am."

"Yes, I have," he said as he lightly stroked her cheek. "You saved my life even before you had the scar. You are still beautiful, my precious Zhanna."

"Anatoly, I will spend the night with you if that's what you desire, but I can only offer you my body. I have never felt love for anyone and I think the Fates will never change their minds. I've always been honest with you about that."

Chapter 41

1942

The Battle for Stalingrad in the Soviet Union

The Germans had the city surrounded.

The Battle for Stalingrad had raged since July. It was now November with no end in sight. Food had been cut off and the citizens of Stalingrad were living off the last of the potatoes in their cellars. For those families that had already run out of potatoes, they survived off the flesh of dead horses, dogs, and even cats—any animals that had been killed in the streets during the constant artillery shelling by the German Sixth Army.

Colonel Anatoly Trukhin had been assigned by General Zhukov to defend the southeastern quadrant of the besieged city. This was an important assignment as this area of the city outskirts was where much of the German Sixth Army lay encamped. Much of the German shelling came from this edge of the town.

Winter had made an early appearance, even for a city accustomed to harsh winters like Stalingrad. The howling winds, overcast skies, and deep snow had aided the Russians, bringing the German Luftwaffe and the supplies it delivered to a virtual halt. So it was not only the citizens and Red Army in Stalingrad who suffered from lack of food stuffs and medical supplies but the Germans, as well. Both sides had to endure cruel conditions but the battle continued. Hitler had ordered the city be taken regardless of cost; Stalin issued a mirroring directive that the city not be taken despite the loss of lives—civilian or military.

Normally, a Red Army colonel would not be expected or encouraged to join his men in the field. Someone with the rank of colonel, if captured, could reveal much information under torture. Yet Anatoly Trukhin ignored this protocol more often than not and he would assume command of one of the diminishing number of T-34 tanks into the field to try and knockout German artillery positions. Many of the Russian T-34s had been destroyed in the fighting; some sat quietly in Stalingrad for lack of fuel.

This November, during one of Trukhin's forays into German territory, his T-34 had not made it very far out of the city when his tank came across one of the newly developed German Tiger tanks just outside the city limits. The T-34 could compete in head-to-head battle with any German tank including the Nazis Tiger. That is if the crew was capable. A large number of Soviet tankers who had been stationed in Stalingrad were dead. Trukhin found himself with an inexperienced and not very well trained crew.

Trukhin's tank got off the first shot which missed. The Tiger fired and hit Trukhin's T-34, blowing off the tank's starboard track, rendering it immobile. Trukhin's cannon loader was slow and a second shot from the Tiger found the engine and gas tank just behind the turret. The T-34 rapidly began going up in flames.

Trukhin ordered his four-man crew to evacuate. All made it out in relatively good shape except for the driver. The tank driver sat lowest in the tank and it always took him the longest to exit. He suffered third degree burns on his legs and found it difficult to walk.

Trukhin and his tank crew knew they couldn't run away. They helped the injured man as they tried to find somewhere to hide, but the Germans arrived too quickly and Trukhin and his men were taken captive by five German Wehrmacht soldiers. The Russians were disarmed and ordered to hike in single file with their hands on their heads. The Germans quickly understood the burnt man could not keep up so they shot him and left him where he fell in the snow. Trukhin knew they would all die soon. The Germans would take them to some command post, interrogate them then they would be shot. Intelligence had told him this was standard procedure by the Germans as they had less food than they needed for themselves and certainly not enough to feed prisoners or war.

After an hour of trudging through knee-deep snow in -10° Fahrenheit temperatures, they entered a stark valley void of trees surrounded by small hills. Suddenly the crack of a rifle shot from long distance sounded out. The distinctive German helmet of the sergeant in charge flew off from a head shot that entered his body directly through his ear. The other Germans stopped for a moment and this cost them another soldier. This one to another head shot. The remaining three Germans, all wearing white camouflage parkas, dived into the deep snow seeking cover as did Trukhin and his remaining two men. The Germans frantically looked around trying to find a target but the only possible location a Russian sniper could be working from was from one of the hills nearly a half kilometer away.

The snow was not enough to hide them from the sniper's higher vantage point. Within two minutes the remaining three Germans were dead. There had been five shots that rang out from somewhere in the far distance and now five Germans were dead.

Trukhin ordered his men to begin running as best as they could back to Stalingrad, three kilometers away.

◊ ◊ ◊

Anatoly Trukhin and the remaining two members of his tank crew eventually made it back to Stalingrad and to Trukhin's command post that was set up in what had been a furniture warehouse before the war. A building that was now heavily sand-bagged from street-level to just below the roof.

Trukhin and his men were half frozen. The tank's gun turret canon loader had three frostbitten toes that would have to be removed.

After the lifesaving heat from the building's coal boiler had warmed Trukhin to the point where he could speak without shivering and his teeth chattering, he summoned his second in command.

"Was you mission a success, Comrade Colonel?" the major asked.

"Does it look like it was a success, Major? We left this morning in a tank and we return on foot with frozen balls. What would be your guess?"

"I'm sorry, Colonel, but at least you made it back alive."

"Major, I want you to contact Captain Uritski. He is in charge of our snipers here in Stalingrad. I want to find out which one was assigned to a position about three kilometers west of the southeastern sector today. He saved our lives, killing the Germans who captured us with shots a half kilometer away. I want to meet him."

"Yes, sir. The phone link to Uritski's bunker is still in working order. I'll call him this evening."

"Call him now."

"Yes, of course." The major offered a snappy saluted and left to fulfill his orders. He returned after fifteen minutes.

"Colonel, Capitan Uritski informed me the sniper was a woman, Zhanna Rogova. Apparently the myth is flesh and blood, Colonel. He will send her to you as soon as she returns to the sniper bunker for food and more ammunition. That should be tonight."

The surprise showed on Trukhin's face. The Red Army was known for its excellent snipers, many of whom were women. Yet like the major and most of the Red Army, he was under the impression that the super sniper they called Zhanna was a fable. Propaganda created to shore up Red Army morale and to force Germans to watch their backs.

"Very well, Major. Be sure the tank crewmen who returned with me are attended to and fed. That will be all for now."

"Yes, sir." The major saluted again before leaving.

Chapter 42

Washington, D.C.
Thursday, 26 December 1946

Grusha had requested a meeting with the Russian ambassador. It took two days, but the meeting was finally granted. Now she sat in the office of Ambassador Extraordinary and Plenipotentiary Nicolai Vasilevich Novikov.

"Thank you for granting me this meeting, Comrade Ambassador," Grusha started out.

"That's fine," said Novikov. "I'm busy. What is this all about?"

Grusha got right to the point. "For the past two nights, a high-priority prisoner has been the overnight guest of Minister Trukhin in his quarters."

"And you think I'm not aware of this?"

A surprised Grusha paused. "I wasn't sure, Comrade Ambassador."

"I know who you are and I know of your role in apprehending Zhanna Rogova. That should be enough for you. You'll receive the proper accolades when you return to Moscow. I'm also aware of Zhanna Rogova's importance. We have a plan for her."

"I want to know that plan," Grusha demanded.

The ambassador's face turned dark. "You forget who you're talking to," Novikov barked.

"*May* I know the plan, sir?" Grusha amended her wording.

"No, you may not. You will be informed on a need-to-know basis. Just follow the orders given you by Minister Trukhin. For now you are to serve as her chaperone. She is not to be interrogated by you—I have been told of your techniques—and she's to receive good treatment. If that is all, get out."

[same day—The Pentagon]
Erika had been studying the blueprints of the building that was now the Soviet embassy. The blueprints were easy enough to attain as they

were on file with the D.C. Housing Authority since the days the building served as a private residence owned by an American. She and Al Hodge now sat in Leroy Carr's office.

"It's curious why Zhanna is allowed to walk the grounds of the Soviet embassy," said Erika. She had spent time the past two days working with the surveillance team that kept track of who entered and who left the consulate. Yesterday, Erika saw Zhanna walking around with Grusha and two men in black suits following closely behind.

"Leroy, I think I've found a way to get into and out of the embassy without the Russians knowing."

"Erika, I know you've been studying the blueprints, but an operation to break into the Soviet embassy would have to be cleared by the Secretary of State, and he wouldn't give the okay unless he checked with the president first to cover his ass. So for all intents and purposes, approval would have to come directly from the White House and that's not going to happen. Truman doesn't give a rat's behind about Zhanna. He might not even know about her even though she's been in many of my reports. White House aides read a lot of the truck loads of reports from different agencies that arrive at the White House every day. Some get passed on to the president and many don't.

"If something were to go wrong and the CIA were discovered to be behind it there would be hell to pay and international repercussions like you wouldn't believe."

"Then will you at least try to get permission? I can do it, Leroy. I just need one person who is good that I can trust for a two-man team."

"And who would that be? It can't be Sheila, she's an Army major and the Soviets could declare it as an act of war."

"Is Kathryn Fischer still teaching at that war college in Rhode Island?"

(Erika, Zhanna, Sheila Reid, and Kathryn had worked together on the last mission that rescued the genius inventor/Hollywood movie star Hedy Lamarr from the Russians).

"Yes," Carr answered, "Kathryn is there, but I'm afraid I have to decline your request for now."

Erika said nothing.

"Are we clear, Erika?" Carr asked firmly. "I know you sometimes go off and cowboy on your own. We can't have that here. Is that fully understood?"

Erika paused, and then finally nodded.

"I need to talk to Al about another matter," Carr said. "That will be all for now, Erika. Thank you."

As soon as Erika left the room, Hodge said, "You know she's going to do it anyway, Leroy."

"I know. We have to stop her, Al. She still has charges against her here in the States pending because of her wartime activities for the Germans. Take charge of arresting her. Unfortunately, I think locking her up is the only option we have. Take her to the brig at Fort Dix."

Chapter 43

1942

Stalingrad, Soviet Union
Same day in November, 1942—that evening

It was nearing nine o'clock when Trukhin's aide reported back. Everyone was still on duty. There was no off-duty time during the Battle for Stalingrad. Everyone assigned to Trukhin's headquarters had a cot on the second floor of the building and it was here they stayed 24/7 unless sent out on an errand or mission by Trukhin. Any hours not spent sleeping were hours on duty.

"The woman sniper has reported, Colonel," the major said after a salute.

"Bring her here to my office."

"Yes, sir."

In a few moments the major escorted in a beautiful woman dressed in a Red Army uniform. Her jet hair and striking eyes enhanced her classic features. There was no rank on the uniform which for snipers was standard procedure. They worked alone and were not to be under the authority of anyone except the sniper commander. Right now that man was Captain Uritski, but sniper commanders came and went quickly. In a month it was likely this woman and the other Russian snipers in Stalingrad would have a different commander. The Soviet high command considered the snipers a clandestine force, and decided it best that no one commander get to know his charges too well.

"Comrade," the major said to Zhanna, "I present you to Colonel Anatoly Trukhin, commander of the southeastern quadrant of our defenses."

Zhanna said nothing and looked around with suspicion.

"Salute the Colonel, Comrade!" the major thundered.

Trukhin stepped in. "That will be all, Major, you may leave us now."

"Please have a seat," Trukhin told Zhanna as the major left and closed the door.

"I'd rather stand."

"Humor me and sit down . . . please."

Zhanna looked around again before sitting.

"I'm afraid you might have the wrong impression," Trukhin said. "I brought you here to thank you."

"For what?"

"You saved my life and the lives of two of my tank crewmen today if what I've been told is true, that you were the sniper working about three kilometers west of the quadrant boundary."

"That was you?" Zhanna asked. "What is a colonel doing commanding a tank crew?"

"Never mind that. So it *was* you behind the rifle?"

"Yes."

"And you are the famous Zhanna Rogova?"

She was tired and hungry. She paused and looked at him without responding.

"I'll repeat," Trukhin said patiently. "Are you Zhanna Rogova?"

"That is my name."

"Have you eaten since returning from the field?"

"No." She was quite thin as were all the Soviet troops in Stalingrad.

"What do you normally eat at the sniper bunker?"

"We are issued a small tin of American SPAM each day along with flat bread if there is any."

Trukhin sounded a buzzer to summon the major.

"You will dine with me tonight," Trukhin said to her. "Don't expect too much, but I can offer you a better meal than SPAM and fried flour."

"I'm instructed by my commander to report back to the bunker as soon as this meeting is over. Captain Uritski is under the impression this would be a short meeting."

"My aide will inform Captain Uritski that you will be here until I have one of my men drive you back to the bunker."

◊ ◊ ◊

The very late night meal was ready just before midnight. On each of the two plates sat two roasted doves that had lingered in Stalingrad too long this fall, a small red potato, real bread, and even butter, something Zhanna had not tasted in two years.

The ravenous sniper dived in. Trukhin ate along but slower, spending much of his time watching Zhanna shovel in the food.

During the meal, Trukhin made an effort at small talk.

"I had heard that the great Zhanna Rogova, if indeed she was real, had blue eyes."

Her eyes were dark and hypnotizing.

"Is that what they say?" was her only response. She continued to concentrate on the food on her plate.

In the scheme of filling, fine dining it would never qualify, but Zhanna's stomach had shrunk to the point that she felt full.

"Thank you, Comrade Colonel," Zhanna said after scrapping her plate for any remaining remnants of food.

"I can see you enjoyed it," Trukhin commented. "I'm glad."

"Now I must return to the bunker," Zhanna said.

"Of course, I will have one of my men drive you there. It is too far to walk in this ungodly weather."

[December 1942—Battle for Stalingrad]

For almost a month since the day Zhanna Rogova saved Anatoly Trukhin from capture, torture, and certain firing squad by the German Sixth Army, he had ordered her to his command post about twice weekly for a meal and conversation. Eventually, he had told her to call him by his first name if no one else was around. They usually ate and stayed in his office, one of the few places they were afforded a measure of privacy.

"Where is your family, Anatoly?" Zhanna asked one night.

"I have a sixteen-year-old son and thirteen-year-old daughter that I managed to get to the safety of Archangel after their mother, my wife, was killed by the SS in one of their Einsatzgruppen sweeps through Smolensk, our home town."

Zhanna said nothing.

"And you, Zhanna. Your family?"

"I have none. I was abandoned as a baby and raised in a State run orphanage in Leningrad. I escaped from there when I was fourteen."

"How did you live after that?"

"I lived on the streets of Leningrad until the war broke out, then I joined the army."

"So you have no family that you know of?"

Zhanna shook her head.

"Well, I think we deserve a brief respite from all of this, and from the war. I have saved this for a special occasion." Trukhin reached into one of his lower desk drawers and brought out a bottle of Napoleon brandy. He poured them both a measure into two tin canteen cups, the only cups available.

A week later, Zhanna Rogova and Anatoly Trukhin began spending one night a week together. Trukhin wished her stays could be more often, but always looming was the battle of annihilation just outside the city limits.

Trukhin became very fond of Zhanna during their nights together—perhaps he loved her. For Zhanna, she held no feelings for Trukhin other than he gave her a few hours of pleasure during a ghastly war where they could all die at any moment.

Chapter 44

Washington, D.C.
Saturday, 28 December 1946

"How's Erika doing?" Leroy Carr asked Al Hodge. They were waiting on their breakfast to be brought to their table at Hamilton's Restaurant in Arlington. Hamilton's was a popular place that served good food. Carr and Hodge had met there often, going back to the early years of the war when they teamed up in the OSS. As they waited, they drank coffee and smoked.

"She's not too happy up there in New Jersey behind bars at Fort Dix," Hodge said and then roared with laughter.

"I hate that we had to do that to her," Carr said.

"Not me." Hodge laughed again. "As far as I'm concerned, it's nice to get a little pay back for all the crap she's put us through the past two years." Hodge, a chain smoker, was still chuckling as he lit another Lucky Strike. "Arresting Lehmann has made my week. Thanks, Leroy."

"I never asked you: any problems during the arrest?" Carr inquired after a sip of coffee.

"I took five MPs with me and I warned them ahead of time about her. There was a big scrape but they finally got the cuffs on her. She bloodied a couple of noses and blacked a couple of eyes. She also wrenched one guy's arm badly, but she got a few bruises herself so it worked out fine."

"Geez Louise," Carr said softly, as if he talked to himself.

[later that morning—Soviet consulate]
"I trust that your breakfast was acceptable, Zhanna," said Anatoly Trukhin. He and Zhanna sat alone in his embassy office.

"It was very nice, Anatoly. I remember all those years during the war when an egg was worth its weight in gold. If we were lucky, we got perhaps one every other month."

"Yes, I remember. I want to again apologize that you are housed in a cell for much of the day and take your meals there except when I get the opportunity to have you dine with me."

"I understand, Anatoly. I have been treated very well under the circumstances and I know that's because of you."

"Zhanna, I had you brought to my office today because I have important news for you. News that I am very pleased to tell you."

Zhanna just nodded to signal she was listening.

"I have an offer to make you. This is something I suggested to the ambassador the day after Grusha delivered you here to the embassy. I waited until now to tell you because the ambassador and I needed approval from Moscow. That approval came in last night.

"We will drop all charges against you—wipe the slate clean, as the Americans say—and reinstate you in the NKVD at the rank of captain. As you know, that's a promotion. You held the rank of senior lieutenant when you disappeared and began work for the CIA."

Zhanna replied, "This sounds like generosity one normally doesn't see from the NKVD and the Politburo. I assume it is the Politburo you refer to when you say 'approval from Moscow.'"

"Yes."

"And in return for my earning this generosity, I will be expected to do what, Anatoly? Surely the NKVD has enough assassins. I'm sure Grusha must be very good."

"But she's not a Zhanna Rogova. Our friend Grusha is very good but could never fill your shoes. Nevertheless, that is not part of the deal. In return for clemency and reinstatement in good standing, your assignment will be to return to the CIA and continue to work there, but now as a double agent reporting to us."

Zhanna thought for a moment. "The Americans are clever. I will have to tell them I escaped from here. They'll be suspicious of that."

"You will not have to escape. We will arrange a trade with the Americans. Their CIA has already contacted us with an offer. The offer was initiated by their side, not ours. This should belie any suspicions on their part. My dear Zhanna, it's either this or be returned to the Soviet Union to await execution. That is something I don't think I could bear. You saved my life once. Now it's time for me to repay my debt. If you agree, as I trust you will, I'll set things in motion."

Chapter 45

Washington, D.C.
Monday, 30 December 1946

This time it was Leroy Carr who strolled into Al Hodge's Pentagon office.

"Hey! Leroy," Hodge exclaimed. "I have a laugh for you. Yesterday, Lehmann was let out of her cell to take a shower in the stockade shower room. She somehow managed to get the shower head off and turn the arm toward the bars. When she yelled to the guards that she was finished, they went to get her and she sprayed them with boiling hot water."

"Why did she do that?" Carr asked.

"What do you mean? She did it just to be a bitch is what I figure. When they got her out she kicked one of the MPs in the nuts, and used the shower head to bash one over the head. She was just wearing a towel, and it came off during the struggle to get the cuffs back on her. Some more jailors arrived with nightsticks. They got to wrestle with a naked woman so they're not complaining."

"Holy cow," Carr shook his head. "Well, she'll be happy tomorrow. I need you to go to Fort Dix, Al, and get her released. Bring her straight to my office."

"What do you have going?"

"The Russians have agreed to a trade for Zhanna. You know I've been working on that."

Hodge nodded. "Who are we trading?"

"The Russians named three men the FBI has charged with spying. Two are Russians and one is an American."

"Three for one," said Hodge. "Pretty good deal for the Russians, but I'm still surprised they'd give up Rogova."

"Me, too. All I can figure is that one of the captured Russians must have friends in high places in Moscow. That would explain it."

Hodge nodded. "I assume this trade won't take place here in the States."

"Right, it will take place in Potsdam, Germany. There is a bridge there over the Havel River. It's a restricted border crossing. One side of the bridge is in the Soviet zone, the other side serves as entrance into the American sector."

"I assume we're taking Lehmann because she speaks German and Russian."

"Right."

"Who else are we taking?"

"Sheila and Kathryn Fischer," Carr answered. "That will give us two more German speakers. We'll take the Army Ranger, Stephen Floyd, and three CIA operatives who can handle themselves and offer good backup. I haven't decided who they'll be yet; I'm still reading files."

"Do we have a day for the trade set yet?" Hodge asked.

"No, tomorrow morning I'm meeting with the Russian Minister, Anatoly Trukhin. Both sides need time to prepare. I'm guessing the trade will take place sometime next week."

Al Hodge wasn't enamored with Erika, but above all, he was a professional. That's why Carr valued him so much as his sidekick. "Okay, I'll leave early tomorrow morning. Fort Dix is a three-hour drive each way. I should have her here by one or two in the afternoon. I'll need the paperwork for her release."

"Sheila is already processing it. She'll have one of her aides drop it off to you this afternoon."

"Anything out of Cuba about the Mafia conference?" Hodge asked.

"That's not really our concern since the mob has completed its business with the Soviets, but I've got Marienne Schenk down there now keeping her eyes and ears open."

Chapter 46

Fort Dix, New Jersey
Tuesday, 31 December 1946

Al Hodge reported in with the sergeant-at-arms of the Fort Dix stockade at just after nine that morning. The last thing Al expected was a lecture.

"Master Sergeant, my name is Albert Hodge." Al showed his State Department identification (the CIA had yet to issue I.D.s since technically it had yet to be approved by Congress). "I'm here to pick up a detainee, Erika Lehmann." Hodge handed the release paperwork to the master sergeant. The man rudely snatched it from Al's hand and looked it over quickly.

"Why the devil did you bring that woman here?" the master sergeant asked irritably. "I know you guys have government jail cells in Washington."

"This is where Mr. Carr, my boss, wanted her, that's why." Hodge was starting to get irked at the man's surly attitude.

"Well, tell your Mr. Carr thanks a million. I don't know how I can return the favor other than send him a vile of the black plague. She's been nothing but trouble since the minute she got here. I want that pain in the ass out of here and off the base as soon as you can get her butt loaded into a car. And don't bring her back unless she has specific charges filed against her. I'm not running a hotel here."

The man summoned a jailor who sported a black eye.

◊ ◊ ◊

Erika Lehmann had finished the breakfast brought to her cell an hour ago. Now she was doing pushups with her feet propped on her bunk to make them more difficult. When she heard the cell block door down the corridor being unlocked and opened, it naturally perked her interest as she was the only prisoner in that block.

She stopped her workout and sat on the edge of her bed. In a moment, Al Hodge and the MP jailor with the black eye stood in the corridor outside her cell.

"Hello, Erika," Hodge offered stoically.

"Well, if it isn't my old friend, Herr Hodge. What brings you here, Al?"

"You're being released."

"Is that so? You're telling me I'm suddenly back in Leroy's good graces. Why is that?"

"Don't push your luck, Lehmann. I'll explain everything in the car on our way back to Washington."

Hodge nodded to the jailor to unlock her cell door.

"Goodbye, darling," Erika said to the MP as she stepped out of her cell. "You can keep that black eye as a going away present from me."

The jailor walked Erika and Hodge to the brig's entrance.

The master sergeant watched through his window as Hodge and Erika got into Hodge's Plymouth.

"Well, there she goes, Kowalski. The beer is on me tonight at Finnigan's."

"Where did they ever find a woman like that, Master Sergeant?"

"My best guess would be about the 8th or 9th level of Dante's Inferno."

[same morning—Washington]

Anatoly Trukhin was not about to invite the second man in command at the CIA to a meeting in the Soviet embassy. Likewise, Leroy Carr did not want the Soviet minister to be escorted through the Pentagon.

Subsequently, they now sat in a suite at the Mayflower Hotel. On a large coffee table between them sat a carafe of coffee, some fruit, and assorted donuts and Danish breakfast sweets.

The two men had already exchanged a cordial handshake. Both Trukhin and Carr had brought the agreed upon one 'aide' a.k.a. bodyguard. Both were now stationed outside the room in the hallway. Carr and Trukhin sat alone in the room.

Carr offered Trukhin a cigarette.

"Thank you, Mr. Carr," Trukhin said as he accepted it. "I will admit that you Americans and the Turks make the best cigarettes. Your Kentucky Bourbon is also very good."

"So you drink Bourbon?"

"On occasion."

"I'll send over to your embassy a case for you," said Carr.

"That's not necessary."

"It would be my pleasure."

Trukhin lit his cigarette, took a puff and exhaled. "So now, Mr. Carr, we get down to our business. I'm here to confirm that our deal is set and to confirm that the bargain has been approved by your government."

"Yes," Carr answered. "We will exchange the three arrested spies whose names you sent me in exchange for Zhanna Rogova."

Trukhin nodded.

"And I will ask the same question," Carr said. "The agreement is approved by the appropriate Soviet authorities in Moscow."

"Yes."

"May I ask you one more question? I'm a bit curious why the Soviets would exchange anyone for Rogova, knowing how highly she is wanted by your secret police, the NKVD."

"One of the men we are exchanging for has high friends on the Politburo. Need I elaborate?"

"No, I understand," said Carr. "I had even thought something like that might be what's entering in here."

"Then we understand each other and it looks like we have a deal. You and I have already communicated through diplomatic couriers and agreed on the location of the trade in Potsdam. Now we need to agree on a date."

"We can be ready by next Tuesday—one week from today," Carr announced.

"We can also be ready by that date. Our business is now settled except for the details of the physical trade itself," Trukhin commented.

"Mr. Minister, I propose we don't set a limit on the number of aides each side brings to the bridge, but everyone on each side must remain on their bank. One person from each side will walk the persons we're exchanging to the middle of the bridge and go no farther. The 'walkers' will wait until the prisoners meet in the middle of the bridge and then your walker will escort your exchangees back to your side of the bridge and ours will do the same."

"I have no problems with that proposal. It sounds fair and effective," Trukhin responded.

The two men exchanged a handshake to seal the deal. Trukhin left quickly. Neither he nor Carr had drunk any of the coffee nor eaten any of the fruit or Danish.

Chapter 47

Hotel Nacional, Havana
Same day—Tuesday, 31 December 1946

A riotous New Years Eve party was currently underway at the Nacional even though midnight was still five hours away.

Marienne Schenk sat beside her husband at the main casino bar sipping a Bucanero cervesa, an expensive but popular beer at the hotel named in honor (or dishonor) of the many pirates who used the island as a gathering point and resupply station back in the old days. Several Havana pubs near the water proudly advertised that Edward Teach himself—Black Beard—had downed some pints there.

However, Marienne wasn't there to study Buccaneer history. Leroy Carr had sent her.

During the war, Marienne worked for the OSS. Leroy Carr considered her the best shadow he had ever had, and although she was now a private citizen living in Pittsburgh, Carr couldn't help himself from calling her on occasions he needed her unique skill— Marienne Schenk could tail anyone and they'd never know it. Marienne's husband, Harold, understood. He had served as a Marine during the war and although he worried about his wife's occasional forays for Leroy Carr and his new agency, he understood commitment to one's country. Marienne had asked her husband to come along this time so she would be accompanied by a man and not have to deal with turning down never-ending pick-up attempts by the vultures that quickly swooped down on single women in a casino. With her tough Marine husband at her side that concern was annulled.

Marienne had already been in Havana for a week. Her assignment was to hang around the Nacional and keep an eye on the top gangsters who were assembled there for the mob conference. Especially, Carr wanted her to keep an eye on Albert Anastasia, who Carr doubted would take the disappearance of his two female crewmembers lightly.

Chapter 48

Washington, D.C.
Same day—Tuesday, 31 December 1946

At eight o'clock this morning Zhanna had been brought from her cell to Trukhin's office.

"Yesterday, I met with a highly placed CIA officer—a Mr. Carr," Trukhin said as he poured Zhanna a cup of coffee. "Do you know him, Zhanna?"

"Yes, he was my supervisor and also the supervisor for the German, Erika Lehmann."

Trukhin nodded. "Yes, we assumed as much."

The Colonel took a drink of coffee and continued. "All of the particulars of the exchange are set. We will give you over to the Americans next Tuesday in Potsdam, Germany. There is a bridge there that spans from our sector to theirs.

"I have agreed with this Mr. Carr that one agent from each side will escort the exchanging prisoners. Grusha Mustafina will walk you onto the bridge."

"Why her, Anatoly? I'd prefer someone else. I don't trust her."

"We are expecting no problems, Zhanna. The agreement with the Americans is that the 'walkers' for both sides will not be armed. We'll have snipers nearby to make sure Grusha stays keen to her orders. Those orders will be to do nothing more than walk you to the middle of the bridge, turn you over to the American 'walker,' then escort the three men we are exchanging you for back to our side of the bridge."

"These three men the Americans are exchanging for me; I'm a bit surprised the Americans aren't suspicious of this deal, even though it's three for one. They know how highly I'm wanted by the NKVD."

"I told Mr. Carr at our meeting that one of the men has high friends on the Politburo. This is not true, but this Carr fellow has no way to verify it, and that should be enough to convince him of why we are agreeing to this trade."

Zhanna went back to talking about Grusha. "It is my understanding that Grusha refuses to fly."

"She is leaving tonight on a motorized Greek yacht that is docked in the Chesapeake Bay," Trukhin explained. "It's manned by a Greek crew and the Americans are not aware that we use it on occasion. This yacht can cruise at 27 knots. When the ship docks in Hamburg, Grusha will board a train to Berlin. A train will get her to Berlin faster than a car. The German autobahns still have much damage from wartime bombing that has yet to be repaired; the train from Hamburg to Berlin is now again in service. Potsdam is just outside Berlin. Grusha will be there in time."

[that afternoon—Pentagon]

"What the heck, Erika?" Carr said loudly as Al Hodge escorted her into his office. "Why all these bad reports from Fort Dix?"

"I shouldn't have been there; it wasn't fair, and I was mad."

"You were mad? Al and I both knew you had made up your mind to break into the Soviet embassy, and we knew you would ignore my orders not to do so. Your track record speaks for itself. Now, sit there and tell me I was wrong."

Erika said nothing for a moment and then asked, "Do you have a cigarette?"

"That's what I thought," Carr responded. He laid a pack of Pall Malls on his desk in front of her. "But we don't have to worry about breaking Zhanna out of the embassy anymore. I'm sure Al explained everything to you in the car during the drive back from Fort Dix."

Erika nodded as she lit a Pall Mall. I'm familiar with the Glienicke Bridge in Potsdam. I've crossed it many times."

"Good, that's just another reason why you'll be our 'walker.'

"And I'll be unarmed, I'm sure."

"Yes."

Chapter 49

Atlantic Ocean
Thursday, 02 January 1947

The 80-foot Greek yacht was named *Maia,* after the Spring Goddess and the oldest and most beautiful of Atlas's daughters who made up the Pleiades. The ship's apolitical Greek owner didn't particularly like dealing with the Russians but they paid well. Allowing Russians or any nationality to charter his ship was not illegal in the United States, so he took the jobs to help offset the incredibly expensive task of maintaining the yacht. He and his crew (mostly his sons) performed the jobs and then returned to Maryland where most of them now lived after having fled from the Germans in Crete. Luckily, his wealth enabled him to secure entrance visas to their new homeland without too much trouble. Once in the States, he set up *The Athena,* a Greek restaurant in Baltimore where wives and daughters worked the kitchen and the men served as waiters. During extended jobs like this one—five days across the Atlantic and five days back—the overworked women at the restaurant had to handle everything. Luckily, there were a few cousins that could usually help out as waiters on a temporary basis.

Now two days out to sea, the speedy ship should have its cargo of one woman to the Port of Hamburg by Sunday morning. He would be glad to be rid of her. She was a large, intimidating being who made it clear she wanted to be left alone. She had turned down the customary invitation to dine with him—the captain—and usually ignored the crew if given a "Hello" or "Good Morning." Getting her to Hamburg and off his ship couldn't happen quickly enough as far as he was concerned.

◊ ◊ ◊

As the sun began to drop below the horizon behind the *Maia,* Grusha sat in a deck chair at the stern drinking an American Hamm's beer and smoking a Cuban cigar as she watched the wake from the ship's screws churn the blue sea white.

It boggled her mind that General Pozlin and the Politburo had agreed to this trade. Although she knew it wasn't her fault, Grusha now knew she made a colossal mistake taking Zhanna to the Russian Embassy in Washington. Had she known Zhanna had a former lover who was now consulate minister, she would have diverted her instead to Central America. There were small, but solid Soviet cells scattered helter-skelter in several of the Central American countries. From there, she could have spirited Zhanna to Moscow on a freighter without interference.

That was water under the bridge now. The only thing Grusha had on her mind was the certainty that she was not going to allow Zhanna Rogova to leave the bridge in Potsdam alive.

[same day—Washington]

The buzzer on Leroy Carr's desk went off.

"Yes, Sheila."

"Marienne Schenk is returning your call, sir."

"Put her through."

The phone clicked and Carr said, "Marienne, is that you?"

"Yes, Leroy. I'm returning your call."

"Anything new from Cuba?"

"The mob meetings are about over. Most of the men on our lists have either packed up and returned to the States or will do so shortly. Of course, I wasn't privy to any meetings, so I don't have anything for you there, but I did find out that Albert Anastasia and his men are leaving for Bayamo tonight. From listening to bar talk by some of his men, I think he's going there to confront the Russians about Zhanna and Erika disappearing. Sounds like trouble. Do you want me to follow them there?"

"No, if there is trouble between the Soviets and the mob that might rend the sheets of the bed they obviously share, then that's good for us. The FBI can deal with that mess.

"Get back to D.C. immediately, Marienne. I need you here. I've already sent a plane from Miami to pick up you and Harold. It can fly you directly to Washington non-stop from Havana. It should land at any minute at the Havana airport if it hasn't already. You should be in Washington by seven or eight this evening. I've reserved you and Harold a room at the Mayflower for tonight, registered in your name. I'll see you in my office at seven o'clock tomorrow morning."

Chapter 50

Carr's Pentagon Office
Next morning—Friday, 03 January 1947

Leroy Carr had one of his typists bring in two carafes of steaming hot black coffee, along with sugar and cream. The female Army private set it all up on a small, portable table in the corner of the room.

"Thank you, Private," Carr said.

The woman nodded and said, "Yes, sir," before leaving the room.

Extra chairs had been added. They were occupied by Al Hodge, Erika Lehmann, Marienne Schenk, Sheila Reid, Kathryn Fischer, and a U.S. Army Ranger—Stephen Floyd. Carr had used the tough and capable Floyd on two previous missions.

Carr repeated the essence of the current mission mainly for Marienne Schenk's sake who had not yet been fully briefed, then he addressed her first. Her husband, Harold, had left early that morning to return to Pittsburgh and the river barge business he and Marienne owned and managed.

"Marienne, we've learned that Grusha is on her way to Hamburg by way of a Greek yacht called the *Maia.* You'll fly to Hamburg and be there when that ship arrives and shadow Grusha. Since she has been suddenly dispatched to Germany it can only be because the Soviets intend for her to take part in some way in the exchange. She will be easy to spot; she's nearly six-feet tall and you've been given the photographs we took of her on the grounds of the Soviet embassy."

"I understand," Marienne said. "How will I contact you?"

"Al and I, and the rest of us, will be staying in Berlin at the Kempinski Hotel on the Ku'Damm. It's only 25 miles from Potsdam. Al and I will be registered using our real names. There is nothing to be gained from aliases since the Soviets know we are coming there for the exchange. The hotels you will use will depend on your shadowing of Grusha. As always, Sheila will make sure you have the money you need for trains, taxis, hotels, meals, etc.," Carr replied.

Carr turned to the decorated Army Ranger. "Sergeant Floyd, your job is simple. You'll be armed and will accompany me as backup."

"Yes, sir," the D-Day and Battle of the Bulge hero stated.

"For everyone else, Al will take to Berlin the prisoners and three capable CIA men on hand to guard the prisoners later—probably Monday. Al and I will be working on whom to name to that team today.

"Sheila, you speak fluent German and will stay by my side as my interpreter.

"Kathryn, Erika requested you and I agree that you are right for this team. You're a native German and can serve as an additional interpreter. You will room with Erika at the Kempinski."

"Erika, you are the only one amongst us who speaks Russian. You will be our 'walker' on the bridge. You will be unarmed and I expect nothing from you other than to walk the three men we are exchanging for Zhanna to the middle of the bridge then turn them over to the Soviet walker when they have delivered Zhanna. Then you will walk her calmly back to our side of the bridge. Is that completely understood?"

"Of course."

"Any questions?" Carr asked of them all.

No one responded.

"Very well," Carr continued. "Then I assume we all understand our assignments. There is a winter snow storm forecast to move into D.C. tomorrow morning. We don't want to be delayed by that. We all need to get to Germany in time for preparation. We'll fly out tonight at 2:00 a.m. in order to beat the storm. An Army vehicle will be sent to all of you at your various locations and pick you up at 1:00. Be packed and ready. Try to get some rest before then. We'll go over more details about the mission when we're in the air."

Chapter 51

Crossing the Atlantic
Saturday, 04 January 1947

Flying out of Andrews Air Force Base in Washington at 2:00 a.m. succeeded in allowing the CIA group to avoid the snow storm that the weather forecasters got right this time. By 9:00 a.m. the runways were slick with ice and snow and planes were grounded.

The DC-3 cruised at 220 mph but even with the extra fuel tanks that this particular plane had been fitted with for trans-Atlantic flight it could not make the 4200-mile journey to Berlin without refueling. That would be taken care of in Shannon, Ireland.

The relatively low cruising speed and the stop in Ireland meant the journey to Berlin would take about 22 hours. That would put them in Berlin late Saturday night, giving them two days onsite to prepare for the early Tuesday morning exchange on the Glienicke Bridge.

On board the plane were Carr, Erika, Kathryn, Sheila, Marienne, and Stephen Floyd. Marienne would board a different plane in Shannon to take her to Hamburg.

Noticeably missing was Al Hodge. As Carr had informed everyone at the meeting, Al would bring the three prisoners and his team of CIA agents to Berlin later, arriving Monday morning. Carr wanted to avoid guarding the prisoners in Germany any longer than absolutely necessary.

During the flight, Carr went over the preparation and plan of exchange so many times the women began to finally tune him out. He realized this and to him that was okay. At least there could be no excuses for any of them not knowing their role.

With the six-hour time change, it was nearly four in the morning local time when the group's plane sat down at Tempelhof in Berlin. The weather here was cold and blustering, but without the snow of Washington. Two Army sedans were waiting to drive them to the Hotel Kempinski, located in the American sector of Berlin. After they checked-in at the desk, Carr told the group they could sleep in until lunchtime then he ordered them to meet him for lunch at noon in the hotel restaurant.

[Noon—the Kempinski restaurant]

A lunch of assorted sausages: Bratwurst, Knockwurst, Bockwurst, Knackwurst, and Teewurst were delivered to the table family style piled up on one large plate placed in the middle of the table. The traditional sides of Rotkohl, assorted cheeses and black bread sat alongside. Each person had a liter Maß of beer delivered, of course. This was Germany after all.

The women and Floyd dug in. Even a hungry Leroy Carr took generous helpings. He gave the table some time to eat before getting to the point of why they were meeting.

"Tomorrow we'll take a trip to Potsdam and check out the bridge," Carr said. "I want everyone to stay in their rooms tonight—not going out on the town and getting into trouble like in Bamberg. Is that clear, Erika and Kathryn?" Al Hodge had to bail Erika, Kathryn, and Zhanna out of jail and hide them out in the American Embassy after a 'night on the town' in Bamberg during the last mission.

Both women had their mouths full, but nodded that they understood.

Carr didn't have anything else for now and they all finished lunch and filtered back to their rooms. Carr called Sheila aside.

"Major," Carr said to her. "I know Erika and Kathryn will ignore my orders and sneak out of the hotel tonight. You're one of the Shield Maidens—their partner. They will ask you if you want to go with them. I want you to accept. Don't wear your uniform, of course. Just go along and keep an eye on them. Above all, keep them out of jail. Call me if you need assistance and I'll bring Sergeant Floyd with me."

"Yes, sir. I understand."

Leroy Carr knew less about his executive assistant than he thought he did. Sheila Reid had never been opposed to letting her hair down anymore than Erika or Kathryn.

[that night]

All three women spoke German. Erika and Kathryn, born in Germany, spoke as natives. Sheila spoke the language fluently but with an American accent. There would be no language difficulties or translations needed. Not wanting to use the elevator in case Leroy Carr was lurking around the lobby or sitting in the lobby bar, the three used the Hotel's stairwell and left from a rear door that opened into an alley.

The Hotel Kempinski was located on the Ku'Damm. It was considered the posh street of Berlin. A long street lined with expensive shops, coffee cafés, restaurants, and many bars and clubs. The women would have no need for a taxi. Everything women such as these needed to get them in trouble was readily available on the Ku'Damm.

They stopped in for a drink at the first bar they came to. It was a laid-back atmosphere with most of the clientele middle-aged German couples. They had a good time but stayed for only one drink before moving on.

The next bar was filled with American G.I.s. The women enjoyed the drinks bought them by the single American men, but when two of them sat down at their table and refused to leave the women got up and left.

"Be wary of American soldiers," Erika warned the others as they continued down the Ku'Damm. "There is no wilder bunch than them. Many have been in Europe for the entire war, they are war weary and want to go home, but in the meantime they drink too much and cause trouble while they're on weekend leave."

"Erika's right, Sheila," Kathryn confirmed. "We found that out in Bamberg during the last mission."

They walked a block and the next place they stepped into was a nightclub called *Der Morgan Denach,* meaning 'The Morning After.' It was a nightclub popular among the French troops in Berlin.

For awhile, they enjoyed themselves. Erika was the only Shield Maiden who spoke French. She translated when necessary, but many of the Frenchmen spoke some English. Even if most of it was grammatically incorrect, usually the meaning could be deciphered. Kathryn and Sheila danced with some of the Frenchmen. Erika, widowed just last summer and still mourning the loss of her husband, refused dance requests but enjoyed watching her friends having a good time. Here again, the women had no need to take out their money as their drinks were bought for them.

It was only later that the trouble started.

[next morning—Sunday]

Today was the day reserved for their scouting trip to the Glienicke Bridge in Potsdam where Tuesday's exchange would take place. Carr had called for an early morning breakfast meeting before they departed for Potsdam.

"I got a call from the French garrison commander this morning," Carr started out after the women had finally come down from their room. "He figured out that you three were probably my personnel since Erika is the only one who speaks French, but does it with an American accent, and one of his soldiers you messed up told him one of you spoke German but with an American accent. That would be you, Major Reid. I am extremely disappointed in all of you."

"I kept everyone out of jail," Sheila said. "Those were my orders, Mr. Carr."

"It's not Sheila's fault," said Erika. Kathryn confirmed this to Carr.

"I don't give a rat's ass whose fault it is," Carr said, perturbed. "Why can't you three do what other women do if a guy gets out of line—slap him across the face and walk away? No, you can't do that. You have to break noses and hit people over the head with liquor bottles. Erika here apparently felt she had to fracture a bone in one of the French soldier's legs."

The women said nothing.

"And you disobeyed my orders. I told you to stay in the hotel."

Carr was glad that at least he wasn't forced to bail them out of jail, like Al had to do in Bamberg. For that he gave Sheila credit although he would never tell her.

"I'll deal with your punishments when we return to Washington," Carr warned. "For now we have to stay on mission. We leave for the bridge at eight o'clock. Carr looked at his wristwatch. Finish your breakfast and meet me in the lobby in forty-five minutes. And clean yourselves up for Heaven's sake!"

Part 5

Valhalla [noun]: hall of the slain. The great hall in Norse mythology where the souls of heroes slain in battle are received.

— Merriam Webster's Collegiate Dictionary,
Tenth Edition

Chapter 52

The Glienicke Bridge over the River Havel
Sunday, 05 January 1947

The Army personnel carrier that showed up at the Kempinski was actually a bus that would seat twenty-six. It was a bit of overkill to transport the five-man team of Carr, Stephen Floyd, and the three Shield Maidens. The driver told Carr the bus was all they had at the garage that morning beside sedans that could not transport them all in one vehicle.

"That was on the order sheet, Mr. Carr—a vehicle that could transport five people together," said the driver, a corporal.

"Yes, but I was expecting a six or eight passenger van, not an olive drab school bus. Never mind Corporal, you did well. Getting there and back is all that matters. Let's get going."

The River Havel south of Berlin served as a natural dividing line between East and West. The Glienicke Bridge that spanned the river connected the now Soviet controlled historic town of Potsdam on the eastern river bank to what was now part of the American sector on the western bank.

The Glienicke was a steel truss bridge painted a bluish/green about 300 meters in length from bank to bank and about 50 feet over the Havel. The bridge was located at the mouth of the Havel River where it fed into a large lake. The bridge was rarely used by drivers as the guard shacks on both sides stopped every car to check the driver's paperwork that he or she had permission to cross into the other sector. Not many received that permission.

The American guard shacks on their side were manned by Army MPs.

The drive from Berlin was short. In about 25 minutes the Army bus pulled up and stopped just before reaching the guard shacks.

Carr got out of the bus and told the others to stay put. An Army lieutenant came out from one of the shacks to find out why an Army bus was there.

"Hello, Lieutenant Wallace (Carr read the officer's name tag), my name is Leroy Carr. I'm from the State Department. Carr took out his I.D.; Wallace took it from him and looked it over closely before returning it.

"What can I do for you, Mr. Carr?"

"First, I find it surprising that an officer is assigned duty at a guard shack. Aren't most guard shacks at crossing points under the command of a non-com?"

"This one was until two days ago when I was given this duty."

Carr and Wallace both had suspicions why but neither elaborated. Carr assumed someone privy to the situation at the Pentagon wanted higher command of the shacks for the exchange. Wallace had yet to be told anything about a spy exchange, but he assumed something out of the ordinary was in the works and that this Mr. Carr from the State Department probably had something to do with it.

"Lieutenant, I have some personnel with me who would like to see the bridge more closely. To do this they will need to walk out on the bridge. Will this cause any problems with the Soviets on the other side?"

The lieutenant responded, "There is a white line painted across the road at the exact center of the bridge. If they don't cross that line there should be no problems. If they do cross it, the Reds will come out of their shacks with their rifles and approach them."

"I'll tell them to not cross the line. Thank you, Lieutenant."

[meanwhile]

Marienne Schenk stood out of sight behind a stack of shipping crates when the *Maia* docked in Hamburg. When Grusha disembarked, Marienne spotted her easily enough. Grusha would be hard to miss.

Two men wearing business suits were there to meet her. They looked like NKVD to Marienne.

The men led Grusha to a car parked in a small dock parking lot, loaded her bag into the trunk, and got in the car. Near the dock was a line of taxicabs that camped out at the dock to take passengers to hotels, homes, or, if their journey was to continue, to the train or bus station.

Marienne ran from taxi to taxi until she found a driver who spoke English. She jumped in the backseat and told the cabbie, "Driver, there is an extra twenty Marks in this for you if you do not lose that green sedan coming out of the parking lot." Marienne pointed to the car to make sure the driver knew the correct one.

"Did you say a twenty Mark tip?" he asked.

"Yes."

"Got you covered, sister." The driver's American slang that he had probably picked up from a G.I. sounded comical with his heavy German accent.

Marienne was an expert on all forms of shadowing. "I don't want them to know we are following them. Don't get too close. Stay at least thirty meters behind the car and turn the taxi light on your roof signaling you are available."

"You mean turn it off," the driver responded.

"No, turn your 'Vacancy' sign *on;* just ignore any passengers who try to flag you down. If the sedan driver we're following happens to see us in his rearview mirror from thirty meters behind him, he'll assume no one is in the cab."

[back at the bridge]

All five of the CIA team stood just to the west side of the white stripe looking over the bridge. They could see Russians on the other side watching them with binoculars but since they had remained on the American side of the stripe the Russians had not left their bank.

"Once I jumped off a bridge that was at least twice as high over the river as this one," said Erika. "This jump would be an easy one."

"Yes, I know," said Carr. "I'm well aware of your escape from the bridge over the Ohio River in Evansville. Hopefully, this time there won't have to be any bridge jumping."

Carr ended the talk of former times. "Erika, I like this white stripe. It gives us an exchange point that's not subjective. You'll walk the three prisoners to the stripe, stop, and wait for the Soviet walker to bring Zhanna if they're not already here waiting. Simple enough, right?"

"It sounds very simple, Leroy. I hope things go smoothly. You promised me I can layover in London and visit Ada on the way back to the States."

"Yes, the rest of us will return straight back to the States with Zhanna. I can give you a week in London to be with your daughter and grandparents. But you have to promise me you and your girlfriends will get in no more trouble while we're here."

Erika nodded. Kathryn and Sheila also told Carr there would be no more trouble. They knew how important it was to Erika that she be allowed to see her daughter.

Chapter 53

Train to Berlin
Sunday, 05 January 1947

The train ride from Hamburg to Berlin took only three hours. Marienne sat in a seat directly behind Grusha and one of the agents who had picked up her in Hamburg. This was another of Marienne's little tricks. On a bus or train, many times it was better to be close instead of several seats away. Most people looking out for someone following them would assume the tail would be farther away. By sitting just behind Grusha, Marienne was invisible in plain sight.

About halfway into the train journey, Marienne, now wearing a Red Cross nurse's cap, sat reading a three-day old copy of the London Herald. From where she sat she could listen in on any conversation. She found out the agents that picked up Grusha in Hamburg were not Russian NKVD, but from the East German secret police the K-5. Since Grusha's German was weak, and since the German K-5 agent did not speak Russian, their conversation had to be in English.

"I expect the woman Zhanna Rogova is in Berlin by now," Grusha stated.

"Yes, she's been locked up and under guard in the Russian zone of Berlin since she arrived by plane on Friday night. Both the K-5 and the NKVD are guarding her."

"Anything else I need to know?" Grusha asked.

The man said sotto voce. "I'm assured that the American the CIA is turning over to you has some of their atomic secrets."

Even though he had whispered it, Grusha winced. "I wasn't asking about that, you damn fool. Never say something like that in a public place." Grusha looked around her. The seats directly in front were empty. An elderly couple occupied the seats across the aisle. She turned around. A nurse sitting behind them had dozed off. Farther back, people were engaged in their own conversations.

[later that day]

Marienne Schenk was waiting at the Kempinski Hotel when the group returned from the Glienicke Bridge.

They all went to Carr's suite for a meeting where Marienne filled them in.

Carr, who rarely issued vulgarities, couldn't help it this time. "What the hell? All three of these prisoners we're exchanging were vetted for what exactly it was that they could offer the Russians. One of the Russians was simply used for message dead drops. The other Russian was just a radio operator. They didn't care about getting those guys back—not enough to offer up Zhanna Rogova. It was the American they were after all along. They just stuck in the two Russians to make it look good."

"That explains our suspicions of why the Russians would make the trade for Zhanna at all," said Erika.

"Yeah, we have to give those damn Russians credit. Kuznetsov pulled the wool over my eyes telling me one of the Russian prisoners had friends at high places and I swallowed it. And Grusha sent you and Al on a wild goose chase to Iceland. They're smarter than some people in the State Department want to give them credit for."

"When the CIA vetted the American, what was the story on him?" Marienne asked.

"The FBI arrested him for taking photos of the submarine pens at New London, Connecticut. That was it. There was no indication he worked anywhere where he had access to atomic secrets. I'll take the blame for all this; the Russians have outmaneuvered us at just about every turn. It's my job to make sure that doesn't happen."

"If the American prisoner had no access to atomic secrets," Erika asked, "How did he get them?"

"It's obvious there's a Russian mole somewhere in the system. The work on the Bomb takes place at several facilities across the United States. At one of these places the Russians must have a spy— probably another American communist sympathizer. The spy, probably a scientist, is the one who fed the American prisoner the information. By giving the information to a flunky to relay, they could protect the important mole by not getting him involved. That's the only scenario that makes sense. Al is still in Washington. He's scheduled to fly out with the prisoners in three hours. I'll call him right now and have him go to work on this guy and get to the bottom of it. If he has to delay his flight so be it."

"You think the guy will crack?" Kathryn asked.

"He'll crack. Al makes them all crack."

Erika asked what they all wanted to know. "Are you going to cancel the trade, Leroy?"

Carr thought for a moment. "We're not turning over to the Russians anyone with atomic secrets, that's a given. If that guy does have that kind of information, he'll never leave his prison cell in the States, and probably be hanged before too long. I'll wait to hear from Al before making the decision whether or not to continue with the exchange."

Chapter 54

Berlin, Germany
Monday, 06 January 1947

The call from Al Hodge didn't reach Leroy Carr until after midnight Berlin time. It had taken longer to make the American prisoner spill the beans than expected but Hodge, who was not opposed to using physical pressure, always got the job done sooner or later. Yes, the American possessed some atomic secrets and, yes, he had been sent them by a scientist somewhere in the atomic research system. The man didn't know which facility the spy worked at, nor did he know his name. He told Al the man sounded like an American, but he only knew the spy by the codename *Rollo.* He had no contact information for *Rollo.*

The secrets the prisoner possessed concerned the plutonium trigger that set off the Bomb's chain reaction. That information would not give the Soviets everything they needed to make their own atomic device, but it was nevertheless something that could put them closer.

Carr told Hodge to inform the FBI of the new charges that should be added to those already listed against the man and leave him locked up in Washington for FBI pick up. Then, Carr told Hodge to get on a plane with his team and the two Soviet prisoners and fly out for Berlin. Even with the delay, they could still reach Berlin by this evening.

The CIA deputy director was irked with himself. He had been out-foxed, something he wasn't used to, and he didn't like the feeling. He thanked his stars that he had brought Marienne Schenk onto the team or tomorrow morning they would unwittingly turn over to the Soviets a prisoner with nuclear secrets.

Carr was determined that the Soviets were finished with their lucky run. It was now time for him to turn the tables. He had received an ample amount of criticism for keeping Erika Lehmann around despite all the trouble she had caused him and others. There were those who argued vehemently that she should be turned over to the Justice Department for her crimes in the United States.

What only she could do tomorrow morning on the bridge was the reason why Carr ignored the criticism and kept her close.

◊ ◊ ◊

The CIA team met in Carr's suite just after lunchtime.

"I hope you all had a good night's rest. I decided to let you sleep in because we have to get up very early tomorrow morning. Has everyone had lunch? If not, I'll order something from room service."

Everyone had already taken their lunch.

"Good," Carr said. "We'll get directly to business. I spoke with Al late last night. The American prisoner does have some minor atomic secrets. He won't be coming to Berlin."

"So the exchange is cancelled?" Kathryn asked. "The Soviets aren't going to trade Zhanna for a couple of low importance workers like a dead dropper and a radioman."

"True," Carr affirmed, "but the exchange is not cancelled. Al has been in the air now for over thirteen hours. Despite the delay, he can still be here with the Soviet prisoners and their guards by this evening. Here's the new plan."

[same day]

Grusha had requested a private dinner with Zhanna Rogova—a last dinner, so to speak. Zhanna was brought from her cell at the Russian garrison to the Hotel Berlin where Grusha stayed. The hotel was located in the Soviet sector. They would dine in one of the small, windowless private rooms adjacent to the hotel restaurant with a bevy of NKVD and K-5 guards standing vigil just outside the room. The two women had already ordered their dinners and now sat at a small table drinking vodka martinis. They spoke in Russian.

"It's nice to see you again, Zhanna. You don't know this but I have always held you on a pedestal as my inspiration for what I do. You were the best. Everyone knows that—the best sniper during the war and then the best assassin for SMERSH."

"Is that what they say?"

"You know it is," Grusha answered with a roguish grin. "Is it not true?"

Zhanna shrugged, "That's for others to decide, but I always tried my best at what I was assigned to do."

The waiters were allowed in the room. Both women had ordered a house specialty—a traditional German meal of a liver dumpling in broth, and wild boar. The waiters also sat two more martinis on the table in front of the women. Grusha waited until they left the room to continue.

"Tomorrow you'll be a free woman, Zhanna. Free to go back to being a traitor to your country."

"My country turned its back on me and sent you to cancel me ('cancel' was the word used by SMERSH for assassinate), but I don't feel the need to explain my actions to you."

"I'm not asking you to. It's enough for me to tell you what I think of you—a combination of admiration for what you did during the war to disgust at going over to the capitalists. Nonetheless, let's not let this ruin our dinner. I love wild boar."

Grusha had her own plan in place. That plan was to eliminate Zhanna Rogova. She knew for her to do this and survive retribution by her countryman, Grusha still had to deliver the American with the atomic secrets. For that reason, she could not kill Zhanna before the meeting at the middle of the bridge. Grusha had a strong feeling that Erika Lehmann would be the "walker' for the Americans. The German spoke Russian and could easily identify Zhanna by sight. Grusha had convinced the NKVD that she should be the walker for their side using similar reasoning—she knew Erika.

The one very important piece of top secret information Grusha had not been told was that Zhanna had agreed to become a double agent for the Soviets and they were determined to make sure she was handed over to the Americans. To trick the Americans into handing over a spy who possessed nuclear secrets, and at the same time insert a double agent into the CIA had already prompted the Politburo in Moscow to order the champagne and Siberian caviar for the celebration.

Chapter 55

Potsdam, Germany
Glienicke Bridge over the River Havel
Tuesday, 07 January 1947

The exchange was scheduled for first light. This time of year in northern Germany that would be around 7:00 a.m. The CIA group met in the hotel lobby at five. This would give Carr time during the trip to Potsdam to explain the significant changes in the original plan, which had been tossed out the window. Along with this, Carr wanted to get to the bridge at least an hour early to watch what was going on over on the Soviet side.

For this trip, the bus that Carr complained about on the scouting trip would be needed. There were twice as many people and he wanted everyone in the same vehicle so he could go over the plan. He ordered the same driver that took them to the bridge Sunday.

At 5:15 a.m., Carr stood by the open door of the bus.

"Another trip to the bridge, hey, Mr. Carr?" The corporal said with a happy-go-lucky smile. "You all must admire that bridge."

"That's right, Corporal," Carr said with a rascally grin. "We're big fans of bridges. We visit them everywhere we go."

Carr waited at the door while Al Hodge, the three prisoners and their CIA guards stepped up into the bus. Then Erika, Kathryn, Sheila, and Marienne loaded in. Carr stepped onboard last. He had been informed that the U.S. Army would have an extra contingent of MPs stationed at the bridge overnight. Carr imagined that the Soviets would also have extra people on hand. It was shaping up to be a crowded morning on the banks of the Havel.

As soon as everyone was aboard, Hodge placed heavy-duty ear protection used by artillerymen and hoods over the heads of the two Russian prisoners so they couldn't see where they were going or hear anything discussed on the bus. This did not apply to the American prisoner who was a CIA agent. To make him look like the real American prisoner, who was bald on top with a horseshoe ring of hair around the sides of his head, the top of the CIA man's head had been shaved on the airplane. He also wore a fake goatee like the real prisoner's goatee. He was very close in height and weight to the man the Soviets thought would deliver atomic secrets. Whoever the Soviets chose to be their 'walker' Carr felt confident that person had never actually seen or met the American prisoner. They would have to trust the walker to identify the man through photographs.

During the ride to the bridge, Carr again went over the new plan.

◊ ◊ ◊

A half-hour later the bus approached the bridge—at least it got close to the bridge. It took a while for the bus to wend its way though several MP check stations where the bus was forced to stop and where Carr had to show his I.D.

"Wow!" Al Hodge joked. "It's like we're trying to get a bus through a crowd to a Frank Sinatra concert."

Finally, the last of the guard stations opened to let the Army bus through; the driver stopped and parked about twenty yards from the foot of the bridge.

"Everyone can get out except the prisoners and their guards," Carr instructed. "They stay on the bus, and keep their hoods and hearing cancellers on until we're ready for the trade." Carr addressed the driver, "Corporal, stand outside your bus, by the door. I will signal you when I want the guards to bring out the prisoners. Understood?"

"Yes, sir," said the young corporal who seemed very nervous now that he knew what this bus trip was about.

Carr, Hodge, and the women got off the bus. It had taken so long to work through the MP guard stations, first light was only minutes away, and when it made its appearance Carr and the others stood at the foot of the bridge. The skies were gray, and a thick blanket of fog shrouded the river, but the river fog did not interfere with views on the bridge. Still, a blustering cold wind made it uncomfortable if not dressed properly. The Americans had anticipated the worst as far as cold and were bundled up sufficiently. Carr immediately asked for a set of binoculars. A nearby MP took his set off from around his neck and handed it to Carr.

The Soviet side of the bridge was as crowded as the American side. Unlike the American side where only woods and farmland served as a backdrop, on the Soviet side in Potsdam several buildings loomed—some as high as four or five storeys. Carr noticed that some windows were open. For windows to be open in January, in this cold, could only mean to Carr that snipers were stationed.

The agreement with the Soviets included a meeting at the middle of the bridge prior to the exchange. One person from each side would meet and make clear that all arrangements had been agreed to and were in place. For the Americans, this would be done by Al Hodge. Leroy Carr had been ordered not to step foot on the bridge during the exchange by the CIA's new director, USAF General Hoyt Vandenberg. As Vandenberg's second in command at the new agency, the general didn't want Carr on the bridge.

A flare gun from the Soviet side of the bridge sent a burning red flare skyward. It was answered by a flare from the American side.

"Al, you're on," Carr said to his buddy.

Al's walk was about the length of one-and-a half American football fields to the white stripe painted at the center of the bridge. Carr monitored everything with his binoculars. When Al started his walk, a Russian in a Red Army uniform began walking from the opposite bank.

Al and the Russian met at the center of the bridge at nearly the same time.

The Russian extended his hand. "My name is Major Kir Volkov. I represent the government of the Union of Soviet Socialist Republics."

Hodge shook the man's hand. "I'm Albert Hodge, representing the United States government."

Volkov knew Hodge was CIA; Al knew Volkov was NKVD.

Volkov said, "We have everything in place for the prisoner exchange our governments agreed upon."

"We're ready, as well," Hodge confirmed.

"Then you and I will return to our side of the bridge and send out the prisoners. We agreed on only one 'walker' for each side. We agreed the prisoners would be shackled during the walk but will be unshackled when they meet here, in the center of the bridge."

"That's correct," said Hodge.

"Very well. When I get back, we will send up another flare to signal our walker has begun escorting the prisoner to this point."

"We'll send up a flare to acknowledge, and then send out our walker with the three prisoners."

Chapter 56

The Walk

When Al Hodge returned to the American bank, he told Carr things seemed to be in order. Carr signaled the young corporal standing at his bus to tell the guards to bring out the three prisoners. Carr ordered the hoods and ear protection be taken off but the handcuffs remained. The cuffs on the CIA agent impersonating the American prisoner were faux cuffs that looked real but he had to only yank hard to free himself.

The two Russian prisoners began talking amongst themselves in their native tongue; Carr immediately ordered them to shut up. There would be no talking.

A flare went up from the Soviet side. The Americans acknowledged with their own flare.

"Okay, Erika, it's showtime!" Carr said, trying to lighten the mood.

Erika turned to the prisoners. "I will lead. Stay behind me but do not fall more than two paces behind." She repeated the orders in Russian to the Soviet prisoners. All of them nodded.

Erika stepped onto the bridge and began her slow walk. Through his binoculars, Carr spotted Zhanna in handcuffs and the Soviet walker. "Erika!" Carr said before she was too far away. "Grusha is the Soviet walker."

The 150 meters that each side had to walk seemed to take an excruciatingly long time, especially for Carr, Hodge, and Marienne who watched from their end of the bridge—all of them feeling helpless as there was nothing for them to do until after the trade. Major Sheila Reid and Kathryn Fischer had disappeared.

Fog still blanketed the river below, but the view on the bridge was adequate. Unfortunately for the Americans, the sun was now peeping over the eastern horizon, behind the Soviets. Carr cursed silently to himself. He thought the trade would be over before sunrise; otherwise he would have insisted on a mid-day trade or an evening trade when it would be the Soviets who would be looking into the sun dropping in the west.

Erika and her three prisoners reached the white line first, but only by a few seconds. Grusha smiled, "Hello, Erika, it's lovely to see you again." She spoke in English. Besides having Zhanna in handcuffs, a wide piece of tape covered her mouth.

"Let's cut the crap, Grusha, and get this over with. You take the handcuffs off Zhanna, and that piece of tape. Gagging the prisoners was not part of the bargain. I'll take the cuffs off these three men."

"Very well." Grusha roughly yanked the tape from Zhanna's mouth—a painful move but Zhanna gave no reaction other than to glare at Grusha.

Erika began removing the cuffs of the Russian prisoners.

Before she had removed Zhanna's cuffs, Grusha suddenly produced a dagger she had hidden on her, moved behind Zhanna and held the knife to her throat.

"You! The American," Grusha yelled. "Cross the line and run to our bank. Go now!"

Before the man could move, Erika grabbed him and produced her own knife. Both Grusha and Erika had broken the "unarmed" part of the deal.

"Grusha, you're breaking the deal. Release Zhanna or I'll cut his throat!"

The two Russian prisoners were aghast at what was happening and in fear both began running toward the Soviet side. Erika let them go.

Suddenly, shots rang out from the Soviet side. Carr was right about the snipers. A bullet grazed Grusha in the arm. She pushed Zhanna away, but before she did Zhanna managed to snatch the handcuff key from Grusha's hand. Erika sliced the American's throat and threw him over the side of the bridge. In a few seconds they heard his body splash.

Grusha thought Zhanna was the target and one of the snipers had aimed badly, but then another bullet grazed her left outer calf.

When Grusha realized her comrades were shooting at her, she climbed over the guard railing and jumped. Zhanna unlocked her cuffs and went after her.

"Zhanna, NO!" Erika shouted, but Zhanna jumped from the bridge anyway. Erika had no choice but to follow her.

Erika had jumped from a bridge once before, one that was much higher over the river then this bridge, but that had been in the summertime. The temperature of the waters of the Havel River in January hovered around 34° Fahrenheit. One could not survive long in such waters.

Carr got on his walkie-talkie and pressed the talk button. "Sheila, are you there?"

"*Yes, Kathryn and I are ready.*"

"They have all jumped—Erika, Zhanna and Grusha."

"*What are our orders?*" Sheila came back.

"Stay where you are until I get back to you."

"*ROGER that.*"

Sheila and Kathryn sat in a wooden speed boat just around a close bend in the river on the American side.

The CIA agent whose throat Erika had misleadingly slit wore a wet suit under his clothes which helped him with the cold waters. The cut Erika had made was into a piece of rubber made to look like human flesh with a slim sack of Hollywood blood behind it. As soon as he hit the water, a U.S. Navy Frogman surfaced and grabbed him within seconds. The Frogman helped the CIA agent to the American shore where two MPs dragged him out of the water. The river fog made this impossible for the Russians to see even if they had been looking for it. They weren't, thinking the American was dead after watching Erika cut his throat.

As far as the women, Zhanna was the first to surface. She twirled around in the water looking for Grusha but saw no sign of her. Erika popped up next and then two more Navy Frogmen wearing underwater breathing tanks, masks, and heavy cold-water wetsuits, unlike the light wetsuits the CIA agent and Erika wore under their clothes. The thin wetsuit helped with the cold, but only to a slight degree. Plus, the suit did not cover her feet, hands, and head. She was freezing.

Fog works both ways—restricting vision from both sides. Erika called out, "Zhanna!" There was no answer. "Zhanna!" she repeated and this time she heard "Over here."

Erika and the Frogmen swam toward the voice. It took two more shouts by Erika and faint replies by Zhanna before they reached the nearly frozen Russian.

"Who has the walkie-talkie?" Erika asked the Frogmen.

"I do," said the one.

"Radio Mr. Carr and tell him we have Zhanna and to leave the boat where it is. We should be able to get her to the boat without risking it coming under fire." Even if the fog helped camouflage the boat, Erika knew the engine would be heard easily enough. "Get her to the boat quickly," Erika told the two Frogmen. "She won't last long in water this cold. I'll follow you."

Chapter 57

The frogmen swam like dolphins and dragged a semi-conscious Zhanna downstream through the cold river to the boat around the bend in about ten minutes. They were now out of sight from the Russians. During the swim, Erika kept up. She was a champion swimmer who some in Germany felt should have competed in the swimming competitions at the 1936 Olympic Games in Berlin when she was a teenager. Yet none of that protected her from the cold. She wasn't in as bad a shape from the cold as Zhanna, who had no wetsuit; however, Erika still suffered greatly.

At the boat, as soon as Sheila spotted them coming she fired up the engine. Kathryn stood with an M-1 rifle looking for Grusha or any other Russian who had perhaps been brave (or stupid) enough to jump from the bridge into the frigid water in pursuit.

There was no Grusha or any of her comrades in the water as the frogmen reached the boat. Sheila and Kathryn dragged a by now unconscious and nearly frozen Zhanna Rogova onto the boat, stripped off her wet clothes, and covered her with multiple blankets. They laid her over the engine hatch that radiated heat. Erika was the next one the frogmen helped onto the boat where she stripped down to her wetsuit and also wrapped herself in blankets. The Navy frogmen disappeared under the water. Their boat waited for them out in the lake.

Sheila got behind the wheel and gunned the engines, bouncing the boat over the waves and down the western shore of the Havel and out into the large lake it fed. Over the walkie-talkie, Kathryn updated an enormously relieved Leroy Carr that Erika and Zhanna were onboard and they were underway.

"Al, let's get out of Dodge fast," Carr told Hodge. Marienne was not clear why Carr had brought her along since he had not assigned her a role in the exchange mission, but she knew that was not for her to question.

Carr, Hodge, Marienne, and the CIA bodyguards loaded onto the bus. Carr told the corporal to step on it. Their next stop would be Neu

Fahrland on the other side of the lake six miles away. Al Hodge handed the corporal a map.

"I know where it is, Mr. Hodge."

The speed boat was waiting at the appointed place on the shore at Neu Fahrland. Zhanna had warmed by now to the point where she was conscious but still weak and groggy. The four women in the boat loaded onto the bus.

'Okay, corporal, take us back to our hotel in Berlin. And turn the heat up full blast."

In twenty-five minutes the bus pulled up in front of the Kempinski where the group stepped off.

Before they left, Carr told the corporal bus driver he did a good job, but Al Hodge approached the young serviceman and made him sign papers stating he would never discuss what he had witnessed that day. If he did so he would be court marshaled and prosecuted by a military tribunal. Without delay, the terrified corporal signed the papers, jumped in his bus, and began high-tailing it back to his Army carpool unit. Tonight he planned to drink a great quantity of German beer and forget everything he saw.

◊ ◊ ◊

Carr knew that a firestorm over the way the exchange went down would engulf the State Department. The powers there would not be happy. Their thinking would be that a shootout during an agreed upon exchange could put the kibosh on any future exchanges. He hated appearing before committees, but he knew a committee and an investigation would surely follow. The best thing he had in his defense was that the Soviets started the commotion. He simply had been ready for such a scenario. They couldn't blame the CIA for that. In addition, they had not delivered over a spy with atomic secrets and at the same time rescued Zhanna Rogova. Carr hoped that would be enough to weather the tempest back in Washington.

◊ ◊ ◊

The ride from the bridge back to the Kempinski got them there just before 11:00 a.m.—the entire affair having taken less than half a day. The CIA agent who had impersonated the traitor needed medical attention. Erika had sliced through his neck rubber a bit too deep in two places and four stitches were needed, two in each location her dagger slightly dug into his flesh. Erika apologized to the man.

Carr called a meeting in his suite for three that afternoon. This would give Zhanna and Erika time to take hot baths, time for everyone to eat lunch, and time for those with family to call home.

Carr called his wife, Kay, letting her know he would be home soon. Al Hodge was divorced, but he called his 67-year-old mother just to say hello. Marienne called Harold, who was now back in Pittsburgh running the barge company. Erika called her grandparents in London and spoke with her six-year-old daughter, Ada. Kathryn thought of calling her parents in Nüremberg but decided against it, thinking she'd just cause them worry when they found out she was back in Germany. Members of the Gestapo were still being hunted. Zhanna had no one to call.

[that afternoon]
"I assume everyone has eaten lunch, and that Zhanna and Erika have thawed out," Carr said to the group of Al, the four Shield Maidens (Erika, Zhanna, Kathryn, and Sheila), Marienne and the CIA operatives Al had brought over from Washington. The Frogmen were gone, disappearing as quickly as they had appeared.

Everyone nodded or said they were fine.

Carr continued, "The mission was messier than we had hoped for, but the job got done. I'll just warn you beforehand that you will all be extensively debriefed when you return to Washington and some of you might be called before a State Department committee. I'm hoping that will be just me and Al, but I can't guarantee that. You never know who these committees might subpoena."

Zhanna held little interest in this talk about committees. "Do we know what happened to Grusha?"

"No." Carr said truthfully.

Al Hodge saw that his old buddy didn't want to address questions about Grusha from Zhanna Rogova, so he steered the conversation another way. "Leroy, if things are taken care of here, when are we heading back to the States?"

"All of us fly out tomorrow except Erika," Carr answered. "She'll take a train to the Channel coast and cross over to England. I promised her a week with her daughter."

"I'm not going anywhere until I find out what happened to Grusha," Zhanna insisted belligerently. "If she made it out of that river, I want to go after her."

"You *are* going somewhere, Zhanna," Carr fired back. "You're going back to the States with us tomorrow. That's an order. You'll be under guard tonight and confined to your hotel room. If you try to escape, the guards have orders to take whatever action is necessary to stop you."

[that evening]

Carr requested a meeting with just Erika. After their separate dinners, they took a walk down the street in front of the hotel.

"Well, I was wrong," Carr said. "You're bridge jumping days were not over after Evansville."

"Couldn't be helped after the Russians starting shooting. I'm glad you had made the preparations with the Frogmen and the boat, Leroy. The wet suit helped a little also, although not as much as I thought it might."

"It had to be thin so it wasn't obvious under your clothes. You couldn't very well walk out on the bridge wearing a thick Frogman suit with the hoods, flippers, and all of that," Carr joked.

He offered Erika a cigarette. She politely declined. He really didn't want one either so he put the pack back in his suit jacket pocket.

"I know you're looking forward to seeing Ada," said Carr.

"I can't wait," Erika beamed. "I'm leaving early tomorrow morning from the Bahnhof. My ferry across the Channel departs at 3:00 p.m. This time tomorrow night I should be with her. I wanted to ask you Leroy, may Kathryn go with me?"

"Kathryn, why?"

"She wants to go and has been there with me before. She's my only real friend and I trust her."

"Let me think about it," was Carr's answer. Then he said, "Keep an eye on Zhanna tonight. The CIA agents Al brought will take shifts outside your hotel room during the night. But you room with her and for that reason you're in the best position to monitor her."

"Where is the Army Ranger, Floyd? Why was a tough guy like that not at the bridge today?"

"I promised his commander I wouldn't keep him longer than necessary, and since I brought in the Navy Frogman team, I sent Sergeant Floyd back to Fort Benning. He flew out yesterday."

"I will keep an eye on Zhanna," Erika said, "but I know I could do a better job of it if you allowed Kathryn to go to London with me."

Carr laughed.

Erika added, "Zhanna had a legitimate question, Leroy. What happened to Grusha?"

"None of us know. Her body is either rotting away, trapped in debris under water in the Havel, or she managed to get to a bank."

"You do realize the Soviets were shooting at Grusha, not at Zhanna as I would expect."

Carr was puzzled. "What do you mean?"

"The sun was in your eyes and you were probably too far away to realize it, but I was standing right there. The Russian snipers were obviously shooting at Grusha, not Zhanna."

Carr thought for a moment "So that's why she jumped. I figured she jumped after you slit the throat of their prize; she knew she had blown the assignment. The Russians usually have little patience or mercy on their agents who blow critical assignments."

"No, the snipers began shooting at Grusha as soon as she grabbed Zhanna and put a knife to her throat. It's as if they were protecting Zhanna to make sure she fell into our hands."

◊ ◊ ◊

[that night]

After Carr's conversation with Erika earlier that evening, he called Marienne Schenk in her hotel room and asked her to join him in the hotel bar. It was late—about 10 p.m.

When Marienne sat down at Carr's corner table he asked her what she wanted to drink.

"Bourbon and Coke," she answered.

Carr already had his gin and tonic sitting in front of him. He got the attention of a waiter and ordered Marienne's drink. Carr waited until her drink arrived then said bluntly, "Marienne, I know you work for us only part-time now, and at your discretion. I also know you want to get home, but I have to ask you to stay here for a few days and not return to the States with us tomorrow. I want you to see if you can get any leads about what might have happened to Grusha. Try to find out if she made it out of the river alive. Erika told me the Reds were shooting at her, not at Zhanna. If that's true, which I have no reason to doubt, Grusha would not have returned to the Russian side. If she made it out of the river, she would have swum to somewhere on the American bank. With the river fog, it wouldn't be hard for someone to exit the river and disappear into the forest without being seen."

Chapter 58

Berlin
The day after the bridge exchange
Wednesday, 08 January 1947

Erika and Kathryn left Berlin first. They checked out of the Kempinski Hotel at 5:30 in the morning and took a taxi to the Berlin Bahnhof. Their train ride would be a non-stop to the English Channel coast at Calais, France, with only a brief stop in Paris to disembark some passengers and take on a few more. From Calais, a ferry would take them across the Channel to England.

Marienne had agreed to stay behind to search for any clues that might help reveal what happened to Grusha. The Frogmen team had not yet left Berlin, and Carr kept them at Marienne's disposal at least long enough to search the river for a submerged body.

The rest of the group: Carr, Hodge, Zhanna, the CIA agent who had posed as the American traitor, and the other agents who had served as bodyguards, flew out from Tempelhof on an Air Force DC-3 at 11:00 a.m. They would be back in Washington by tomorrow morning. They couldn't get back fast enough for Carr; he would meet with J Edgar Hoover and turn over to him everything they had learned about *Rollo,* the scientist who had supplied the American traitor with atomic secrets. This was the FBI's jurisdiction—finding traitors within America.

◊ ◊ ◊

Marienne wasted no time. Carr had ensured that she had an Army driver and an unmarked sedan at her disposal. She was at the Glienicke Bridge even before the group flew out for D.C. The Frogmen had returned to their boat in the Havel lake. To remain inconspicuous, the Navy had rented a fishing boat large enough to contain sleeping quarters for the small Navy crew and the Frogmen.

Before noon, the Frogmen were in the water and searching for a body in the river under the bridge.

Around the American guard shacks, extra military personnel still lingered. Through an open window in one of the shacks, binoculars allowed Marienne to observe the Soviet side of the bridge. There seemed to be little activity and the horde of Russians who manned their side of the bridge yesterday were nowhere to be seen, which surprised her. Things seemed to be back to normal on the other bank, as if yesterday never happened.

The Navy Frogmen were forced to change their oxygen tanks three times as they spent the entire afternoon searching for a body. Finally, the Navy ensign in charge of the crew gave his report to Marienne. The man still was not sure who this woman worked for; all he knew was he had been ordered to follow her instructions.

"Ma'am, we searched out into the lake that the river feeds. There is practically no debris in the lake that could hold a body underwater. The lake bed is pristine sand with a few rocks here and there. The river under and around the bridge has plenty of submerged tree branches and thick, tall growth that could snag a body but we found nothing. We searched under the bridge, and for nearly a half-mile upriver. Even though it would be impossible for a body to float upstream we searched anyway. Then we searched downriver to the lake. No body. We are sure of that."

"Thank you, ensign, for everything—yesterday and today. You and your men are dismissed now with a job well done. I'll make sure my supervisor informs your commander of the exemplary work you and your team did here."

[same day—Moscow]

Soviet General Polzin, head of the NKVD, sat before the Russian Politburo at their headquarters in Red Square.

"I'm pleased to announce that our mission was mostly a success," Polzin told the group of six men.

"Mostly a success?" asked one of the officials. "Explain yourself, General."

"We did not recover the American who held the atomic secrets," Polzin explained. "However, our mole within the American atomic program is still secure. We will send a more qualified agent to work with him. Our real success lies in the fact we inserted a double agent into the American CIA."

"Zhanna Rogova," one of the other officials said. "I read the preliminary report."

"Yes, Zhanna Rogova," Polzin confirmed.

Another member of the Politburo asked, "Who is this 'more qualified agent' who will work with *Rollo* in the United States?"

"Grusha Mustafina."

"Your report informed us that our men shot Grusha in order to keep her from killing Rogova."

"That's true, but her wounds were superficial—we did not have a sniper with your skill shooting at her. We fished Grusha out of the water and offered her a deal: return to Moscow for execution, or bring *Rollo* to Moscow and be reinstated in good graces. She wisely chose the latter."

[same day—Ireland]

As the DC-3 sat on the tarmac in Shannon, Ireland, waiting to be refueled for its leg across the Atlantic, Zhanna sat resting with a pillow behind her head—resting but not sleeping. She had a decision to make: tell the Americans everything, or become a double agent for her homeland. Zhanna decided to bide her time before making that decision. She looked at a ring on her right middle finger. It was a ring all the Shield Maidens wore. Erika had presented each of them the rings after their last mission together in Poland last spring. Erika had told them the story behind the ring. It was a Viking ring called the Valringr, meaning "Ring of the Slain." The ring was silver with a black onyx stone and two Norse symbols engraved on the sides. According to the Norse legend, the ring was worn by Viking warriors and when they died in battle the Ring would signal the Valkyries that here lies a true warrior whose soul should be escorted to Valhalla—the Viking Heaven. For that was the objective of all Viking warriors—to die bravely in battle. It was their hope for Valhalla.

Chapter 59

Berlin
Next day—Thursday, 09 January 1947

Marienne spoke acceptable "tourist" German but she was glad her Army driver spoke the language fluently. The CIA shadow spent all of this day, from 7:00 a.m. until dark, combing the countryside on the American side of the Glienicke Bridge, knocking on farmhouse doors and showing the farmers and their wives a photograph of Grusha that an Army Signal Corps photographer had taken with a long distance lens when Grusha stood in the middle of the bridge talking to Erika before things blew up. The photo was surprisingly clear and showed her face well.

None of the farmers had seen the woman in the photograph. Marienne kept checking, even checking at cottages and farmhouses she knew were much too far from the bridge for a wet, frozen woman to reach, but she knocked on those doors anyway for the sake of being thorough.

When she finally returned to the Kempinski at 7:30 that evening, she called Leroy Carr. The time in Washington was only 2:30 in the afternoon so Marienne knew she should be able to reach him at his office.

Carr answered the button on his desk. Al Hodge sat across from him.

"Yes, Sheila," Carr said into the squawk box.

"Marienne is on the line, I'll put her right through."

"Marienne, thanks for checking in," Carr stated.

"I trust your flight went well, Leroy."

"It was fine—very little turbulence. We landed at Andrews around 11:00 this morning." Carr flipped the switch to speaker phone so Al could hear.

Marienne knew that was enough chit-chat and got down to business. *"Yesterday, the Frogmen conducted a long and extensive search of the river and lake. No body was found. They even searched upriver. Nothing, Leroy."*

"So what's your take?" Carr asked.

"Looks like she made it out of the river. I visited all the farms and cottages near the western bank today, showing them her picture. I even went farther inland than I know Grusha could have reached. None of the locals had seen her. I even asked them if someone in the area was missing, thinking Grusha might have carjacked someone driving down the road. Nothing there either."

"Could someone have been lying?"

"Possibly, but I doubt it. They were all simple farm folk and if Grusha was inside threatening them I don't think they could have pulled off a good enough acting job to hide that they were terrified."

Carr paused for a moment. "It wouldn't make any sense for Grusha to return to the Soviet bank. They were trying to kill her."

"In my opinion, that's the only solution, Leroy. I'm confident she's not dead in the river, and that she didn't leave the water on the American side."

"Hang around Berlin for a couple more days and visit the bridge a couple more times. Keep an eye on the Soviet side."

"They've all left—all the extra personnel, anyway. The guard shacks are back to normal procedure on their side. I dismissed the Navy guys and told them you'll contact their commander and recommend commendations for them."

"Okay, I'll do that, but hang around until at least this weekend. Check in with me every day for any updates. I'll let you know when to come home."

When the phone call ended, Carr asked Hodge, "What do you think Al, Marienne is seldom wrong."

"If Grusha returned to the Soviet side of the river her life expectancy is that of a house fly, that's what I think. They shot her because they didn't want to allow anything to hinder them getting their hands on the American with the Bomb secrets. We already discussed that, Leroy."

Carr took a moment to think about what Erika had said, that is seemed as if the Soviets were determined to make sure Zhanna got back into American hands. Then he nodded.

"When do you meet with Hoover about this *Rollo* that needs to be found?" Hodge asked.

"In one hour."

"Oh, and I have an interesting piece of information out of Cuba," said Hodge. "An asset I developed down there tells me Albert Anastasia has taken a hostage—the major who heads the Soviet NKVD in Cuba."

"You're not talking about Kir Volkov?"

"Bingo. Volkov must have flown directly back to Cuba after the exchange on the bridge."

Chapter 60

Havana, Cuba
Next day—Friday, 10 January 1947

Albert Anastasia was too wily to take his hostage to The Hotel Nacional, the first place the Russians would look. Instead, he had one of his men rent a small abandoned warehouse in the industrial section of the city.

NKVD Major Volkov sat bound to a chair in the middle of the skeleton-like structure. Anastasia had a longshoreman from Russia on the mob payroll who worked the New York docks flown down to serve as an interpreter.

"I want to know what happened to the two women on my crew, you commie rat bastard," Anastasia said with a fiendish look. "I know you Russian fucks are behind this. Zhanna disappeared while going to the can with that Bride of Frankenstein you used as an interpreter. The other one, Erika, vanished the next day."

"I don't know anything about it," Volkov said forcefully.

"Of course you don't. No one remembers anything without some persuasion. I'm very good with persuasion. I've had lots of experience. I've found out that beating the pulp out of a guy with a bad memory, or pulled teeth, takes too long. A blowtorch to the balls works the fastest." Anastasia nodded to his men. One pulled down Volkov's pants and underwear, another lit a blow torch.

"Okay, okay!" Volkov shouted. "I'll tell you what I know. The two women are not who you think they are. They are both CIA agents sent here to spy on your organization and mine! You were duped!"

Anastasia pulled out his Colt 1911 and fired three shots into Volkov's chest.

"Take this piece of shit deep into the woods and dig a deep hole," Anastasia ordered his men. "I don't want a body to be found."

One of Anastasia's men asked, "Boss, what about the women? What if they were feds like the guy said?"

"The Russians captured them. If they were feds, the Ivans probably already have them buried in a swamp somewhere, or they're fish food at the bottom of the Caribbean. Let's just get our asses back to New York. I'm fed up with this fucked up island."

[same day—London]

Erika and Kathryn had enjoyed two wonderful days in London with Erika's maternal grandparents and especially with Ada, Erika's daughter. Erika and Kathryn had taken little Ada shopping each day and had visited some of the famous sites: Big Ben, the Tower of London, Westminster Abbey, and Buckingham Palace where they watched the changing of the guard. Tomorrow they planned to take a bus ride to Stonehenge.

Dinner tonight would be at Erika's grandparents' home in Kensington, an upscale neighborhood on the West End. The home was elegant but small, with Ada taking up the guest bedroom. Erika slept with her daughter. Kathryn got the parlor sofa. When Erika, Kathryn, and Ada arrived back home from their day out and about, Erika's grandmother told her Mr. Carr had called twice that day from America asking for Erika. Finding her still not there the second time, he asked for a call back as soon as she returned. Erika looked at Kathryn and sighed. Leroy Carr would not call twice trying to get in touch with her to ask if she were having a good time.

Before dinner, Erika went to the study and called Carr.

"Leroy, this is Erika."

"Erika, I apologize for this but I have to cut your London visit short. I know I promised you a week and it's only been two days. I will make it up to you with another trip."

"What going on, Leroy?"

"We've got several new developments. Grusha survived the river. Marienne tracked her down and followed her to Copenhagen where she boarded a cruise ship with a final destination of New York City. Marienne is on the same ship keeping track of her. Also, your old buddy Albert Anastasia kidnapped Major Volkov in Cuba and Volkov hasn't been seen since, but that's not our number one priority. Things like that happen in countries on the brink of revolution, and as long as the CIA can't be tied in, we're in the clear.

196

"Our main concern is Grusha. I need you and Kathryn to be on a plane to the States tomorrow morning. Sheila has already made the arrangements. An Air Force plane will be waiting on the tarmac for you tomorrow at 8:00 a.m. at Heathrow. Check in at the military desk and ask for a Captain Crider. Grusha's cruise ship will take at least five days to reach the New York harbor. You and Kathryn will be there when her ship arrives. There will also be FBI there to monitor all the exit planks."

"What about Zhanna and Sheila?"

"I don't trust Zhanna not to kill Grusha the moment she steps off the ship. The FBI wants to use Grusha to lead them to Rollo. As far as Sheila, I'm assigning her to work with Marienne. Marienne is head and shoulders above any FBI shadow. We'll be following Grusha as well without the FBI knowing."

"I thought that was illegal, Leroy, for the CIA to conduct operations inside the States that are the responsibility of the FBI. At least that's what I read in the CIA charter."

"You Germans really go by the book, don't you?"

"You learned to go by the book in the Third Reich if you didn't want to end up in a concentration camp, Leroy."

"Well, this is America. Do both of us a favor, Erika. Quit reading that charter."

Chapter 61

Atlantic Ocean
On the cruise ship Drammen
Tuesday, 14 January 1947

Confident that Grusha wasn't dead after the Frogmen's search, and doubtful that the Russian swam to the American side of the Havel after her own hunt through the farms and countryside, Marienne entered the Soviet zone of East Berlin on Saturday (in 1947, still a relatively easy thing to do). Leroy Carr had told her that Grusha stayed at the Hotel Berlin, and sure enough, Marienne spotted her in the hotel restaurant having dinner that evening with several Soviet military men.

Marienne lost a lot of sleep watching the hotel that night, but that next morning, Grusha and her bags were loaded into a sedan that delivered her to the Berlin Bahnhof. She boarded a train for Copenhagen. Marienne, of course, boarded the same train, this time sitting in the back of the train car, much further away from Grusha than on their previous train ride together. In Copenhagen, Grusha took a taxi to the docks and bought a ticket on a Norwegian luxury cruise liner, the *Drammen,* which sailed out of Oslo with a final destination of New York City. Marienne hustled to buy her own ticket. The only cabins still available were first class. Marienne grinned as she thought of Leroy Carr's face when she turned over that bill. While passengers waited to embark, Marienne managed to place a quick phone call to Carr (she didn't mention the $900 first class cabin; that fun could wait until she got back to the States).

Marienne hadn't had time to return to the Kempinski to retrieve her things, so she boarded the *Drammen* with just the clothes on her back. She bought a suitcase, a few clothes, and toiletries on the ship at one of its three shops. That would be another nice bill for the still not authorized by Congress CIA's tight budget.

Shadowing someone on a ship was an easy matter, at least a lot easier than tailing them on land where you couldn't let them out of your sight. On a ship at sea, the mark had no place to go, so the shadow didn't have to keep an eye on them every second. In fact, Marienne knew it was best not to be within eyesight too much. A wily mark might finally spot someone who was around too often. Marienne caught up on her lost sleep aboard the *Drammen* and now stood on the deck wrapped up against the cold breeze. It was Tuesday, nearly half way into the journey. Marienne knew Grusha was below deck drinking in one of the ship's lounges.

[same day—Washington]

Al Hodge, Erika and Kathryn were once again in Leroy Carr's Pentagon office.

"The ship is scheduled to arrive in New York Harbor at 2:30 p.m. on Saturday," said Carr. "Erika and Kathryn, an Army driver will take you to New York tomorrow and you'll stay at the Waldorf. It's a fancy hotel but they offer very good government discounts. Small, double rooms we get for half price."

"No suite?" Erika joked.

"Sorry, no suite. You two have slept under a tarp in the freezing woods. I think you can make do in a room with double beds at a place like the Waldorf=Astoria."

Carr continued. "The only problem I foresee is the two of you having two free nights in New York City. I'm warning you right now, ladies, if there are any problems I'll pull you off the assignment and make sure you take a long vacation in a stockade. Don't make the mistake of thinking you are irreplaceable."

"There won't be any problems, Leroy, right Kathryn?"

Kathryn Fischer had been looking out the window. She turned back and said, "Ah, yes, that's right. No problems."

Carr stared at them both for a long moment. "I'm serious ladies. It's the stockade for both of you if you cause any havoc. The only reason I'm sending you early is so you can get your bearings in New York. I know neither of you know the city."

Both women nodded.

"Al and I will get to New York on Friday. Turn in your handguns now. You'll get them back when the rest of us get to New York on

Friday. Ladies you're dismissed. Report to Sheila, she'll give you hotel confirmation numbers and expense money. Be frugal with it, it's all you're going to get."

Erika and Kathryn laid their handguns on Carr's desk, left the room, and reported to Sheila.

"Al, I've had it with those two," Carr told his old friend. "I allowed Kathryn to go with Erika to London because I knew there would be no problems there because of Erika's daughter. But now we're back to the old story of them running around on their own. If they cause any trouble in New York in some bar or nightclub I want them arrested and locked up. Technically it's the FBI's case as soon as Grusha gets to the States so we're off the hook, anyway, and we still have Sheila, Marienne, and your men we can count on if we decide to stay involved."

"ROGER that, Leroy," Hodge said with gusto.

Chapter 62

New York City
Thursday, 16 January 1947

Erika and Kathryn had been good girls in New York. After arriving on Wednesday, on Thursday they braved the freezing wind at the top of the Empire State building for the spectacular vista. They walked Times Square and they even took the ferry out to Liberty Island where they climbed the steps all the way up to the torch.

Tonight they had tickets for a popular Broadway play called *Oklahoma!*

The women had gone out on the town last night but no altercations had occurred in any bars or clubs. Men offered to buy their drinks, and the women allowed those men to sit with them. Luckily for the men, none of them went too far with demands or expectations. A wise move for the men who never suspected the former Nazi spy and the former Gestapo officer they flirted with were each armed with a small, slim dagger in a garter belt sheath, and that both were very adept on how to use it.

[next day—Friday]
Leroy Carr and Al Hodge arrived at the Waldorf at noon on Friday. Carr left Al's team in Washington to save money. They would drive to New York tomorrow morning. Carr called Erika before he left D.C. that morning and told her they would meet in his room as soon as he arrived so her orders were to be in her room and waiting for his call.

When they had all assembled in his room, Carr began the meeting by addressing the women, "Well, we received no reports from the NYPD that they had two CIA agents in jail, so does that mean I can assume you didn't hit anyone over the head with a chair?"

"No trouble, Leroy," Erika said as she looked around the room. "I figured you'd be in a grand suite."

"Until we get an official charter from Congress with a budget, the Director has to ask the State Department for nickels and dimes. I'm just trying to save money so Al and I will billet together in a small room. We've stayed in filthy hotels and even taken turns sleeping in cars during stakeouts for multiple days. Any kind of room at the Waldorf=Astoria during a mission is a luxury for us."

"Do you have our handguns?" Erika asked.

Carr nodded at Hodge who opened his briefcase and handed the guns to the women along with extra clips of ammunition. Since the time of year would demand a coat or jacket that would conceal a shoulder holster, he handed each of them such a holster.

"Our job when the ship arrives tomorrow is simple," Carr stated. "The FBI will be at the dock in force. Marienne will follow Grusha off the ship and identify her to the FBI. They will arrest her and then we're done with this mission. You two, Al and I, and Al's men will be there to supply backup but will remain in the background unless needed. This is the FBI's jurisdiction. Originally, Hoover had considered letting Grusha disembark and follow her, but he and his advisors came to the conclusion that losing her was too high of a risk. Their plan now is to arrest her on the docks and get the information by grilling it out of her. Any questions?"

Both Erika and Kathryn said no.

"Okay, meet me and Al in the lobby at seven o'clock this evening. We'll go somewhere for dinner. I know you'll go out anyway, but this time you'll be with us. There have been no problems so far and I don't want you blowing it on the night before the last day of the mission."

[that evening]

A taxi delivered Carr, Hodge, Erika, and Kathryn to *Louis's Sicilian Ristorante* in the Bronx at 7:30. The restaurant was crowded on a Friday night but Hodge had called ahead for reservations.

When the four were seated, Carr ordered a bottle of house red for the table and everyone was handed a menu.

When the wine was delivered, Carr asked the young waiter, Carlo, for a few extra minutes for everyone to look over the menu.

"Our veal is the best in town," Carlo bragged before he walked away.

Carr poured everyone some wine and made a toast. "Here's to tomorrow and the hope that everything runs smoothly so Kathryn can return to Rhode Island and Erika can return to London and finish her stay with Ada."

Everyone lifted their glasses. Then Carr delivered his bombshell.

"Erika and Kathryn, a mobster by the name of Paul Villano was murdered on the street in front of this place in October after having dinner here with two men. We think the killing had something to do with Cuba and that Albert Anastasia's Murder, Inc. crew carried out the hit. I didn't tell you this during our meeting this afternoon, but Al got to New York this morning about four hours before I did and he came here to talk to the owner. Al pressured the man for information, threatening deportation back to Sicily. That did the trick. Al found out that Anastasia and three of his men have reservations for dinner here tonight at eight o'clock—about twenty minutes from now."

Erika said, "Leroy, you know that Anastasia will recognize me immediately."

"That's why I brought you here," Carr answered. "I want to talk to Anastasia."

"I should have known your offer of dinner wasn't just a happy gesture," Erika replied. "There is always a hidden reason behind everything you do, isn't that true, Leroy?"

"Usually," Carr answered.

"I couldn't figure out why you'd bring me back from London just to watch the FBI arrest Grusha. I knew there had to be something else up your sleeve."

"Well, we don't have to worry about any trouble tonight," Carr promised. "Even a goon like Anastasia knows he can't kill federal agents. Now let's order dinner. That veal sounds good to me."

Chapter 63

New York City
Louis's Sicilian Ristorante in the Bronx
Same night—Friday, 17 January 1947

About fifteen minutes after eight, Albert Anastasia and three of his bodyguards entered the restaurant through the kitchen door off an alleyway and were lead through the kitchen to their table by Louis. It took about thirty seconds for Anastasia's and Erika's eyes to lock on each other in the small eatery.

Anastasia immediately rose from his chair and headed toward Erika's table. His men stood up to follow but he told them to stay put.

"Erika, what happened to you and Zhanna?" Anastasia asked. "Did these jokers have anything to do with your capture? If so, we can take care of that right now." He looked at Carr and Hodge. Albert Anastasia didn't have to try to look menacing, he was always so.

"Zhanna was captured Albert, I wasn't."

Carr interjected. "Mr. Anastasia, please have a seat. We have business to discuss."

"Who are you? And why the cheap suit? Don't you know how to dress, you dumb fuck?"

Erika had to work hard not to laugh.

Carr and Hodge produced their State Department identification. "We are federal agents, Anastasia."

"That explains the Sears & Roebucks suit." Anastasia sat down in one of the table's extra chairs. "I know a lot of Jews in the garment district—high end stuff. I'll get you a discount on some new threads so you two guys don't look like a Hillbilly from Stinking Creek getting married in the same suit he'll be buried in."

Erika again suppressed a laugh, but Kathryn wasn't as successful. She kept her laugh to a soft chuckle. It was the best she could do.

Kathryn's chuckle diverted Anastasia's attention to her. "Who's the new broad?"

"We're all federal agents, Anastasia," Carr said.

The mobster looked at Erika. "You're a fed, too?"

"Yes, Albert," Erika answered. "And so is Zhanna."

"That's a shame. You two could have made a lot more money working for me than for these clowns." He turned to Carr. "You have nothing on me. Nothing happened here in New York. Everything happened in Cuba. And by the way, nothing happened there. My men and I were just taking a vacation."

Now it was Carr's turn to laugh. "Right, nothing happened. A pool hall gets shot up and burned down, and an important Soviet official has mysteriously disappeared, but for now we'll go with what you say.

"Anastasia, I've heard through the grapevine that you've vowed to find Erika and Zhanna. Here's my deal: you call off that search, and I won't investigate what happened to Major Volkov. I can't tell you the Russians won't investigate because you and I both know they will, but I can promise you the United States won't, and I think that's what should concern you the most. Am I right?"

Anastasia looked around the table then back at Carr. "I never heard of this Volkov, but I accept the deal."

"Albert," said Erika. "I want to thank you for that night at the pool hall."

Anastasia stood up, looked at Erika and said, "I don't know what you're talking about." Then he returned to his table.

Not wanting to interrupt, Carlo waited until the conversation was over then brought the food immediately to Carr's table.

Albert Anastasia sent a bottle of expensive Sicilian ruby Marsala to Erika's table. Erika turned around and raised her glass of wine to Albert Anastasia. The head of Murder, Inc. returned the salute.

She turned back to the table. "Leroy, you always have a plan, as I said earlier, but they are not always nefarious. I apologize. I know now you are trying to protect us."

"Hopefully, all this will be over with tomorrow," said Carr. "If everything goes according to plan, the FBI will have Grusha in custody and we'll be done. There is a mission in South America that I've had other agents working, but since the war, so many German speakers have arrived in South America that it's really a perfect assignment for you two. But you'll still get your makeup time with Ada, Erika, before we start something new."

"I'm still unclear why the Soviets would send Grusha back here to the States so soon," Kathryn commented.

"Has to be one of two reasons," Al Hodge said. "She's coming back to complete her mission to eliminate Zhanna, or, as the FBI is hoping, she's here to contact *Rollo* and obtain the Bomb information."

Part 6

If I cannot bend heaven, I'll stir up hell!

— *Vergil (ca. 20 B.C.)*

Chapter 64

New York City docks on the Hudson River
Saturday, 18 January 1947

The *Drammen* was scheduled to tie up to Dock 42 at 2:30 p.m. Slow boat traffic up the Hudson turned 2:30 into 3:15, but the *Drammen* finally came into sight for the thick throng of friends and loved ones who had someone onboard they were there to welcome. Family and friends standing on the dock were shoulder to shoulder.

The *Drammen* had three gangplanks. Passengers could use the one of their choice to disembark. This meant the FBI was forced to station a team of agents at each location. Leroy Carr had met with the FBI Special Agent in charge that morning and told him since Grusha might be wearing some type of disguise, the focus would be on spotting Marienne. Marienne would be wearing a green hat and would disembark down the same gangplank as Grusha, staying just a few passengers behind.

Carr told the FBI agent that since it was possible other women could be wearing green hats, and since the FBI did not know Marienne by sight, he would station Al Hodge at one gangplank, Kathryn at another, and Erika at the third. They would identify Marienne, who would remove her hat when Grusha stepped off the gangplank and onto the dock.

Hopefully all would go smoothly and the CIA could return to Washington and be finished with this affair.

It took another thirty minutes for gangplanks to be lowered, tied up and secured so the passengers could begin disembarking. Hundreds of people walked off the ship before Kathryn spotted Marienne and her green hat coming down the gangplank that she had been assigned to monitor. Kathryn told the FBI agent who had stayed by her side that she had identified Marienne. He radioed his team.

Marienne removed her hat when the fourth person in front of her stepped off the gangplank. The FBI swooped in and surrounded Grusha, who was not in disguise.

"You're under arrest," said one of the FBI agents. "What is your name?"

"Grusha Mustafina, and you are making a big mistake," she replied. "I am here to report to the Soviet Embassy in Washington as an interpreter. I have diplomatic immunity." She produced her paperwork.

"We'll see about that," said the agent. They hustled Grusha into a private room in the dock building. The agent called his boss.

"Mr. Hoover, this Grusha woman has all the correct paperwork for diplomatic immunity. What are you orders?"

"Bring her to me."

"Yes, sir."

Twenty minutes later the Special Agent in charge met with Leroy Carr.

"Everything is under control, Mr. Carr. We're taking the prisoner to FBI headquarters. Thank you for all your help."

This was a great relief for Leroy Carr.

◊ ◊ ◊

Instead of the delay of the four-hour drive from New York to Washington, the FBI flew Grusha to D.C. Her fear of flying forced a panic attack and she had to be restrained even more. She arrived at FBI headquarters a few minutes after 6:00 p.m. Hoover had her interrogated which revealed nothing. The grilling was as if it was an amusement for Grusha; she constantly laughed at the FBI interrogators attempts to pressure her.

When Hoover was given the interrogation report, he called Secretary of State James Francis Brynes at home.

"What a minute, Edgar," Brynes said forcefully. "You're telling me you're holding a prisoner and have interrogated her—a foreigner with proper diplomatic immunity papers?"

"Yes, Mr. Secretary. We know the papers are a ruse even if they are official. She's here for a purpose that works against our national interests. I'm confident of that."

"Let me make this clear, Edgar. This is a dog fight we want to avoid. You know as well as I that we send many spies and agents to Moscow and other Iron Curtain countries under the ruse of embassy workers with diplomatic immunity. You need to release this woman immediately. In fact, I expect you to apologize to her. Tell her it was some sort of mix up, and have one of your men drive her to the Soviet embassy. I admire the work you've done over the years Edgar, and I always support the FBI when I can, but not on this one. Don't make me go to the president with this because you know you'll lose."

Hoover was beet red and hung up the phone without a goodbye. He was a powerful man unaccustomed to being told what to do. Hoover wasn't about to apologize to anyone, but later that evening Grusha was driven to the Soviet Embassy and released.

Chapter 65

Washington, D.C.
Next day—Sunday, 19 January 1947

"Al, did I wake you?" Carr said into the phone from his home at 9:00 a.m.

"Naw, I've been up for nearly two hours."

"You'll have to make up church later. Meet me at Hamilton's in one hour."

Both men had arrived a few minutes early when they walked into the restaurant across the Potomac River in Arlington. Even before the waitress had time to get to their table to drop off menus, Carr told Hodge the news.

"Grusha is free," Carr said.

"What? What are you talking about she's free?"

"She carried diplomatic immunity certificates on her. They checked out as authentic. Hoover was ordered by the Secretary of State to let her go. She's currently snug as a bug in a rug inside the Soviet Embassy in Washington."

Hodge made no comment, simply throwing up his arms in frustration.

The waitress arrived. "Sherry, I'll have black coffee and scrambled eggs with bacon," Carr told her. Hodge ordered biscuits and gravy.

"And you like your coffee with some cream, right, Al?" the waitress said. The men's first names were all she knew them by.

Al nodded as he lit a Lucky. "That's right, Sherry. Thanks." When she walked away, Hodge said, "Basically, what you're going to tell me this morning is we aren't finished with this pain-in-the-ass assignment."

"I'll bring them all in for a meeting this afternoon," Carr referred to Marienne and the Shield Maidens. "Marienne is the only shadow we have that has a chance of not losing Grusha when she emerges from that embassy. Marienne will have to stay on for as long as it takes. I'll bring Zhanna back in and have the Shield Maiden team in my office this afternoon. I'll call you back with a time so you can go get Zhanna released from the safehouse and bring her to the meeting."

[that afternoon]

At 2:00, Leroy Carr, Al Hodge, and Marienne Schenk sat in Carr's office along with what were perhaps four of most dangerous and tough women in the world. The credit went to Carr who had brought these women together to work for the United States; although doing so had caused him many problems and headaches because of the past histories of Erika, Zhanna, and Kathryn. Nicknamed the *Shield Maidens* after the famous legend of the great Viking female warriors (the Norse version of the Amazons), this modern group of Shield Maidens comprised a list of names such as Erika Lehmann, Zhanna Rogova, Kathryn Fischer, and Sheila Reid.

Before Carr could say anything, Zhanna blurted out, "I want to know why I was held prisoner after we returned to this country!"

"You weren't a prisoner, Zhanna," Carr answered bluntly. "We held you in a safehouse with all the modern amenities. I'm told the place even has one of those new television devices that are becoming available—those things like radios except with a screen where you can actually see the people talking. But to be honest, I assigned you to the safehouse because I didn't want to take you to New York where I thought you might kill Grusha on sight. Tell me I didn't have a legitimate concern and I will believe you."

Zhanna looked away.

"Okay," Carr said, "since that's settled, let's move on."

"By the way," Zhanna said, "those television machines are worthless. By the time they get the antenna adjusted properly the show is half over. Those devices are just another valueless American gadget that will allow the capitalists to squeeze more money from the people."

Hodge quickly grew tired of Zhanna's communist harangue. "Yeah, yeah, Rogova. Leroy, can we move on now?"

213

"Marienne," said Carr. "I'm afraid I have to ask you to stay with us for now. I know you want to get home to Harold and your family. I apologize."

Marienne nodded reluctantly.

"Kathryn, I called your commander at the Naval War College and told him you would be delayed. Erika, you'll have to postpone your return to London but I promise you that you can make up your time there as soon as this mission is over."

"I agree with Al," Erika said. "Let's get to the point, Leroy. What are our assignments?"

"First, we have to wait until Grusha leaves the Soviet embassy. Obviously, Marienne can't monitor all the exits 24-hours a day so she'll have a task force at her disposal of some of Al's best men. We can expect the FBI to also monitor the embassy and we want to avoid them.

"Sheila has a home here in D.C. The rest of you ladies will billet at the Mayflower. As soon as Marienne is told that Grusha is on the streets, she will tail her. Hopefully Grusha will lead us to *Rollo.*"

"I thought you said this was the FBI's job, Leroy," said Erika.

"I received a phone call from Secretary Brynes. He knows of Marienne's reputation and he wants her, and us, in on this. From reading between the lines, I don't think the Secretary trusts the FBI not to lose Grusha on a tail."

"Isn't that breaking the law for us to be involved?"

"You're reading that charter again, Erika. I asked you to lay off. Find yourself a good spy novel to read instead."

Erika was right. It was contrary to the CIA charter to work on American soil. But if it came down to protecting his country, Leroy Carr was willing to ignore the rules.

"None of you have to worry," Carr told the group. "I'll take the heat if it comes down to that. If the horse dung hits the fan, I'll stand in front of the fan. None of you will go down with me, I promise you that."

Chapter 66

Washington, D.C.
Next day—Monday, 20 January 1947

Early Monday morning the meeting that Carr had anticipated became a reality when he and Al Hodge received subpoenas to appear that afternoon in front of a State Department committee assigned to monitor intelligence. Carr breathed a sigh of relief when he found out his hopes had been answered; only he and Al were subpoenaed. The women had been left out. He could only imagine the mayhem that could ensue if Erika and Zhanna appeared before a State Department inquiry board.

[that afternoon]

Leroy Carr and Al Hodge sat at a table in one of the State Department's assigned quarters in the U.S. Capitol building facing eight men sitting behind desks on an oval pedestal that towered three feet higher than where he and Al sat. Carr had been at such venues before, both here and before the Senate, and he always figured the layout was designed to give the impression to the poor soul being questioned that he or she looked upwards to a council of the gods.

Running the meeting and sitting in the middle was Secretary of State James Francis Brynes. Next to him was Undersecretary Tuttle who Carr worked with often. Carr recognized another man who worked at the War Department during the war. The other five he had never laid eyes on, but one was an Army brigadier general in uniform. They were all identified by a name plate sitting on the edge of the pedestal in front of them, but the plates offered up only a name and not a department so Carr had no idea if the men he didn't recognize worked for the State Department or some other agency or department.

"Mr. Carr and Mr. Hodge, thank you for appearing before us today." Brynes gave this traditional welcome even though the subpoenas gave the people being grilled no option of not reporting.

215

"Hopefully we can keep this brief," Brynes stated. "I know you and Undersecretary Tuttle have worked closely together so I'm turning the main questioning over to him. Anyone else on the panel may ask questions at any time, of course."

"Thank you Mr. Secretary," said Tuttle. Then he turned his attention to Carr and Hodge. "You've already stated your names for the record. Tell us your job responsibilities with the new intelligence organization—for the record."

"I'm deputy director of the CIA," Carr answered.

"I'm in charge of counterintelligence," Hodge said into the mike.

Tuttle continued. "As I'm sure you know, we are here to discuss the exchange with the Soviets on the bridge in Germany. In our eyes it can only be considered a debacle that could very well impact any future exchanges. We'd like to hear your comments, Mr. Carr."

"We kept our end of the bargain, Mr. Undersecretary," Carr said. "It was the Soviets who broke their end of the deal by firing onto the bridge and putting our people at risk."

"By our people, I assume you mean the German you now use as an operative, this Erika Lehmann. We have all read your report. She was the only CIA operative on the bridge."

"Yes, that is correct; however, she is still our operative."

"Do you have anything to add, Mr. Hodge?"

"Only that Lehmann has proved her value to the United States, Mr. Undersecretary," Hodge piped in.

"Although you, Mr. Carr, have had this woman locked up on more than one occasion," the one-star general stated.

"All I can do," Carr replied, "is to ask the committee to consider Lehmann's record on missions since she began working for us in late 1943."

Byrnes took back control of the meeting.

"We're all aware of this woman's effectiveness. For that reason we will table this discussion for the present. But make no mistake, Deputy Director Carr, the State Department has reservations about both this woman Lehmann and the Soviet Rogova you have brought into your fold. Then there is this other woman, Fischer, working for you who served as a Gestapo officer during the war. It's not the State

Department's intention to allow the CIA to become a haven for former enemy spies, Soviet assassins, and Gestapo officers. I've directed CIA director Vandenberg to monitor them closely and report to me or Mr. Tuttle weekly. If any of those three women make the smallest of glitches, they are out of the CIA and I'll order them to be turned over to the proper authorities. I just want to be clear about this, Mr. Carr and Mr. Hodge."

[that evening]

"That meeting with those bureaucrats at the State Department this afternoon was the most hypocritical thing I've been exposed to, Leroy," Al commented. Carr and Hodge sat sipping cocktails at *Jocko's*, their favorite pub in Annapolis. "The State Department has brought to the U.S. every Nazi rocket scientist they could lay their hands on, some who have committed obvious war crimes, yet they call us on the rug and break our balls about some former Nazis like Erika and Kathryn. Despite the fact Lehmann grates on my nerves something fierce, she has proven her worth, as has Kathryn and even Zhanna for that matter."

"You're preaching to the choir, old buddy," Carr said as he sipped his gin and tonic. "All we can do is try to keep Erika, Kathryn, and Zhanna out of the eye of the storm for the present. I'm hoping with Marienne's help, the FBI can handle this without us being forced to get the Shield Maidens involved."

Chapter 67

Soviet Embassy
Washington, D.C.
Next day—Tuesday, 21 January 1947

"Are you clear about your mission, Grusha?" asked Anatoly Trukhin.

"Yes, Comrade Minister," Grusha answered.

"I know there is bad blood between you and Zhanna, but if your paths ever cross such as during any future assignments, you are not to bother Zhanna in any way. You've been given a second chance by the Politburo. I need not tell you how rarely that happens."

"Apparently it happened for Zhanna," Grusha smirked.

"Zhanna has her own mission." Trukhin was growing impatient. "Your life depends on you obeying your orders."

"I said I understood. May I ask why the Politburo changed its prerogative so quickly from wanting to eliminate Rogova to now protecting her?"

"No, you may not. That is information above your security clearance level."

Grusha had been told nothing about Zhanna's deal to become a double agent, but she knew her spy world and suspected as much.

"Your focus should now be directed solely to your mission," Trukhin continued. "Locate our asset codenamed *Rollo* and retrieve the information we lost on the bridge. Originally, General Polzin instructed us to take *Rollo* to the Soviet Union, but this has changed. The Politburo overruled him, deciding *Rollo* is too valuable where he is. *Rollo* will hand over the secrets to you on microfilm and you will transport them back to Moscow in a diplomatic immunity pouch. Return here this afternoon for your briefing. At that time you'll be given the name of the facility in the United States where *Rollo* works. You leave tomorrow morning."

[Next day]
While Erika, Kathryn, and Zhanna had been sleeping in the luxury of the Mayflower hotel, Marienne had spent most of her last three nights

drinking strong black coffee to stay awake while sitting in a CIA stakeout vehicle disguised as a plumber's van parked two blocks away from the Soviet embassy. Binoculars allowed her a satisfactory view of the Soviet grounds. She caught up on her sleep after daylight when the FBI shadow team took over and she could return to the comfort of her bed at the Mayflower.

Late that morning the phone call came.

"Agent Schenk, this is Special Agent Carmichael."

Marienne recognized the FBI man's voice. "Yes, Special Agent Carmichael."

"The subject Grusha just left the Soviet grounds in an embassy staff car."

"Make sure your men don't lose her," Marienne said. "I'm leaving right away. I'll be in a car with a two-way radio. Use your radio to keep me updated on her location. We don't want the police hearing our conversations and getting involved so use Channel D." Channel D was a new secure government radio channel that scrambled anything said over the airwaves which in turn could only be unscrambled if the receiving radio was also government issued with the capacity to unscramble the gobbledygook. *"ROGER that."* Carmichael signed off.

◊ ◊ ◊

Leroy Carr called Al Hodge in his Pentagon office.

"Grusha's on the move, Al. She left the embassy about an hour ago."

"Does Marienne have her in her sights?"

"The FBI is following Grusha right now but Marienne is on her way."

"Do we tell the Shield Maidens?" Al asked.

"No, hopefully Marienne and the FBI can get this done without getting all the women involved. I'm sending Sheila along to help Marienne. I can trust Sheila to stay on course, but those other three we have to keep out of trouble for awhile."

Chapter 68

On a Union Pacific passenger train
Wednesday, 22 January 1947

The FBI had kept its tail and radioed Marienne that Grusha had been dropped off at the train depot. By the time Grusha had stood in line and finally bought her train ticket, Marienne and Sheila had arrived.

At the District of Columbia train station, Grusha bought a train ticket for Nashville, Tennessee. Marienne knew this did not mean her destination was Nashville. The train had numerous stops before reaching the Tennessee capital. Grusha could step off the train at any of those stops, or she might reach Nashville and continue on to another destination.

By the time the train pulled out, Marienne and Sheila sat several tables away from Grusha in the train's lounge car sipping on Irish coffee. Grusha sat by herself at the small bar drinking a vodka martini.

Major Sheila Reid was well aware that Marienne was the CIA's best shadow and her orders from Leroy Carr were clear: learn from Marienne, follow her orders and offer any assistance needed. Sheila was especially tasked with protecting Marienne, who was skilled with a handgun but had never undergone close quarters combat training like Sheila. They posed as sisters on their way to a family wedding for any nosey passengers who asked. Both wore brunette wigs, felt hats, and did their makeup in similar fashion. Each wore eyeglasses with clear, phony lenses.

Suddenly Marienne whispered, "We have a situation."

"What situation is that?" Sheila asked.

"See those two men sitting at the table at the other end of the car? One has a mustache."

Sheila scanned for a moment. "Yes, I see them."

"They're Grusha's team of shadow seekers. Their job is to make sure Grusha isn't being followed. They've already made us. We're blown."

"How do you know all this, Marienne?"

"Both of the men have walked by us to another car—probably to the toilets in the next car back. As they walk, they look at everyone except us, avoiding eye contact thinking we won't suspect them. It's an amateur move and a dead giveaway that they know we're following Grusha. They're most likely NKVD from the embassy. At our next stop, call Leroy and let him know that our covers are blown."

"Then what?"

"Since it's obvious the two shadow seekers are inexperienced, we'll keep tailing Grusha as if we suspect nothing until they make their move."

[same time—Washington]

Erika called Carr from her suite in the Mayflower. Carr had reserved them a small suite since she, Kathryn, and Zhanna had to room together.

"Leroy, what's going on? We're going stir crazy here. Has Grusha left the embassy yet?"

"No, not yet," Carr fibbed. "The three of you just stay put until I contact you. Don't leave the hotel."

"So we're prisoners here," said Erika.

"You have the run of the Mayflower Hotel. You can dine in the hotel restaurant and visit the bar whenever you like. I know being ordered to stay at the Mayflower, the best hotel in Washington, has got to be a rough assignment," Carr said flippantly.

"You're a pain in my ass, Leroy."

"The same back at ya, Erika."

[later that day]

Carr called Erika at the Mayflower. None of the women were in their room but Carr had Erika paged. She, Zhanna, and Kathryn were in the restaurant having dinner.

"Hello," Erika said into the restaurant's customer telephone.

"Erika, it's Leroy."

"Yes, Leroy, I recognize your voice after three years."

"Is everyone in the hotel? Zhanna and Kathryn?"

"Yes, those were your orders, Leroy. Do you really think we'd break an order?"

Carr would have laughed if the circumstances weren't so critical. *"We won't get into that now. Al is on his way to pick up you three. Be checked out and be waiting for Al in the lobby in twenty minutes."*

[two hours later]

Things moved quickly now because they had to. Within a couple of hours of Carr's phone call to Erika at the Mayflower, Carr, Hodge, and the three Shield Maidens were in the air.

Carr had not wasted time on the ground briefing the women. He did that now on the plane.

"Marienne and Sheila are tailing Grusha. Currently they are all aboard a train to Nashville. Sheila called me from Bristol, Tennessee, during one of the train's stops. Their covers have been blown by a couple of NKVD shadow seekers. Marienne and Sheila are ignoring the two NKVD men and will keep Grusha in sight as long as possible."

"We don't know where Grusha will get off the train," Carr continued. "The final destination for her ticket is Nashville, but she could get off the train before that or purchase another ticket to continue on to some other place. Marienne knows we need to find that out; she and Sheila are putting themselves at risk for the sake of the mission. This plane will beat the train to Nashville where we'll be waiting so we can relieve Marienne and Sheila—they're in a dangerous situation right now. If Grusha gets off the train before Nashville, I told Sheila to call my wife at home and let her know. Both Sheila and Marienne have my home phone number memorized; I'll check in with Kay every thirty minutes after we reach Nashville. My wife has the proper clearance. She was involved in an OSS mission in Bath, England, during the war."

◊ ◊ ◊

Carr had chosen a Lockheed 10-E Electra for the trip to Nashville. It was the same model of plane preferred by Amelia Earhart. The Electras were smaller and the interior louder and less comfortable than a DC-3, but the Electra could cruise at almost 290 knots at full throttle making it faster than a DC-3.

The group arrived in Nashville around 11:30 that night, an hour-and-a-half before Grusha's train was scheduled to arrive. As soon as the plane touched down, Carr called home from a phone in the airport's only concourse.

"Marienne called about thirty minutes ago, Leroy," Kay said. *"The woman they are following got off the train at Knoxville, Tennessee. Sheila has been captured!"*

When Carr got off the phone, he told Hodge to get out his map of Tennessee. He found Knoxville and saw that Oak Ridge, Tennessee, was only 25 miles away.

"Damn it, Al," Carr said vigorously. "I should have known! Oak Ridge played as important a role in the Manhattan Project as did Los Alamos. *Rollo* must be at Oak Ridge!

"Get everyone back on the plane, now!"

Chapter 69

Knoxville, Tennessee
Next day—Thursday, 23 January 1947

Marienne had come up with a plan in case Grusha exited the train before Nashville. Unfortunately, for the plan to work, Sheila would have to let herself be captured. The brave Army major agreed.

When the train stopped in Morristown, its last stop before Knoxville, Marienne got up and left the lounge car for the next car back; the car with the shower and toilet facilities. This was not suspicious as many travelers used the stops to refresh. Inside one of the cramped toilet rooms Marienne removed her hat, wig and glasses. She scrubbed her face and applied new makeup. She never returned to Sheila's side.

When the train stopped in Knoxville in the dark of night, Grusha and her men disembarked. The men waited for Sheila to step off. The platform lighting allowed a much different looking Marienne, who had stepped off the train from another car, to see that one man held something under a newspaper. It had to be a knife or gun. Sheila was escorted out of the terminal. The capture allowed Marienne just enough time for her quick phone call to Kay Carr then she hailed a taxi and told the cabbie to follow the taxi that had just pulled away. In Grusha's taxi, Sheila sat in the back with a gun poking into her ribs, a gun still underneath a newspaper to conceal it from the driver.

If it were a matter of shadowing a car from another car, Marienne always preferred nighttime. A certain set of headlights among many other sets of headlights were nearly impossible for the person or persons being tailed to spot.

[Russian safehouse]
Sheila Reid sat tied to a chair in a warehouse in the industrial section of Knoxville. Normally, the Soviets would not bother having a safehouse in a place like Knoxville, but this warehouse had been leased by the Russians nearly a year ago under the name of a French

company the Soviets controlled. A safehouse in Knoxville became necessary to serve as a private meeting place with *Rollo,* their mole within the American atomic research facility in Oak Ridge, just a half-hour away by car.

Grusha viciously used the butt of her gun to strike Sheila across the face. Sheila already bled from her nose and a severe cut over her left eye. Her left jaw sported a purple mark from a previous blow.

"I'll ask you again!" Grusha shouted. "Where is the woman who traveled with you?"

"I've told you a dozen times," said Sheila, groggy from being beaten. "She's my sister. She got off the train in Morristown. I don't know what you mean with all this talk that we were following you."

"Does your sister also wear a brown wig to cover her red hair? Quit lying!" Grusha again pistol whipped Sheila. This time the Army major passed out.

"What do you want to do with her, Comrade?" one of Grusha's shadow seekers asked.

"Nothing for now. Her driver's license states her name is Gertrude Banks but that means nothing. It would be protocol to travel under a fake identity. We won't dispose of her until we get the truth, and she might offer us a bargaining chip if indeed she does work for the FBI or CIA."

◊ ◊ ◊

Carr called home as soon as the Electra landed in Knoxville.

"Any new word from Marienne?" Carr asked his wife.

"Plenty," Kay responded. *"Marienne knows where Sheila's being held. Marienne is waiting for you now at an all-night country and western honky-tonk called the 'Red Saddle' in downtown Knoxville. She said it is a half-block down from 19th street on Lake Ave.*

◊ ◊ ◊

[45-minutes later at the Red Saddle tavern]

Carr, Hodge, and the three Shield Maidens found Marienne at a table with a man who had been buying her drinks for the past hour. Erika told the guy to scram.

"What? Who are you, lady?" the man asked, but the look in her eyes convinced him to leave the table.

It was nearly three in the morning, and if loud country and western bands were not playing, the half-drunken crowd made plenty of its own background noise. The group shrugged it off. At least they would not be overheard.

"Sheila was taken to what looked to me to be an abandoned warehouse on Union Avenue, three blocks from Henley Avenue," said Marienne.

"It must be a Soviet safehouse," Carr interjected.

"Right," said Marienne. "We need to get Sheila out of there. She's probably being tortured as we sit here drinking beer."

"Our first objective is to find *Rollo*," Carr responded. "If we move in now, we might never find out who he is."

Marienne and all of the Shield Maidens objected vehemently. Even Al Hodge told Leroy they had to get Sheila to safety.

Erika spoke for them all. "Leroy, what are you talking about? Sheila is one of us! We have to get her back, and we have to act quickly, which means now! They might move her at any time."

Carr thought for a moment. This time he knew the team was right—leave no one behind. "You're all right. We owe it to Sheila. We'll get her back then I'll turn all this over to Hoover. With the kind of leads we can give him, the FBI should be able to mop up all this *Rollo* business pretty quickly.

"We have to find a close hotel where we can change and secure our weapons."

"I saw one a couple of blocks from here," Marienne said. "It looks pretty seedy but all of us have stayed at plenty of those types of hotels. It will suit our purpose."

Chapter 70

Terrible is the likeness of her face to immortal goddesses.

— Homer, (ca. 700 B.C.)

Knoxville, Tennessee
Same night

Carr wanted the advantage of darkness when they reached the warehouse where Sheila was being held. With just a couple of hours left before first light, the team was forced to hustle.

They rented two rooms at the rundown hotel Marienne had referenced—one room for the men and one for the woman. They would be there only long enough to change clothes and put together a quick plan.

Everyone changed quickly into dark fatigues and Army boots that Hodge had brought with him. He also had with him a large trunk filled with heavier weapons such as an assortment of knives, two double-barreled shotguns, two Thompson machineguns, and two M-1 rifles. Hodge had even brought along some grenades.

In the room that the women used, Erika, Kathryn, and Marienne changed clothes quickly. Erika used a sock hat to cover her bright blonde hair. Kathryn used a rubber band to tie her long brown hair into a pony tail to keep it of her face. Zhanna on the other hand spent a long time in the bathroom. Erika pounded on the bathroom door and told her to hurry up. When Zhanna emerged she looked like some frightful apparition from a nightmare. Black eye shadow stretched entirely across her face, from hair line to hair line giving the impression she wore a mask. No lipstick other than three streaks that extended vertically from her lips to her chin. Her scarf was gone, revealing the horrific neck scar from when she was hanged by the SS.

Erika wondered about Zhanna's extreme makeup but there was no time to ask questions. Kathryn entered the bathroom and Marienne was out of earshot when Zhanna whispered a shock. "Erika, my country wants me to become a double agent. But I will not betray you."

Erika looked at Zhanna and thought for a moment. "You'll have to tell Leroy about this, Zhanna, but not now. It can wait until after we've freed Sheila. So for now it's our secret. I trust you."

"I will do what you say, but I want your promise that you leave Grusha to me!" Zhanna said forcefully.

◊ ◊ ◊

The team arrived at the locked-down warehouse one hour before first light. The plan they had quickly thrown together entailed Erika, the best athlete amongst them, gaining secret entry to the facility, give the place a quick once over, and hopefully spot Sheila. Then she was ordered to report back to the team waiting in the shadows of an alley across the street. At that time a rescue plan would be put together.

The three-storey-high building had a fire escape but it only extended halfway up the side of the building. The pull-down ladder to access the fire escape from the street was eleven feet from the ground. Kathryn crossed the street with Erika and boosted Erika up so the ladder could be pulled down quietly. Erika ascended the fire escape quickly. Kathryn, instead of returning to the alley across the street where Leroy Carr, Al Hodge, Zhanna Rogova and Marienne Schenk waited, found a shadow and remained by the warehouse.

A door at the top of the fire escape was locked from the outside. Erika couldn't take the risk of noise by kicking in the door, so like a spider on the wall she began mountain climbing up the building's rough-edged bricks until she reached the roof.

A skylight on the roof enabled Erika to see the weak lighting on the warehouse floor, but she saw no one.

Back in the alley, Zhanna convinced Carr that he allow her to cross the street and backup Kathryn if necessary. Carr agreed, but added, "None of you try anything on your own. Erika's orders are to just give the inside a quick once over to determine if Sheila is in there, then she is to return here and we'll come up with a strategy and all go over together. Got that, Zhanna?"

She nodded and then ran across the street to join Kathryn. Marienne was ordered to remain with Carr and Hodge.

"What's the deal with the war paint on Zhanna's face? What's that all about?" Hodge asked Carr after Zhanna left.

"During the war, some Russian female snipers applied bizarre makeup," Carr answered. "I'd bet it's her Russian sniper face."

"If that's it, it's not working as camouflage. It just draws attention to her face. She looks like one of those creepy vampire women from a Bela Lugosi movie. All she needs is a set of fangs."

Hodge continued, "Why don't you stay put here, Leroy? The CIA Director and the State Department are not going to be happy about the deputy director inserting himself into an active mission and in harm's way. What if you were captured? You stay here and I'll go in with the women. I'm a lot more expendable than you."

"Don't give me any of that horse crap, Al. We've been through too much together."

"And don't think that I'm staying here," Marienne said. "When you guys go, I go."

◊ ◊ ◊

On the warehouse roof, Erika discovered that the skylight was secured by a weak thumb lock. It took her only a moment to quietly jimmy it open with her knife. A rope encircled one of her shoulders; a Thompson machinegun was strapped to the other. She tied one end of the rope to a cast iron plumbing vent pipe extending from the flat roof and began lowering herself down. Without noise, she descended to a steel grate walkway inside the building high above the warehouse's concrete floor. Still, she hadn't spotted Sheila.

The purpose of the grated walkway was to allow workmen to service the lighting and other equipment suspended from the ceiling. It continued around about three quarters of the building. Erika softly walked along the grates until she finally got to a point where she saw Sheila sitting tied to a chair on the warehouse floor. Her head was bent forward. Erika assumed she was unconscious. Grusha and two men stood talking a few feet away.

Erika's orders were to surveil and then report back to Leroy. Instead, she began climbing down the iron work to the next level.

Chapter 71

Warehouse in Knoxville, Tennessee
Same night

In the shadows cast by the lampposts on the street outside the warehouse, Kathryn and Zhanna remained well hidden, crouched beside a trash receptacle in an alley beside the warehouse. Zhanna carried a sawed-off double-barrel 12-gauge shotgun in addition to her pistol and a large Bowie knife. Kathryn, besides her handgun and similar knife, was armed with an M-1 rifle.

"Erika's taking a long time," Zhanna whispered.

"That's because she isn't coming out," Kathryn also said sotto voce. "I know her. If she had to enter the building to spot Sheila she's not going to take the chance of being heard while making her way back out. That's asking for double trouble. Follow me. We'll go around the back and see if we can find a way to quietly get inside. Erika will need backup."

Staying low, and out of sight from both anyone inside the warehouse and from the rest of the team across the street, Kathryn and Zhanna worked their way to the back of the building.

Inside, Erika had lowered herself to the building's second tier and could now hear Grusha and her watchdogs speaking in Russian, yet she was still too far away to make out what was being said. Luckily, the lighting at floor level came from only a couple of low suspended yellow bulbs. The upper regions of the building where Erika perched were bathed in darkness.

◊ ◊ ◊

Across the street, Hodge said, "Leroy, Lehmann's taking a lot of time to do a quick surveillance."

"Yes she is, Al. But finding Sheila in there might take some time."

"These binoculars don't work worth a shit in the dark," Al added. "I haven't been able to spot Kathryn or that zany Russian since they disappeared into that alley."

"That's kind of the point, Al. They're supposed to stay hidden."

"If you ask me, Leroy, that damn broad is disobeying orders again." Hodge referred to Erika.

"We'll give her ten more minutes, Al. Then we'll go ourselves and find out what's going on."

◊ ◊ ◊

At the rear of the warehouse, Kathryn found a window beside the loading dock. It was locked, but a bit shaky. Kathryn went to work trying to crack the window open with her Bowie knife.

"Work faster," Zhanna said quietly.

"Shut up, I'm working as fast as I can without making noise."

Chapter 72

Same time and place

Erika watched from the darkness of the second tier as one of Grusha's men threw a bucket of cold water on their prisoner. Sheila slowly raised her head.

"Now I want the truth!" Grusha shouted in Sheila's face. "Who are you, where is the woman that accompanied you on the train, and who do your work for—the FBI? Tell the truth and I'll make your death painless." Grusha pulled out a stiletto and pressed it to Sheila's throat.

"Okay, okay," Sheila said. "I'll tell you."

"I'm listening," Grusha removed the slim dagger from her throat.

Sheila said, "Untie me from this chair, so I can bend over and you can kiss my ass."

Grusha plunged the stiletto into Sheila's shoulder. The Army major grimaced from the searing pain but refused to scream.

Immediately, Erika jumped from her second storey perch onto one of Grusha's men. The blow to his head delivered by an elbow as she fell on him knocked him unconscious. He fell to the floor with Erika on top of him. It was such a high jump, however, the impact of landing was tough on Erika and she was slow to stand up. When Erika got to her feet, Grusha shouted, "Shoot her!"

The second man raised a gun but just then a shot rang out, striking the man in the knee and shattering his knee cap. It was the best shot Kathryn had as the man's upper body, from her angle, was obscured by warehouse equipment.

The man fell like a building demolished by high explosives. Erika quickly limped over and smashed his face with the butt of her Thompson.

Grusha had a handgun tucked in the back off her pants but decided since there was another gunman somewhere in the warehouse her best move would be to circle around Sheila and hold her dagger to Sheila's throat.

Erika raised her Thompson and aimed at Grusha.

"Those American Thompson's are not accurate and spray everything, Erika," Grusha said. "If you pull that trigger you'll kill your comrade." Grusha was crouched behind the still-bound Sheila and tightened her hold.

"You're right," Erika said. "I have another way to free Sheila."

"Sheila! So now I have a name," Grusha smirked.

At that moment, Zhanna Rogova slowly walked out of the darkness so Grusha could see her. The weak yellow lighting made Zhanna's severe makeup look evermore fiendish, like an image from one of Edgar Allan Poe's macabre nightmares.

For a moment Grusha was taken aback by Zhanna's severe manifestation and the smirk disappeared, yet she kept her cool.

"Welcome Zhanna," said Grusha. "This is the moment I have always wished for—the day that I kill you."

Both women spoke in Russian.

"That remains to be seen, doesn't it? Perhaps you have mistakenly looked forward to this day." Zhanna laid her shotgun and handgun on the floor. She brought out her knife, "It's now between just you and me, Grusha."

Just a couple of seconds later, Kathryn emerged from the darkness with her M-1 zeroed in on Grusha.

"How do I know your comrades will not get involved?" Grusha again applied pressure to Sheila's throat with her stiletto.

Erika dropped her weapons to the floor. She put a hand on Kathryn's shoulder as a sign that she should do the same. Kathryn wavered for a moment, but eventually bent over and placed her rifle on the floor.

"Other weapons on the ground!" Grusha barked.

Erika and Kathryn laid their handguns and knives on the floor.

"Step away!" Grusha ordered.

The two women took several steps backwards.

Now Grusha addressed Zhanna. "Kick those weapons over to me or your comrade dies!"

Zhanna did so, then said, "Can we get down to our purpose tonight—you and I? Both of us want the same thing—that one of us dies before the sun rises." Zhanna dropped all her weapons to the floor except her knife, which she held at her side.

"So it is a knife fight you propose," Grusha sneered. "I salute you for not bringing your sniper rifle with which you are famous."

Grusha released her grip on Sheila and with the thin but twelve-inch-long stiletto in hand, walked out into the brighter light to wait for Zhanna.

Chapter 73

Same time and place

When Carr, Hodge, and Marienne heard the gunshot from Kathryn's rifle, they immediately ran across the street toward the warehouse's heavy double doors.

Inside, Zhanna and Grusha stepped into battle. Grusha drew first blood when a swipe with her dagger put a deep slice into Zhanna's left forearm. Zhanna was not a small woman at 5'8" and with an equally-sized opponent, she would have used the opportunity to rush Grusha, but a trained assassin like Zhanna has to know her mark's strengths and weaknesses. At nearly six-feet tall and heavier, Grusha was physically stronger than Zhanna, so she avoided rushing Grusha and possibly ending up in close hand-to-hand combat. On the other hand, Zhanna was quicker and more agile than her opponent.

Grusha realized that Zhanna was going to keep her distance, so she tried to rush her. It was a mistake. Although Grusha managed another glancing strike, this one opening a small cut on Zhanna's cheek, Zhanna plunged her Bowie knife into Grusha's right leg. Unfortunately for Zhanna, she missed the femoral artery. Grusha was slowed for a moment but showed no signs of pain. In fact, she smiled and kept trying to close in on Zhanna.

Just then a loud explosion rocked the warehouse. At the other end of the building, Carr and Hodge had set grenades and blew off the warehouse's heavy steel doors.

Zhanna and Grusha ignored the tumult and kept their attention focused on each other.

Grusha kept stepping toward Zhanna. Zhanna kept up her strategy of keeping her distance.

"What's the matter?" Grusha growled. "Is the great Zhanna Rogova afraid?"

It was the opening Zhanna had waited for. Talking during any kind of fight diverts the talker's attention and slows reaction, if only minutely. Zhanna sprang toward Grusha like a cheetah onto a wildebeest. Zhanna had been fighting with her knife in her right hand.

She brought that hand around in a stabbing motion. Grusha blocked the thrust, but the knife was not there. Zhanna brought her left hand around and buried the knife deep into Grusha's chest, under ribs and up into her heart.

Grusha was quickly dying with a look of utter surprise on her face, but in the few seconds she had left she managed one last swipe of her knife. Zhanna was able to deflect this one and Grusha's last act managed to put only a cut in Zhanna left ring finger.

It was as if Grusha refused to die. Even with her heart penetrated she remained standing. Zhanna kept trying to push the knife deeper. Finally, Grusha dropped to her knees, looked at Zhanna and then fell forward on her face, dead.

Carr and Hodge finally found the women in the expansive building, and with Marienne alongside, they rushed up fully armed and ready for whatever was to come. They were too late. The fight had taken no more than ten minutes.

"What in the hell happened?" Carr asked. His eyes scanned from Grusha's body to the two unconscious men several yards away on the floor.

No one answered. Erika and Kathryn untied Sheila. Erika still limped from the twenty-foot-high leap from the second tier, but she ignored it and removed her shirt. She tore off a sleeve and used it to apply pressure to the profusely bleeding knife wound in Sheila's shoulder. Luckily, the bleeding had been slowed somewhat by the frigid temperature inside the unheated building.

"Leroy, we have to get Sheila to a hospital," Erika said calmly. "Zhanna needs some attention, too."

Carr sent Hodge to the car to radio for an ambulance.

◊ ◊ ◊

Leroy Carr spent much of the rest of the day in a hospital waiting room. Sheila needed the most attention but Zhanna required several stitches to the various knife wounds. Erika's ankle was X-rayed and even though she had not fractured anything from the high jump, her ankle had suffered a stretched ligament and she left the hospital with a heavily taped foot and ankle.

Al Hodge spent his day ensuring Grusha's men were properly turned over to the FBI. It also fell on Hodge to stay in Knoxville and deal with the police until Sheila was able to fly home.

Carr, Erika, Zhanna, Kathryn and Marienne flew back to Washington that evening.

"We'll all meet tomorrow morning at ten," Carr told them on the plane. "I realize Erika's injury makes it tough for her to walk and Zhanna has a lot of stitches. I'll get you all another room at the Mayflower and we'll have the meeting there so all of you don't have to walk the long halls of the Pentagon."

Chapter 74

Washington, D.C.
Next day—Friday, 24 January 1947

The team (minus Al and Sheila who were still in Knoxville) arrived back in D.C. late that night. As promised, Carr got the women a suite at the Mayflower, told them to get some sleep, and that he would return at ten the next morning.

'Next morning' was now.

Carr knocked on the women's door and Kathryn opened it. They all ended up sitting on sofas and chairs in the suite's parlor.

"I'll start off with the good news," said Carr. "Sheila needed some blood pumped into her but she's doing amazingly well. Al has turned over Grusha's men to the FBI. The man Erika smashed in the face with the butt of her Thompson is a mess, but Al told me the doctors said the guy should survive. I sent Hoover a full report of everything we learned about *Rollo*—that he's working at Oak Ridge, etc. The FBI should be able to wrap up *Rollo* quickly.

"The doctors want Sheila to spend one more night in the hospital in Knoxville. So if all goes as expected, Al and Sheila will be back here sometime late tomorrow."

"You said you'll start with the good news, Leroy," Erika said. "That tells me there must be some bad."

"The bad news is you can bet your rear end that there will be another hearing by the State Department or Senate into why a person protected by Russian diplomatic immunity was killed on American soil. But that's for me to deal with."

"Can't you just tell them the truth?" Kathryn asked. "That Grusha was a Russian spy sent here to steal atomic bomb secrets."

"I'll certainly try the truth, Kathryn," Carr responded. "Sometimes with these government investigation committees the truth works and sometimes it doesn't. You'll have to wish me luck that the truth works this time."

"So what's next?" Erika asked.

"What's next is that Marienne, you are free to return home to Pittsburgh." Carr handed her an envelope containing a sizable pay check for dangerous mission work as a civilian. "Your flight leaves this afternoon at 2:00. You'll be home for dinner. Tell Harold I said he should take you out to eat," Carr smiled, "but don't send me the bill. I'm already over budget for this mission.

"For the rest of us, we'll wait until Al and Sheila get back to town. We'll gather again after that happens."

[that evening]
Erika, Zhanna, and Kathryn sat in a booth in the larger of the two Mayflower Hotel lounges. Carr had left. They were alone. All had drinks in front of them.

"I wish Marienne could be with us," Erika said before she took a sip of her brandy.

"She has a husband to return to; who can blame her?" Kathryn immediately regretted her words, remembering that Erika had lost her husband only last summer.

"I'm sorry, Erika," Kathryn apologized. "That was a stupid thing for me to say."

Erika shook her head slowly. "It's okay, Kathryn. You also know how it feels to lose someone." Erika referred to Stephanie, Kathryn's sister, who died a hero during a mission with Erika during the war.

The visible evidence of Zhanna's fight to the death with Grusha was a bandage on her cheek covering the four stitches, and a Band-Aid around her left ring finger. The bandage covering her severest wound—the deep slice in her forearm—was covered by a long-sleeved blouse. The Russian smacked down half of her vodka and moved the conversation to another zone to relieve the awkwardness. "How much do you two think Grusha's men will know about her involvement in her atomic bomb mission?"

"Probably not much," Erika answered. "My guess is they know nothing and were assigned to Grusha as nothing more than shadow seekers, but I might be wrong. As far as *Rollo* is concerned, the FBI has extensive files on any American involved in any type of top secret

239

work, and I've heard that the FBI is very good with interrogations. If the men know anything, the FBI should be able to extract it. I think Leroy is right; I think the FBI will find *Rollo* pretty quickly."

The conversation turned lighter from there. They talked about humorous things and banal thoughts about the latest Hollywood movies. Yet in the back of Erika's mind lurked the necessity for Zhanna to tell Leroy Carr about the real reason the Soviets agreed to the trade on the bridge over the Havel—for her to become a double agent for the USSR. Erika knew Zhanna had to fess up. If she didn't and Carr found out on his own later, Zhanna would surely be imprisoned or perhaps even executed.

[next morning—Saturday, 25 January]
Leroy Carr had not planned to bring the group together until after Al and Sheila made it back from Tennessee, but Erika placed an early morning phone call to his home. Erika was glad Leroy answered and not Kay, who held Erika in low regard because of past history during the war.

"Hello."

"Good morning, Leroy. I hope I didn't wake you."

"Are you kidding? Do you think I get Saturdays off? I'm already dressed and have eaten breakfast. What's up, Erika?"

"Zhanna and I would like a private conversation with you."

"About what?"

"It's not something to discuss on the telephone," Erika said.

"When do you want to do this?"

"This morning."

"I was just about to leave for my office. I'll meet you there in an hour."

[60 minutes later]
Erika and Zhanna sat in chairs across from Leroy Carr and a smiling Harry Truman whose portrait hung on the wall behind Carr's desk. When FDR died shortly before the end of the war, many in the

Washington crowd wrung their hands and said things like, "Lord help us, we now have a country bumpkin from Missouri taking control of the White House." Since then, Truman had made mistakes (many people pointed to the Potsdam Conference where Truman didn't stand in the way of Stalin's plans for Poland, a move that vexed Winston Churchill greatly). On the other hand, Truman had made some wily moves to ensure access to Berlin by the West. And it was on Truman's shoulders that the decision laid to drop two atomic bombs on Japan—a cruel and heavy weight to bear for any president, especially one who had held the office for just a few months. Most Americans believed it was the right decision, one that surely saved countless American lives by avoiding a D-Day-style amphibious invasion of the Japanese mainland, and ending the war for a war weary world.

So Truman had, so far, fought to at least a draw with the early croakers of doom.

"Okay, Ladies," said Carr. "What is this meeting all about?"

Chapter 75

Washington, D.C.
Wednesday—29 January 1947

Carr had given the women a few days to heal, especially Sheila who Al had brought back to D.C. Saturday evening. Sheila's injuries were severe. Her left shoulder was heavily bandaged and her arm in a sling. Cuts on her face, some that had required stitches, and facial bruises moved Carr to leave it up to Sheila to decide when the team could meet. She called from her home yesterday to let him know she was ready. (Actually, Carr had brought in Zhanna for a private meeting on Monday, but this was the first time since Knoxville that the entire team was back together.)

There was one person missing, however. Marienne Schenk was back home in Pittsburgh. Marienne had worked for Carr and the OSS full-time during the war but now had moved on and worked for him only occasionally—when Carr needed an expert shadow for a tough assignment. As soon as those jobs ended, Marienne returned home to her family. That was the agreement she had made with Carr.

Now the four Shield Maidens and Al Hodge sat around a table in a Pentagon conference room, along with the ever-present portrait or photograph of a smiling Harry Truman whose image hung in nearly every room of the Pentagon alongside the limp Stars & Stripes affixed to a standard. Other than those ubiquitous accoutrements, the windowless and soundproof room was very white and very spartan— like a hospital operating room void of equipment. Each of the four Shield Maidens wore on their right hand a silver ring with a black stone and Norse engravings. It was the Viking Ring of the Slain Erika had presented to them all after their first mission together last spring.

"I called Marienne and her husband yesterday," Carr started out. "Marienne's glad to be home."

"She's amazing," said Erika. "We never had a shadow as good as Marienne in the German Abwehr. I can see why you still ask for her help on tough jobs, Leroy."

Al Hodge added, "I second that. We'd have been screwed on this mission if it wasn't for Marienne and the things she found out while tailing Grusha in Germany. Also, Marienne is the one who discovered Grusha was still alive after the leap into the river."

Carr nodded then moved on. "So, let me ask, how are your injuries? Sheila, let's start with you?"

"I'm doing better," said the Army major. "The worst part is not being able to shower, and even bathing is a chore with all these bandages I have to keep dry. The doctors tell me the sling might come off next week. I hope to return to work then."

"No hurry, Sheila" said Carr. "Getting you healed up is all that counts. Zhanna, how about you?"

"My stitches will be removed Friday," Zhanna answered.

"Erika?"

"My ankle is still sore but getting a little better every day. I'm fine, Leroy. I'm ready to return to London to be with my daughter as you promised."

"I'll get to that in a moment," Carr responded. "Sheila, whenever you're ready, report back to work. If that's next week as you mentioned, that would be wonderful, but take the time you need."

Sheila replied, "As soon as the sling comes off, Leroy, I'll be back. I can't wear my uniform correctly with this sling, and I don't want to report back until I can show up in appropriate uniform. Again, if the Walter Reed doctors are right, that should be next week."

"Very good," said Carr. One thing he admired about Sheila was she was U.S. military to her core. Other than a few female doctors who served during the war, only a small number of women in the Army had risen to the rank of major.

Carr turned to the uninjured Kathryn. "Kathryn, you'll report back to the Naval War College in Rhode Island and resume your job as an instructor. I promised your commandant I would return you there as soon as possible.

"Erika, since you said you are ready, I'll get you an Air Force transport flight to London. I still owe you five more days with your daughter. You might fly on a plane filled with equipment being delivered to the UK, but it will get you there a lot faster than a ship."

"That's fine, Leroy. I don't care what type of plane it is. I can leave tomorrow."

"Al," said Carr, "find out when the next equipment transport plane leaves from Andrews and get Erika on it."

Hodge nodded. "I'll find out this afternoon and let you and Erika know."

"Okay," Carr said. "I've kept my promises. There is another possible mission waiting in South America but we're not ready for that yet. It will take Al and me some time to formulate how we want to go about it, if we want to get involved at all. Maybe we won't. For now you can all go about your personal or professional business."

"What about Zhanna?" Erika asked.

"Zhanna knows what she has to do. This meeting is over. Thank you all. Dismissed."

Chapter 76

Washington, D.C.
Next day—Thursday, 30 January 1947

By nine o'clock this morning Kathryn was on a train back to the Naval War College in Newport, Rhode Island. Sheila was at home healing.

Al Hodge found out that an Air Force C-47 cargo plane was scheduled to leave Andrews Air Force base for London at noon. Erika was on it, sitting on a metal chair bolted to the floor surrounded mostly by oak barrels of whiskey being exported to England from Kentucky and crates of eggs from Oklahoma tightly packaged to help minimize breakage if the flight was shaky.

Zhanna, on the other hand, still had a mission.

When she informed Carr that the Russians wanted her to work as a double agent within the CIA, he immediately knew this gave him an opportunity to double cross the Soviets and work Zhanna as a triple agent. Carr knew he would have to occasionally supply Zhanna with some valid information to keep the Soviets happy, but he would keep that information to low-level intel that couldn't hurt the CIA or the United States badly. Then, when an important occasion arose where Carr could supply the Russians false information that could really deliver a blow, he would have the perfect conduit—Zhanna.

[that morning—Carr's Pentagon office]

"I understand why you didn't set a tail on Rogova, Leroy, but I'd feel better if we knew how things went down from a second party."

"Too risky, Al," Carr said from behind his desk. "If the Russians even suspect a tail it will blow up everything. As far as Zhanna is concerned, she has nowhere to go. Heavens knows she can't turn herself over to the Soviets."

"How about Grusha?" Hodge asked. "Any squawking from the Soviets about Knoxville?"

"Nothing yet, but we'll probably hear a complaint pretty soon. I'm hoping it won't be too bad. Grusha betrayed them during the exchange on the bridge, and the Russians got what they really wanted, a double agent inside the CIA. The American traitor they thought they were getting was in the end secondary to them. They know they still have *Rollo* inside our nuclear research program, and can still access him with other of their agents."

Hodge looked at his wrist watch. "You said Rogova was meeting with Trukhin at eleven o'clock this morning. It's eleven now."

◊ ◊ ◊

Anatoly Trukhin, Minister of Affairs for the Soviet embassy in Washington, approached a short walkway bridge over a stream that ran through the gardens of Dumbarton Park. Surrounded by cherry trees, which at this time of year were devoid of leaves, the bridge was a popular rendezvous point for lovers. Today it would serve as a secure place for two Russians to meet. Trukhin wore a black great coat over his suit and a black fedora. The sun shone brightly but still a cold breeze demanded appropriate cold weather attire. Because the bridge was well shaded by trees, the sun had yet to melt the slush still remaining on the wooden bridge. The slush forced Trukhin to watch his step as he walked to the middle where he stopped and waited.

About five minutes later, Trukhin saw Zhanna approaching from the opposite side of the bridge. He was sure she had been watching him. She wore a light gray, lamb wool-lined jacket and a black knitted mink hat with a fox trim.

"Zhanna, my dear," Trukhin greeted her when she stopped at his side. "It is wonderful to see you again."

"It's nice to see you, Anatoly." They both spoke in English. Speaking in Russian would draw attention in a public venue.

"How did you hurt yourself?" he saw the small bandage on her cheek.

"I killed Grusha in a knife fight, Anatoly."

"We know Grusha came to an abrupt end but we didn't know the particulars. We found her body in the warehouse. You have nothing to worry about, my dear. To the Americans we will act outraged. It would be suspicious if we didn't. But we'll drop it after a short time. Grusha's death will convince the Americans even more that they can trust you."

"I imagine you don't have much time," the Russian minister continued. "I just want to say how happy I am to be able to work with you. This will give us some opportunities to be together."

Zhanna looked at him and smiled.

"I have worked out a way for you to quickly contact me with dead drops," said Trukhin. "I don't trust the Americans to not have listening capability to our embassy telephones, so even if you called me from a public telephone booth it might not be safe. Dead drops will protect you."

"Anatoly, I am not going to be a double agent for you. I told the Americans about your plan and they want me to do it but as a triple agent for them."

"You told them?" Trukhin looked totally stunned. "Why did you do that?"

"Because I want out of this life, Anatoly. The only way for me to get out is to disappear—try to find a place where the NKVD and the Americans cannot find me."

"Let me try to work something out, Zhanna," Trukhin pleaded. "Perhaps I can . . ."

Zhanna interrupted him. "There is nothing you can do to protect me from the NKVD if I refuse to work as a double agent, you know this is true, Anatoly. In the same light, if I return to the Americans and tell them I want out, I've been threatened with prison. Or they'll use me as trade bait in another trade and then I'd be in the hands of the NKVD and executed probably before that day is out."

"So you are not returning to the Americans?"

"No. They will never see me again." Zhanna kissed Trukhin on the cheek. "This is the only way. Goodbye, Anatoly."

Still staggered by the outcome of this meeting, Trukhin watched her walk off the bridge and fade away into the stark trees around a bend on the thin trail.

Chapter 77

Washington, D.C.
06 February 1947

Under cloudy skies, Erika's plane skidded to a twilight landing at Baltimore's airport instead of Andrews Air Force base. This made for a longer journey to D.C. but Baltimore was closer to where she lived—a sailboat she shared with Zhanna docked in the Chesapeake Bay near Havre de Grace, Maryland. The sailboat belonged to William Donovan, OSS chief during the war. Back then Donovan was Leroy Carr's boss; now Donovan was retired, but the two men remained friends. Last spring, Carr asked Donovan if the two women could billet on his boat for a time because of the severe housing shortage after the war.

Erika had not spoken to Carr while she was in London, but she was told before departing to meet with him the day after she returned. Instead of taking a train to D.C. and spending the night in a hotel, she headed to Havre de Grace. She would travel to D.C. tomorrow morning.

There were no bus rides available that would pass through Havre de Grace until tomorrow, so Erika took a taxi. It was an expensive ride, as the drive was an hour long, but it was worth it to her to get home. She paid for the taxi with her own money.

She had enjoyed the wonderful time with her daughter and maternal grandparents and promised herself she would do everything in her power to return sooner. Maybe even bring Ada to the States with her for awhile. Carr had mentioned that a mission in South America was only in the consideration stages. Perhaps that mission wouldn't happen, and she could settle in for a while doing her job as a trainer at the CIA 'Farm' at Camp Perry. If that happened, maybe Ada and her great-grandmother could visit. Marie Minton was Erika's grandmother but still only sixty-seven years old and spry.

Hard, freezing rain had begun falling on the taxi about ten minutes before Erika arrived home. Now at the dock, she could see from the well-lit platform the solid rain strike the Bay as if Atlas threw handfuls of sand into the water. She threw her bag onto the boat's deck and climbed aboard while being attacked by the stinging rain. When she got below she noticed Zhanna was not onboard. Only eight o'clock, Erika assumed she was in town having something to eat or sitting in a bar.

When she got to the sleeping quarters below deck, the frozen rain pelted the deck above her and the waves thumped the wooden hull as Erika took off her wet blouse and wrapped a towel around her shoulders. She began unpacking, laying her things on her bunk when she noticed the envelope on her pillow. Inside was a Ring of the Slain. Erika had presented one of the Rings to all the Shield Maidens. Along with the Ring was a note written in Russian.

Erika, I'm leaving this for you while you are in London. If you have spoken to Mr. Carr you know by now I've been missing for a few days. If you haven't spoken to him, tell him I no longer want to be part of this life where I have to betray my homeland, yet I also don't want to betray America, which I have learned to appreciate. If I stay, there is no way I could avoid being forced to do one or the other. I leave behind the Ring. I no longer deserve to wear it. Because of the things I have done in my life, I have no hope for a warrior's Valhalla or a Christian Heaven. Unlike you, I have no love in me. If ever I had any, it left me when I was a small child. Also, unlike you who have killed only as a soldier, I have killed people I didn't have to kill, and some who did not deserve such a death.

Goodbye, Erika. I wish you the best. Please tell Kathryn and Sheila I said goodbye.

Zhanna

Historical Notes

Lucky Luciano

Unable to return to the United States from where he had already been deported, the Cubans eventually deported the mob boss, Charles "Lucky" Luciano, back to Italy, where he spent the rest of his life. Luciano suffered a fatal heart attack and died in Naples in January of 1962.

Meyer Lansky

Meyer Lansky built a mob empire in Havana that did not end until Fidel Castro's coup d'état in 1959. In 1970, Lansky tried to immigrate to Israel but that country had strict immigration rules prohibiting criminals and Lansky was turned down. He returned to the United States where for years he battled criminal charges. Finally the United States judicial system gave up on trying to put Lansky behind bars and he died in Miami Beach at the age of 80.

Benjamin "Bugsy" Siegel

Bugsy Siegel, "The Man Who Made Las Vegas," was brutally murdered in his longtime girlfriend's Beverly Hills home (actress Virginia Hill) on June 20, 1947. Suspected by his fellow mobsters and investors that he was skimming funds, Siegel was sitting on the couch when a fusillade of bullets crashed through the living room window. Two bullets struck Siegel in the head, one blowing out the mobster's left eye. His killers were never caught.

Albert Anastasia

In 1951, Albert Anastasia, "The Lord High Executioner," had his crime family boss, Vincenzo Mangano, killed and Anastasia took over the family. Anastasia's reign would not last long. On October 25, 1957, Anastasia was getting a shave in the Park Sheraton Hotel in New York City when two masked gunman entered and killed Anastasia in a hail of gunfire. The murder of Albert Anastasia inspired a scene in the movie *The Godfather*.

◊ ◊ ◊

The Glienicke Bridge

The Havel River on the outskirts of Potsdam, Germany, provided a natural border separating Soviet controlled Potsdam from the land on the river's opposite bank that was controlled by the USA. The Glienicke Bridge over the river was used throughout the Cold War as a place for clandestine, face-to-face meetings between East and West. Still to this day, many local Germans refer to the bridge as "The Bridge of Spies" instead of calling it the Glienicke Bridge.

In 1962, American pilot Francis Gary Powers whose CIA U-2 spy plane had been shot down over Soviet airspace was exchanged for Soviet KGB Colonel Vilyam Fisher, known as "Rudolf Abel" who had been captured by the FBI then tried and imprisoned for espionage against the United States. The exchange took place in the middle of the Glienicke Bridge.

Powers was criticized by some for not taking the lethal cyanide pill the CIA provided him for the mission.

The 2015 Tom Hanks Hollywood film *Bridge of Spies* deals with the exchange for Francis Gary Powers on the Glienicke Bridge. Scenes were shot for the movie on the real bridge on the outskirts of Potsdam.

Shield Maidens

The legend of the Viking warrior women called *Shield Maidens* dates back twelve centuries—from the earliest times of the Vikings. According to Norse lore, the Shield Maidens were great female warriors who fought bravely, and just as enthusiastically and skilled with weapons as many of their male Viking counterparts.

For centuries this legend of the fierce Shield Maidens was held to be just a myth.

Recent excavations in Norway have uncovered graves of Norse women buried with weapons and shields, the same burial ritual the Vikings held for their venerated male warriors.

Acknowledgements

First I have to thank my wife, Sandy Whicker, who has supported my writing from the start along with all of my family. A family is the greatest blessing God has given any of us.

I thank my attorney, David Jones, who wears many hats when it comes to my novels. David is not only a great friend, but helps me with research and offers me sound advice if I'm getting off track. And thanks to Lauren Jones for all her help over the years.

Thanks are due to my proofreaders, Tim Heerdink and Erin Whicker. With their keen eyes they spot my pesky little faux pas here and there in the early drafts.

Thanks to my daughter, Savannah Whicker, a U.S. Army veteran who spent three years in a war zone in Iraq during the Iraqi War. Savannah would fit in nicely on the *Shield Maidens* team. She posed as Zhanna Rogova for the book cover. Professional makeup artist Crystal Smith did an out-of-this-world job recreating Zhanna's WW II Russian female sniper makeup and her neck scar. And my good friend, Amanda Reising, owner of Hår Salon in Evansville, did an incredible job on Zhanna's (Savannah's) hair for the climactic battle scene between Zhanna and Grusha in Part 6.

The Erika Lehmann Series

Book 1: *Invitation to Valhalla*
Book 2: *Blood of the Reich*
Book 3: *Return to Valhalla*
Book 4: *Fall from Valhalla*
Book 5: *Operation Shield Maidens*
Book 6: *Hope for Valhalla*

Other books by Mike Whicker:
Proper Suda
and
Flowers for Hitler: The Extraordinary Life of Ilse Dorsch
(a biography)

All books are available in print copy from Amazon.com, bn.com, and electronically from Kindle. Signed copies are available from the author.

Author welcomes reader comments
Email: mikewhicker1@gmail.com

Hope for Valhalla

Hope for Valhalla

Notes

(a place for readers)

Hope for Valhalla

CPSIA information can be obtained
at www.ICGtesting.com
Printed in the USA
LVOW03s0637101217
559270LV00003B/12/P